FOUR FURLONGS

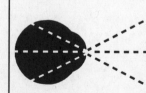

THE CHINA BOHANNON SERIES

FOUR FURLONGS

CAROL WRIGHT CRIGGER

WHEELER PUBLISHING
A part of Gale, a Cengage Company

Farmington Hills, Mich • San Francisco • New York • Waterville, Maine
Meriden, Conn • Mason, Ohio • Chicago

GALE
A Cengage Company

LIBRARY OF CONGRESS CATALOGING-IN-PUBLICATION DATA

Names: Wright Crigger, Carol, author.
Title: Four furlongs / by Carol Wright Crigger.
Description: Large print edition. | Waterville, Maine : Wheeler Publishing, a part
    of Gale, Cengage Learning, 2017. | Series: The China Bohannon series | Series:
    Wheeler Publishing large print western
Identifiers: LCCN 2017019095| ISBN 9781432842239 (softcover) | ISBN 1432842234
    (softcover)
Subjects: LCSH: Women detectives—Fiction. | Horse racing—Fiction. |
    Murder—Investigation—Fiction. | Spokane (Wash.)—Fiction. | Large type books.
    | GSAFD: Mystery fiction.
Classification: LCC PS3623.R595 F68 2017 | DDC 813/.6—dc23
LC record available at https://lccn.loc.gov/2017019095

Published in 2017 by arrangement with Carol Wright Crigger

Printed in the United States of America
1 2 3 4 5 6 7 21 20 19 18 17

To Mom and Dad, who were great readers and instilled the love of books in me and my siblings. Bet you never thought I'd stay the course and become a writer! Joke's on you.

PROLOGUE

"What's your son think he's doing?" Louis Duchene's eyes narrowed, straining against distance and a pileup of colors and motion. Dust boiled from under the hooves of the eight horses racing down the track, raising a cloud that obscured details such as showing which horse led.

"Sonuvabitch," he added.

Duchene chewed on the unlit cigar clamped between his teeth, his jaws moving like a clockwork mechanism. One fist pounded the wagon's thick edge in a nervous tattoo.

"What do you mean?" Hazel O'Dell, Duchene's daughter and the mother of the lad in question, reefed the soiled hem of her skirt above her knees and clambered into the wagon bed to stand beside him.

"Him and Mercury have run off the track," Duchene said.

"Are you sure?" She squinted, peering

ahead. "I can't tell. The horses are all bunched together at the halfway pole." A small, brown woman as agile as a squirrel, Hazel stepped up onto the cedar tack box and cupped her hands around her eyes in a poor man's version of field glasses. "Dad, I don't see him, anywhere. Robbie must've pulled him off the track in time —" And then, a second later, "Oh, no. A horse is down at the turn. Two horses. One of them —" Her voice broke, then rose. "Dad, one of those horses is Mercury."

"Nooo —" The cigar dropped unheeded from Duchene's mouth. His face turned a pasty shade of beige. "Are you sure?"

Around them, other spectators became aware of the pileup. Some turned to look in their direction. A few muttered disconsolately. A group of three rough-looking characters grinned in blatant satisfaction.

Hazel clutched her father's arm. "I'm sure. And . . . I can't see Robbie. I think . . . I think Mercury has fallen on top of him."

Duchene's face twisted, the expression a mixture of dismay and anger. "Stay here." He leapt from the wagon, stumbling a little as he landed on bad knees, and broke into a shambling run.

Neva Sue O'Dell, Hazel's daughter, wasn't watching the race. She stood at the front of

8

the wagon, unconsciously soothing the two draft horses as they rested in the shade. A bucket of water stood in easy reach of the big horses' heads. She'd just fetched the water from a spigot over by the race course barn. Her mother and grandfather often got so excited on race day they forgot the team doing the heavy work and thought only of the horse on the track. Neva Sue knew how the draft horses felt. Her family forgot her, too, most of the time.

They did, on the other hand, think a lot of Robbie.

And of the wagers they placed.

And of winning. Or losing. Depending.

Just like now.

"Robbie," she whispered, gently pulling the brown horse's ear. "Oh, Robbie, what have you done?"

CHAPTER 1

"Is that him?" I asked my partner, Gratton Doyle. I nodded toward a shifty-looking individual wearing a loud plaid suit who was weaving his way through the crowd lining the rails of the Corbin Park racetrack. The way he moved, slinking like a fox about to attack a henhouse, aroused my suspicions.

Gratton shook his head. "Naw. That's Lucky Parsons. He's known for being the nosiest man in Spokane, but not dishonest. He just likes to eavesdrop on what people are saying."

"Oh." Disappointed, I went back to staring around. The day was ideal for attending the Interstate Fair's annual race meet, and judging by the attendance, several thousand people agreed with me.

Gratton nudged my elbow. "Ladies first."

Ever the soul of generosity, he proffered the brown paper bag of hot roasted peanuts he'd bought from a vendor touting his wares near the horse saddling enclosure. The peanuts' enticing scent rose on the crisp, late September air. My mouth watered. I'd missed lunch, too busy getting ready for this outing . . . er . . . job assignment with Gratton.

"Have a handful." Gratton grinned down at me, his storm-dark-gray eyes squinted against the brilliant sun. "They're good."

Grat is a man who knows how to treat a girl to a good time. Don't believe me? Just ask him.

And maybe he does, I conceded, my heart melting as I removed my gloves and reached into the bag. After all, he had given me my dear little dog, Nimble, the Bedlington terrier who had saved my bacon more than once during the course of my time at the Doyle & Howe, and *Bohannon* — italics mine — Detective Agency.

And Grat's bacon, too, come to think of it.

As my constant companion, Nimble strained at the end of her leash, prancing at my side as we strolled along today. Happy as Mrs. May Arkwright Hutton at a suffragette meeting, she was sniffing at myriad enticing odors along the verge of the racetrack. Horse turds are one of her favorite things.

But in this case, the aforementioned good time meant first crack at the peanuts. I grabbed a large handful while I was at it.

As for me? I am the Bohannon of the Doyle & Howe — and Bohannon — Detective Agency. Miss China Bohannon — spinster, bookkeeper turned detective, and living decoy for mayhem. "Decoy for mayhem" are not my words, by the way. I believe my uncle Monk coined the phrase.

Gratton, of course, is the Doyle, and although he's totally unaware of it, the keeper of my heart. My uncle, Montgomery Howe, with whom I live, is the Howe. Together we are a force to strike fear in the hearts of criminals. At least, I hope we are. Such was Gratton's and my intention today. We were on the hunt for a notorious bunco man reported to be plying his trade at the fair. If we managed to snare him, we'd not only please our specific customer, but those in charge of fair security.

Instead of enjoying the horse races, sunny blue late September skies, and Grat's company, I couldn't help thinking my time would be better utilized at our office on Riverside Street. I should be using my newly acquired typewriting machine — now I was finally gaining some mastery over the pestilent thing and not wasting so much paper — to make out an itemized bill for a major case my uncle had solved last week.

Of course, I'd rather be in on the action of helping Grat catch a bunco man, eating peanuts and watching the ponies run.

In the pursuit of our assignment, we'd kept close to the saddling enclosure during the first two races of the day. This is where the bookies usually set up shop. Well, not shop, exactly, but where they conducted business. I was beginning to think bunco men operated differently.

Nimble barked as yet another horse galloped past. Sighing, I tugged the leash. "Heel, Nimble." I offered a shelled peanut as a bribe. She snatched the morsel, but I fancy she would've preferred the horse apples the horse dropped.

"Look, there's a man wearing a porkpie hat." With a tingle of excitement, I grabbed Gratton's elbow. Grat had told me our quarry always wore the thus-named headgear, a matter of pride. I'd spotted a large fellow in a rather grubby tan-colored suit and a brown porkpie pumping his fist and yelling something about "the odds." He seemed a likely suspect to me.

Gratton shook his head. "Nope. Not him,

either. Jimsy Woodsmith, our target, is the weaselly sort. A little fellow. Got small hands. He picks pockets as well as runs his cons."

"Jimsy?" I gave him a questioning look. "Who'd name their child Jimsy, for goodness sake?"

"Dunno, but wait until you see him. You'll find it suits him to a gnat's nose." Sounding preoccupied, Grat's saunter picked up speed. "Hello. What's this?"

I trotted to keep up with his lengthening stride. We abandoned our watch of the enclosure and headed down the racetrack toward a group of people who stood about haggling in loud, angry voices.

Their situation deteriorated quickly. Shouts carried over the distance. A thrown punch sent someone — a shopkeeper, judging by his clothes — staggering. A white-haired gentleman waved his cane in the air, dangerous to friend or foe alike.

In the center of this conflict, a man not much taller than me seemed to be struggling with a fellow wearing farmer clothes. Did the smaller one wear a porkpie hat? Was he the weaselly sort? I couldn't tell at this range, but Gratton seemed to think so.

"Ah-hah. Stay here." Thrusting the peanut bag into my hands, Grat dashed toward the conflict.

Stay here? Miss all the action? Not likely. Anyway, Nimble, sensing one of her favorite things — a melee, which she seemed to think allowed her to jump and nip and trip with utter immunity of reprimand — jerked her leash from my hand and followed Grat.

So, perforce, did I.

By the time I arrived at the scuffle, Grat had a grip on the person I presumed must be Jimsy Woodsmith. Nimble had managed to wrap her leash around the ankles of the farmer, causing him to stumble. He lashed out at her with his free foot. Since it was clad in a heavy boot, this not only didn't please me, it frightened me.

"Nimble," I called, my voice rising over the grunts of men. "Come here at once!"

Nimble, easily dodging the farmer, ignored my summons. Grat, however, distracted and in danger of being tripped by her leash himself, lost his hold on Jimsy.

Jimsy, grasping his chance, darted behind the cane wielder where he was almost hidden by the white-haired man's bulk. He was also the only person not in danger from the cane wielder, who kept swinging his weapon. To no avail, as one might imagine, but the cane certainly kept everyone else at bay. Including Grat.

What a ludicrous situation. I shook my head in disgust, dodging a thrust of the cane as Jimsy shoved the old fellow toward me.

How rude, I thought, before it struck me Jimsy's maneuver had a determined focus. The little weasel was trying to cause a pileup from which he could make his escape.

Hah! He must've been counting on these men being willing to aid a lady and an old gentleman. More fool he.

The next time the cane came around, I threw the peanuts in the air. Or more precisely, straight into the cane wielder's face. Peanuts flew everywhere. Grat, after all, had purchased the vendor's largest bag.

And don't forget the peanuts were hot, fresh off the roaster.

Stung by the sudden heat, which I suspect felt as though he were being attacked by a swarm of bees, the elderly gentleman cried out, let go of his cane in mid swing and clutched his face. He lurched about like a madman. The crunch of trodden peanut shells sounded even over the noise of the fight.

Jimsy, although he'd lost his shield, was still in danger of making good his escape since I'd conveniently provided him with a diversion. Holding onto his porkpie hat with one hand, he dug in his toes, and took off running.

He hadn't considered that I might have excellent reflexes.

I managed to catch the cane before it dropped, jerking it from the owner's hand. The stick became of real use in my possession. As Jimsy fled past me, I thrust it between his legs.

Down he went, end over end.

As it happened, the fool grabbed on to me and we both tumbled to the ground. Me, with my knees exposed and my hat askew. Nimble, eager to play this game, pounced on top of us.

The farmer and the shopkeeper also piled onto the escaping bunco man before he could squirm free. An elbow in my belly knocked the wind out of me. A fist clipped my cheekbone, setting my head abuzz. The ground shook as several horses raced past, only inches away.

Gratton, his face red, wrenched bodies off until I was uncovered enough to draw breath, but it was Jimsy he helped to his feet. Holding the weasel in a one-handed grasp I'm convinced must've set the bunco man's bones to aching, he produced a set of handcuffs from his pocket and slipped them over Jimsy's narrow wrists.

Someone heavy trod on my hand. "Ouch," I cried.

Grat's fierce glare warned the culprit — the farmer, I believe, judging by the weight that had crushed my hand — to watch himself.

"Stand back, and help this lady rise," he snapped.

I don't know if he frightened them off with his scowl, or if they were just too boorish, but although no one else stepped on me, no one offered aid. I regained my feet by my own efforts. Disgruntled mutters from those around me indicated they intended to take matters regarding Jimsy into their own hands, whether Doyle liked it or not.

"Little twerp ain't been paying the right odds," the farmer said in a loud voice. "Seems to think I'm too ignorant to figure the payoff on me own."

The shopkeeper added, "He's trying to say I bet on a different horse than what I said."

"He's an out-and-out thief," the white-haired man said. "I caught him stealing my wallet." He bent with more ease than I would've expected and retrieved his stick from where it had fallen. His expression indicated he was still thinking of using it to pound Jimsy.

Jimsy shook his head in such a violent manner I felt sure his brains must be addled. "Buncha rubes don't know what you're talkin' about," he said.

"Might be better to keep your insults to yourself." Gratton gave him an ungentle nudge.

"I never stole anything, I tell ya. Never cheated anybody, either. I ain't got but a dollar in my pocket." Jimsy put on an innocent face, but his eyes glittered like blue ice, betraying him.

"Search him," someone yelled.

"Yeah, search him," another man agreed.

"Go ahead," said Jimsy carelessly. "See if I care."

In fact, he seemed to welcome a search. Suspicious in itself, if you ask me.

Gratton, no doubt wisely, stepped aside and let the search begin, the shopkeeper taking charge. For a while it seemed they'd rip the clothes from the little man's body. Fortunately for my sensibilities, they stopped a tad short.

I took the opportunity to straighten my hat, and brush down my skirt, not so easy a task with Nimble running circles around me, stirring up a dust with her leash. Gratton, while he waited for the search to end, helpfully tucked a few stray curls behind my ear.

Sure enough, the only money recovered was a single dollar, a shiny new silver one. Just as Jimsy had said.

My suspicions grew.

"Make 'im tell us where he stashed the rest." The farmer was doing the talking again. Or maybe I should say the rabble-rousing since he said, "Bet a rope around his neck would encourage him to talk."

Jimsy flinched. His eyes widened.

"Nobody is hanging anybody," Grat said. "I'm arresting this man and taking him to jail." Although he lacked the authority, he faced the men — or maybe I'd call it a mob — with confidence.

"We got the detective outnumbered," someone said. "He ain't the law, anyhow. He's just a private detective."

Obviously, Gratton was well-known about town.

Grat touched the pistol in the holster under his arm, a plain indication he'd brook no further interference, and grinned at the man who'd spoken.

The white-haired fellow cleared his throat. "Hold on a minute. Maybe Doyle's right. Get the police on his tail. I've seen gents they've worked over. Give this runt three minutes and he'll be talking his head off."

"Who're you callin' a runt?" Jimsy snarled, buck teeth showing.

In the end, the mob found the white-haired man's words convincing. Grat, careful not to turn his back either on Jimsy or the men, steered his prisoner toward the trolley, which we'd catch to take us downtown to the police station. I ran after them.

Jimsy was still arguing. "The old feller's right. You ain't the law. You can't arrest me." He writhed in Gratton's grip. "You're that digity detective been tailin' me for the last two days."

"There you go talking too much." Grat kept his voice low. Two of the group still followed us. "You better hope nobody else questions my authorization — unless you actually want them to find a rope and a tree."

Finally, a hint Jimsy understood. His struggles subsided. He grabbed at his hat, lifting it from where it had sagged over his ears. "Turn me loose. I'll pay you. I'll pay you fifty bucks."

Grat gave the weasel's shoulder a shove. "I thought you didn't have any money. Isn't that what you told everybody? And what the search was all about?"

"I can get money," Jimsy said.

"Yeah?" Grat said.

"Yeah."

Behind us, the followers, no doubt enticed by the call for the next race, doubled back.

I trotted a half pace behind Jimsy and Grat, watching the top of Jimsy's porkpie hat bob at a level no higher than Grat's shoulder. A sudden urge to giggle came over me. Jimsy seemed to contradict himself, but I rather thought I'd caught onto his trick. The question was, did I want to tell all I knew — or suspected — right this moment, or should I wait until we got to the police station?

All thoughts of Jimsy and money fled from my mind as Nimble stopped in her tracks. She spread her front legs and ducked her head, heaving and gagging. Nothing came up, but she fought for breath, gasps wheezing from her lungs.

"Nimble," I cried.

"What's the matter with your dog?" Grat spun around.

"I don't know." I'm sure my face must've turned white as a cauliflower.

"Do something, China," he said.

I did. Prying Nimble's mouth open, I peeked inside. No obvious obstructions.

She continued to struggle. And heave. And gag.

23

Please, no. Was something blocking the airway to her lungs? Would she die? Tears filled my eyes. With no other remedy occurring to me, I stuck my hand in her mouth. Ignoring her gnashing white teeth, I felt around.

Touched . . . something. Something slimy and unpleasant.

I shut my ears to her whimpers.

Drawing a shuddering breath, despite her strong measure of resistance, I dug between her two back molars with my fingernail. A slippery brown object popped out, landing on the ground at my feet. I bent to look.

Half of a well-chewed peanut shell. It looked every bit as disgusting as it had felt.

Nimble, her agonies relieved, ignored my effort in saving her without so much as a thank-you. She pranced over to Gratton to receive pats on her funny little wedge-shaped head.

Regarding Jimsy and the money? I decided to delay further comment until we got to the police station.

CHAPTER 2

From what I can tell, nothing upsets men more than having their preconceived notions foiled, whether by the law, a private detective, or a bunco man. When foiled by a woman . . . well, let's just say he's not likely to appreciate the woman's efforts, no matter her intentions.

Gratton accepted my company if not complaisantly, at least without objection right up until the three of us, Jimsy Woodsmith, Gratton, and I, stepped from the streetcar. He'd been taking sideways glances at me during the entire ride downtown, and now, on the verge of entering the police station, he stopped in his tracks.

"What's that expression on your face?" he demanded, stepping in front of me to bar my way.

"Expression?"

"Smug," he said. "Like you know something I don't."

"I can't imagine what you mean." I opened my eyes wide.

His mouth twisted, half distrust, half grin. His grip on Jimsy's arm tightened as the bunco man squirmed in a last-ditch effort to escape. "Sure you can. You got it right before Nimble started gagging." He flicked a glance at Nimble. "I didn't give her any peanuts, so don't blame me for her choking spell. She stole it."

"I know she did. I don't blame you." I'd never accuse him of harming the little curly-coated dog.

"Well —"

Jimsy, no doubt aggravated with me because I was the one who had tripped him, thereby enabling his capture, did his part to sow discord. "Don't trust her, Doyle. A hoity-toity miss like her don't have any business showing her face in a police station. What'll all the respectable people think?" He gave his porkpie a jerk, raising it a quarter-inch higher above his ears before it settled down again.

Hoity-toity? Me? Just because I've become a master — or do I mean mistress? — at ignoring people on trains or boats or streetcars who look at me with down-turned mouths. Which is what the passengers had done today when they saw I accompanied a

26

disreputable man in handcuffs.

"Oh, please," I said, disgusted, even though I had half a hunch Grat might agree with Jimsy. In this case and at this moment, at least. "I doubt we'll find many people in the police station whose opinion I need worry about."

Gratton scanned from one side of the street to the other. "Maybe, or maybe not, but he's right about one thing, China. The police station is no place for a lady."

"I dare say I'd as soon not be here," I responded crisply. "However, this man assaulted me and I intend to press charges. Let's get this over with. Maybe I can still get the client's bill out in the afternoon mail."

But Grat was holding back. "Are you forgetting we gotta recover his money first? Lion's share, anyway. It's part of the contract."

Brow arching, I frowned at him. "I know what the contract says. I wrote it."

"Has it escaped your —"

"Don't worry. I believe we're covered," I said.

Jimsy renewed his struggles upon hearing my cryptic reply, so that Grat, in forcing the little man into the station in front of him, failed to keep me out.

27

Sergeant Lars Hansen of the Spokane Police Department, a tall man resplendent in his thigh-length blue coat, crisp white shirt, and luxuriant handlebar mustache, was standing by a much-battered oak desk talking with a beat officer. Sunlight shone through a dusty window, glinting off his slicked-back blond hair.

Two or three other policemen sat at desks, heads bent and pencils in hand, looking as if they were conducting important business. For all I know they may have been, but Lars's presence likely had a little something to do with their activity. Another bluecoat loomed threateningly over a female wearing a very low-cut frock. She sat on a wooden bench bawling like an orphan left on the church steps, poor young thing. A short, white-haired man with a stethoscope hanging from his neck emerged from a door on our right, reminding me of the morgue located in the basement below.

The officer speaking with Lars opened his eyes wide and nudged the sergeant in the ribs as I elbowed Jimsy aside. It drew Lars's attention. He turned, his blue gaze chilly as it swept over our party.

"Hire a new man?" he called to Gratton, loudly, so everyone in the room could hear. An insult, since everyone there either recognized Jimsy as a repeat offender or knew him for what he was.

Oh, dear. I sighed internally. Here we go again.

Lars and Gratton did not get along. Have I said it plainly enough? Oh, they'd been forced to cooperate on various matters during the time I'd known them, but the truce never lasted more than a day or two. Sometimes only hours. Their trouble stemmed from both wanting the same woman. One who, whether they admitted it or not, played them both false. Each man preferred to blame the other instead of her.

I, of course, was not the woman.

Fools, the pair of them.

"Nah." Gratton's retort boomed louder than Lars's initial comment. "Just out doing your job for you, nabbing outlaws and keeping the public safe. Someone has to do it."

Pin drop, anyone?

Gratton, as one might guess, doesn't have many friends or supporters in the police department. Blame his private-detective status, although his prowess at the game of baseball might be a larger cause.

"Take your prisoner into the back room." Lars cocked his thumb toward a hall leading deeper into the building where the jail cells were located. "You know which one I mean. Ought to, at least."

An implication Grat had been present there in something other than a prosecutorial capacity, I believe.

"You mean the one where three or four bluecoats pound the uh . . . stuffing . . . out of one handcuffed feller?" Grat responded.

Jimsy let out a little moan. Feet shuffled in the background. I began to perspire. My word, they were apt to go on like this all day if I didn't take a hand.

I cleared my throat in an attention-getting kind of way. "We've made a citizen's arrest, Sergeant Hansen, and brought this man to you to hold for trial." Nothing like stating the obvious, but it served to curb their collision-bound train of thought.

Lars made a face. "Oh, you have, have you?" His glance at me seemed barely more friendly than the one he aimed at Grat. "What do you want him charged with, if I may ask?"

"You asleep, Hansen? You've taken our Jimsy in custody often enough to know his methods. Same as usual. A few minutes ago, a certain Mr. Dobbs caught him picking his pocket out at the racetrack. Several men are willing to testify he falsified their bets. Couple others have complaints, too. Should be enough to start with."

"I never did," Jimsy denied firmly.

I was a bit startled when Gratton didn't mention the charge made against the little man by our client, a certain Mr. Mickelson. But then I thought I understood. Gratton wanted first crack at recovering any monies Jimsy may have hidden away before the police got their hands on it. Our fee depended on returning the money.

On further thought, entertaining Jimsy in the back room might be a good idea after all.

"What kind of complaints?" Lars demanded. "Who are these 'others'? Why aren't they here to press charges?"

"I'm here," I broke in, "and I'm telling you he assaulted me, knocked me to the ground."

Lars studied me. "Are you hurt, China? Excuse me . . . Miss Bohannon. You don't look hurt."

"Do I have to suffer visible wounds? Isn't my word good enough?" I fear my expression turned belligerent as I fingered a small tear in my skirt and brushed at some remaining dust particles.

Grat made an impatient gesture. "Get him for disturbing the peace and interfering with the races, if nothing else. He dang near caused a riot down by the track. Officials had to hold up the fifth."

"So what's your horse in this race, Doyle?" Lars grinned at his own witticism. "Seeing as how you're the one bringing him in."

Grat winked. "Just doin' me civic duty," he said, broadening his Irish brogue. A good many of the police were Irish themselves, not that their ethnicity stopped every last one of them in the room from practically busting a gut, to coin a phrase, over the idea of Gratton and civic duty.

"Good one." Lars, face still red from laughing, twirled his lush handlebar mustache like a storybook villain. "So, got any way to prove these pickpocket charges? Or the betting swindle? Need something concrete enough to make it worth my while if you want me to hold him."

This *worth my while* business was one of the things regarding Lars my uncle Monk and Gratton always cautioned me about. He was on the take, open to the highest dollar. And, the good Lord only knows how, he always managed to keep his job, even rising in rank.

"Alls I have in my pocket is a dollar," Jimsy said, possibly sensing a break coming his way. Lifting his cuffed hands, he raised his porkpie hat from around his ears, even though it immediately sank again. "Swear to you, Sergeant. If I'm lyin', I'm dyin'."

"Harrumph," I said before I could stop myself.

Grat shot me a quick look. "I hear you put a bet down on a horse now and again, Hansen," he said. "How would you like it if your bookie stiffed you? Took your money then claimed you bet on a different horse after you won."

I heard a couple strangled gasps, then a fearsome silence lasting a full ten seconds.

"Is this what the weasel's been doing?" Lars shook his head. "He ain't a licensed bookie anyway. Who'd be stupid enough to place a bet with him?"

"From the look of things, several people," Gratton said.

Lars huffed and puffed before giving in. "All right, all right. Take him into the back room. I'll round up a clerk and you and China can fill out some paperwork."

"Thank you," I told Lars and gave Gratton a nudge. "The back room. Come along, Nimble."

My dog came willingly. Jimsy not so much. Gratton wasted a couple of those minutes chatting up a man wearing a baggy suit, its seat thin and shiny with sitting. I was actually breathless with impatience before we finally entered a dark and dirty room measuring about ten feet square. It contained a table and a couple chairs, all of which were on their last legs, and bore a bare electric lightbulb overhead. Nothing else. The place stank of blood, dirt, and fear. The light bulb put forth an annoying hum.

Jimsy, head hanging, sank onto one of the chairs.

"Told you this is no place for a lady." Grat eyed my disgusted expression. "You're not going to faint, are you, or cry?"

"Me?" I was offended. "No. I most certainly am not. Although the sooner we leave here the better. What were you doing, exchanging life stories with that man? Who is he, anyway?"

"Just a fella I know," Grat said. "He's in a position to help us pick up some clients if he puts in a good word. Aren't you the one always going on about the agency needing more work? Best advertisement is word of mouth. I remember you telling Monk and me so. Repeatedly."

I couldn't deny it.

"Although," he said, "unless we can return Mickelson's money to him, could be the word of mouth thing will do us more harm than good.

"Now," he went on, giving me a sharp look when I smiled, "what's up with you,

China. You're jumping around like an ant on a hot stove. I know you've got some devious plan in mind."

His attitude struck me as more apprehensive than anticipatory.

I sat down across from Jimsy and batted my eyes at our prisoner. "I don't know if you've ever heard," I asked him with a simper, "but a gentleman should always remove his hat when in the presence of a lady?"

Clamping his cuffed hands to his porkpie, Jimsy jerked upright. "Huh," he said, "I don't see no ladies here. Alls I see is a wild-haired harridan and her freakish little dog."

Involuntarily, I touched my hair. Blasted man. He was right. I swiveled my eyes far enough to spy brown locks slipping from under my boater and springing out in curls around my ears. Which gave him no excuse whatever to pick on Nimble.

I guess Gratton didn't think so either. "Watch your mouth, you little weasel," he snapped. Before Jimsy could shy away, he flipped a finger and knocked Jimsy's porkpie to the floor.

The hat thumped resoundingly onto the filthy floor. A gold double eagle bounced out, disappearing into a corner of the room.

Jimsy made a curious whining sound and

sent a wary sideways glance at Gratton. Hah. Wrong decision. I was the one who'd caught onto his tells.

"Fetch it," I told Nimble, upon which she pounced on the coin. I smiled as I retrieved Jimsy's surprisingly heavy hat. He moaned and tried to rise from his chair as though to stop me.

Gratton smacked him back down. "What's going on, China?"

"Didn't you notice the way Mr. Woodsmith is forever adjusting his hat?" I hefted the porkpie as though to show its weight. "I began to suspect there was a reason it kept falling over his ears. Gold is heavy, after all. I do believe we've discovered Jimsy's bank." I was willing to share credit with my partner.

Oh, my, Jimsy had quite the vocabulary of curse words. I felt the tips of my ears heat and glow red even as I recovered the first of nineteen more twenty-dollar gold pieces from the partitions sewn around porkpie's headband. Plus a bearer's bond in the amount of ten thousand dollars stuffed in the crown. No wonder our client had been so worried.

"Quick, stow everything in your pocketbook." Grat flashed a toothsome grin.

He didn't need to tell me twice. I'd just snapped my poor stuffed pocketbook's clasp

36

tight around the recovered goods when Lars and his clerk strode in. By this time Jimsy was on the verge of tears at seeing his stolen cache disappear.

Lars cast us a suspicious look. "Get a confession?" he asked. I'm sure he wondered why Gratton smiled like Lewis Carroll's Cheshire cat while Jimsy appeared so woebegone.

Grat offered me his elbow, which I took. "I'm not doing your job for you, Hansen. Beat it out of him yourself. We're leaving. China's not feeling well." His nose twitched. "The stench, I imagine. Sure and it's rank enough in here to choke a hog."

I took Nimble's leash in hand, and the three of us swept out of the police station on a wave of euphoria. We were nearly run down in the doorway as a young officer sprinted in, bouncing off Gratton in his hurry.

"Come quick," he yelled into the room. "There's been an accident at the races. Horses are down and a kid has been killed. There's a fight — a riot — brewing. Big Bill Shannon says we need Sergeant Hansen and all the men he can muster."

Footsteps pounded around us as policemen answered the call. When they had passed, Gratton looked down at me, his face sober. "Jimsy did us a favor."

I didn't understand. "He did?"

"Yes. I'm glad you weren't there to see what happened." He shook his head. "I'm glad I wasn't there to see what happened."

How were we to know we'd soon be knee-deep in the aftermath?

CHAPTER 3

Gratton made no bones about itching to get back to the racetrack to hear about the racing accident. Who? What? How? The incident might even overshadow the derby coming up on Sunday, the final day of the fair.

Even so, he took the time to walk me home from the police station — although the length of his strides meant I barely kept up. He was, he said, unwilling to let me traverse the streets of Spokane while carrying ten thousand four hundred dollars upon my person.

"Don't worry about me," I told him, panting a little between every few words. "I walk alone every day and I've only ever been accosted once."

"You don't carry ten thousand dollars with you every day," he retorted. "And I want to keep my eyes on Mickelson's bearer's bond until it's locked in our safe."

"No one knows I have it." I checked my

purse's clasp to make sure it was still latched. A testament to the purse's sturdy construction considering the weight of twenty double eagles, enough to drag on my arm. It's no wonder I lagged a few steps behind.

Grat took my elbow and pulled me out of the path of a man weaving down the center of the boardwalk. "Some of these yahoos can hone in on money like hound dogs after a cat. And they're not real careful how they treat the person they're stealing from. A man like Jimsy . . . he's meek as a mouse compared to them. I won't have you hurt, China."

A little thrill shivered through me at that. He really did care about me. He just wasn't good at showing it — most of the time. At other times? A bigger thrill shivered.

"Don't worry." I drew my hatpin a few inches from my boater and shoved it back in again. "I do have defenses, if you remember." I referred to the time I'd stabbed this same enamel-headed pin right through the cheek of a very bad man. He'd yelled like a baby right up until the police arrested him.

The reminder drew a grin. "Who could forget?" Grat said. "But you might not always be so lucky."

By this time we were nearly home and I

had no reason to argue further.

Home is a brick building butted right up against others of its ilk. The Doyle & Howe Detective Agency occupies the street level, and consists of the main room, a smaller, private room, and a largish area off the rear entrance. Stairs to the second floor jut upwards from there, with a commodious closet beneath them. The hall, as one might expect, is always dark and gloomy.

We met my uncle Monk, with whom I live on the building's upper floor, just leaving the office as we arrived. Although he was tickled pink to discover how well Gratton's and my operation had transpired, he, too, had heard about the accident at the Corbin Park Racetrack and was anxious to acquire firsthand news.

"May be something there for us," he told Grat as he gave Nimble a pat on her funny little head. "I just got off the telephone with one of the racing commissioners, a feller named Lloyd Branston, a minute ago. He said the race committee heard there might be foul play involved and they want to relieve the public's mind. Says they prefer their own people to look into it. Somebody other than the police. If we work it right, they'll hire us."

Poor Lars. Even on the occasion his

integrity was intact, he and the force were regarded with suspicion. And what did I know? He could even be at the center of this tragedy.

"I'll be right with you." Gratton turned to me, his need for action sparking from his eyes, and written all over his handsome face. "Put the bond and the gold in the safe, China. I'll get in touch with our client as soon as I get back."

I nodded. "I'll prepare the bill for him." It would give me something to do while the men were gone.

"Wait." He frowned. "We need to talk about the charges."

"No we don't. Ten percent. Mr. Mickelson agreed to the deal and he signed the contract."

Gratton enjoyed the fruits of our labor well enough — much increased since I'd taken over keeping the agency's books. He just had a problem with underrating the cost of his . . . our . . . services.

"Leave those details to China," Uncle Monk broke in. "She knows what she's doing. Let's go, Grat. Need to get to the track before Hansen's bunch muddies up the scene."

My uncle is very good about supporting me, bless his soul.

As soon as they left, I let Nimble into the backyard and waved to our neighbor as he dumped an armload of wood shavings atop a steadily growing pile. Cosimo Pinelli, a recent Italian immigrant, had acted as my bodyguard more than once. Judging by the increased sawdust, his cabinetmaking business was picking up as the economy slowly recovered from the panic of 1893.

Inside, I did as Gratton had asked, stowing away the bearer's bond and coins and giving a sigh of relief when they were safe. Only then did I draw the nine-inch hatpin from my hair and remove my boater. Jimsy, I reflected, twisting the pin between my fingers, should've had such an implement to keep his hat in place. Although, for the sake of our detective agency, I was grateful he hadn't. Our client would be grateful, as well.

Suppertime came and went before Monk and Gratton returned to the office. They were as subdued as I'd ever seen them, shaken by the sight of two dead racehorses and the mangled body of one young man.

"Pretty grisly." Monk shook his head in sorrow. "Met the boy's mother and grandfather. Hell'uva deal."

"Sad. I still can't quite figure what happened." For Grat, admitting as much meant a puzzle indeed. "I'm glad you weren't there, China."

Me, too, as I freely admitted.

The annual fall Interstate Fair and Race Meet was supposed to be a time of family fun and friendly competition, although for some, friendly didn't enter into the equation. A good many people took the races more seriously. Look at Jimsy Woodsmith and the folks he'd swindled.

"The jockey was only a kid." Monk corrected himself sharply when he thought I was too busy slamming pots on the cookstove to hear what he was saying. "A boy. Looked about twelve."

"Sixteen," Grat said. "I heard his mother tell Shave Johnson."

"The reporter?" Monk frowned.

"Yes. Funny thing. I talked to Shave myself today, at the station. I wonder . . ." Grat's voice drifted off.

Ah. Now I knew who the man with the worn suit was. I'd seen his byline — and his flamboyantly written version of the news — in the paper quite often lately. As well as being a rather poor writer, he struck me as a rabble-rouser.

"You wonder what?" Monk asked.

Grat's mouth pursed. "What she — the

O'Dell woman — meant when she said, 'This wasn't supposed to happen. They said they'd take care of —.' Then she shut up, real quick-like. She walked away from Shave and wouldn't answer any more questions, not even when he offered her money. And if you noticed, their whole outfit looked like a ragtag bunch of stump farmers who could use any dollar offered. Not like they owned the odds-on Spokane Derby favorite. To-day's race was supposed to be just a warm-up for him."

"So those are the folks who own Mercury, eh? Guess I didn't realize their own kid was riding him."

"Yeah, but they're not husband and wife," Grat said. "Grandfather and mother with some Frenchie-sounding name. I think there's another kid, too."

My heart ached for them.

I laid out plates, utensils and cups on the dining-room table. None of us had much appetite for overcooked food grown dry as chaff. The beefsteak was tough enough to pull teeth.

"Eat up." I slapped a bowl of buttered car-rots on the table beside boiled spuds, milk gravy, and a platter of the beef. It would have to do. The meal had been edible once.

It was the men's own fault if it no longer was.

The thing was, neither Monk nor Grat seemed to notice, chewing methodically and talking between bites. I concentrated on sawing tiny chunks off my steak, Nimble receiving her share under the table, until Monk said, "Branston told me he wants to hire us to prevent any more 'accidents.' He's got to clear the expense with the racing committee, but he says he's had a run-in with Lars Hansen before. He doesn't know who the bluecoats might be working for." He spoke softly, with a sideways glance at me.

My uncle thought I was interested in Lars, silly man. My silly uncle, I mean, not Lars. I knew enough never to tell Lars anything about our business. Lord knows I'd been told often enough. Which didn't stop me from flirting the least little bit with him upon occasion.

Yes. I knew it irritated Gratton. So?

"When will Branston know about the job?" Grat perked up at this news. Never far from any of our minds, the lack of money loomed over our heads. The agency had taken a bit of a hit during our adventure last August. Monk was still recovering after getting shot.

"By morning." Monk shoveled a big bite of spuds and gravy into his mouth, manipulating his fork to keep from smearing gravy into his droopy mustache. "He's worried about something going wrong on the seventeenth. The derby has to go off without a hitch or his name'll be mud and he'll be the one out of a job."

"He will? The racing committee doesn't get paid, does it?" I sipped water, washing down a final bite of steak.

Monk laid his cutlery neatly across his plate. "In a manner of speaking, but they're paid in more than money, lambie. Influence, power, connections. A different kind of currency, one often more valuable than cash."

"Oh, yes, of course." The penny dropped. I should've known. I've learned rich people think about wealth every bit as much as the rest of us, but not necessarily in the same way. "Like Mr. Corbin allowing use of the land the racetrack is on and having people beholden to him."

Monk laughed. "He keeps a pretty close watch on it. You wouldn't think he'd worry about money so much considering the way he acquired the land."

Grat shrugged. "Bought up an unpaid loan. There's nothing illegal about the deal. And he is supporting the racetrack."

"For now," Monk agreed.

Finished with his meal, Gratton pushed back his chair and changed the subject. "Did you get Mickelson's invoice typed out, China?"

"Indeed I did." I couldn't prevent a smug smile. "And not a single error on it."

He grinned back. "Good for you. I'll take the invoice and the recovered items around to his hotel this evening. He should be finished with his dinner, by now."

"Seeing what you have for him ought to aid his digestion." Monk patted his own flat belly, sounding a bit happier.

"Remember the math," I warned Grat, jumping up to begin clearing the table. "Our agreed upon fee is ten percent of the bond and gold pieces, which is fourteen hundred dollars of the combined value. Do not settle for the gold if that's all he offers." It was the best bit of business we'd done since I came to work here, and the easiest to complete.

Gratton, in the act of retrieving his hat from the hall tree beside the apartment entry door, swatted it against his knee. "Doggone it, China, I know. You've told me twice already. And Mickelson will probably do it, too, the cheap son of a gun."

Heat rose in my face. There. I'd gone and

aggravated him again by pointing out the obvious, but really, Gratton was no kind of businessman. And unfortunately, neither was my uncle. On the other hand, they're excellent investigators.

"He'll respond better with a formal bill, the terms set out in black-and-white," I assured him.

Downstairs, in the office, the telephone rang. Being on my feet and the one nearest the stairs, I dashed down the steps to answer the peremptory summons — not to mention escaping a discussion that threatened to become a bit hostile.

"Here is Main five, five," I breathed into the receiver.

"Oh, I was about to hang up," the girl at Central said. "One moment, I'm plugging you in."

"Good evening," a mellifluous voice greeted me. "This is Lloyd Branston. Have I reached the residence of Mr. Montgomery Howe?"

"You have, sir. One moment, please, and I'll fetch him." There wasn't much in the way of fetching. Monk and Gratton had followed me downstairs and stood one on either side of me.

After a beat, I handed the receiver to Monk. He doesn't mind speaking on the telephone; he just avoids answering it.

A low-voiced conversation ensued, during which Grat opened the safe and took out the Mickelson trove. Gold stowed in his money belt, bond in his inside jacket pocket with my typed invoice folded around it, he waited for Monk to finish.

And soon he did, saying, as he replaced the receiver, "We're on. Branston held a special meeting and the committee agreed. Partly, anyhow. We begin tomorrow."

Grat nodded slowly. "Partly? I know Branston is uneasy and suspicious of today's horse-and-rider accident, but what, exactly, will be our job?"

Monk shrugged. "Simple security, he says. See nothing else goes wrong, even if it's something as nonthreatening as a jockey with a hangover and prone to fall off his horse. We're to keep our ears open about betting trends, and our eyes peeled for money changing hands where it shouldn't."

Phooey. I knew the men would never let me anywhere close to the action.

"What can I do?" I asked.

"Mind the office," Monk said. "Answer the telephone."

"Keep the books," Gratton added. "Greet any potential clients with your pretty smile."

Rats! I was back to the small stuff again. I

can't understand why men get to have all the fun.

CHAPTER 4

Uncle Monk awakened me early the next morning — by accident, I think, not design. He was preparing his own breakfast and may have wanted help without actually asking for it. The clatter of a cast-iron frying pan banging onto the stove top was accompanied by a great many *ouches* and *blasts*. Whether he suffered from self-inflicted knife cuts, or scalds from not letting the coffee settle before pouring, I found it wiser not to rise and inquire.

When I heard him leave, I got up, aware there'd be a lengthy session of kitchen cleaning ahead of me.

Nimble, ever helpful, was a dab hand at licking egg yolk from the floor, so I decided against wielding the mop. Monk's lady friend, Mavis Atwood, who doubled as his housekeeper, was scheduled to clean tomorrow. Apparently she liked this type of job. Or maybe she just liked my uncle. I couldn't blame her. I liked him, too, messy though he might be.

Anyway, since Mavis would be there the next day, I simply ran a feather duster over the tabletops, washed up the breakfast things, and called it good. I was happy to get downstairs, unlock the office door and turn the closed sign to open, ready in case any stray business opportunities occurred. I settled behind my desk and turned the ledger page to the current day.

My uncle had filled out one of the expense forms I'd created for him and Grat and put it on my desk. I pulled it forward and began totting up the costs. He universally underestimated the hours he spent on the job, so I added twenty percent to his total and went from there.

Gratton was every bit as careless regarding his timekeeping as my uncle. Sometimes I wondered if he ghosted through his assignments, but his sheet from yesterday's Mickelson adventure looked more realistic than usual. Probably because I'd been with him during the collar of Jimsy Woodsmith.

Although, I noticed, he hadn't charged for my time. I soon corrected the omission and made a note for later reference. Gratton and Monk needed to factor me in. I insisted.

Between the two forms, I was busy at my

Smith Premier writing machine when the door swung ajar. Nimble, asleep at my feet, stirred as I looked up, a smile on my lips.

The door closed, apparently just as it had opened, of its own volition.

Strange. I hadn't realized a breeze had arisen. When I glanced through the plate-glass front window, dust from the traffic on the street rose straight up instead of sideways. No sign of wind there, either.

I'd just settled my fingers on the typewriter keys again when the door squeaked on its hinges, then stopped halfway. A shadow darkened the aperture, but no one appeared.

Slowly, the door began closing again.

"Hi," I called out. "Please do come in. I don't bite." Nimble got to her feet, ambled over and poked her head into the opening. "And neither does my dog." Her whippy tail swished.

"Aren't you a funny one?" a young, female voice whispered. I heard a giggle, hastily muffled.

Nimble's tail beat faster. Whoever the soft voice belonged to must've been getting a licking.

"Come in," I said again.

Nimble nosed the door wide enough to reveal the girl standing outside. A girl, although not a particularly ladylike one, I observed. She was probably an undersized fourteen or fifteen years old and wore loose denim jeans held up by suspenders, a red-plaid shirt, and boots. Hair so dark brown it was almost black hung down her back in a long, thick single braid. Huge brown eyes peeped from within a fringe of dark lashes. Her skin was clear and fresh.

In all, she'd have been quite beautiful even clad in her outlandish male clothes if they'd only fit a little better, or if her hair had been fluffed to soften her hollow cheeks. Or if her eyes had not been red from crying.

Crying.

When ladies enter Doyle & Howe Detective Agency weeping, it generally means a new client and a new problem has arrived on our doorstep.

My interest piqued. "Are you in trouble?" I asked, then chastised myself inwardly for phrasing my question in those words. I hoped she wasn't "in trouble." She was too young and looked too innocent.

She didn't seem to notice my faux pas. "Yes," she said with nary a blush. I got the impression she and I might have different ideas about what constituted trouble. In this case, at least.

"How can I help?" I asked as she finally

worked up her nerve to step inside. I believe if it hadn't been for my dog, she might still have run away.

The girl's small white teeth chewed at her lower lip. She stared around the room, taking in the tin ceiling, wooden floors, and even the typewriting machine on my sturdy oak desk. "I want to see the detective, Mr. Howe," she finally said. Her voice trembled.

"I'm sorry. He's out right now. I'm also a detective." I stretched the truth only a little. "Can you tell me what's wrong?"

"I don't know. Mr. Howe . . . I saw him. He looked kind."

If she didn't stop with the chewing, she'd soon be wiping blood from her chin. A tiny red dot already beaded her lip.

"He is kind," I said. A thought occurred to me. "When did you see him?"

"Yesterday. Last night. After —" Tears brimmed in those beautiful eyes.

My breath caught. Hadn't I heard Grat, or maybe Monk, mention another "kid" belonging to yesterday's horrible racetrack mishap? I'd assumed a boy, but might the kid as well be a she?

"What's your name, if you don't mind me asking?" I patted the chair beside my desk, inviting her to sit. Nimble, no doubt thinking I meant her, came over and jumped onto it. The girl, emboldened, claimed half the chair from Nimble, the pair of them seeming satisfied with the arrangement.

"Neva," she mumbled. "Neva Sue O'Dell."

O'Dell? Hmm. As Irish as Doyle or Bohannon. The men had spoken last night of someone with a French name. So who was this girl? I'd thought at first she must be connected to their case, but maybe not. And what did she want with my uncle? Apparently I'd have to work at drawing her out.

"Neva Sue," I said. "What a pretty name. I am Miss China Bohannon."

"How do you do," she said politely, and glanced at me through lowered lashes. "I don't like the Sue part. Neva is all right."

"Neva. Yes. Sounds more grown up. Although Sue is nice, too."

"My granddad," she said, her outrage plain, "calls me Sue-ee, as if he's calling a pig."

Grandfather, eh? And not her favorite relative. "Maybe he doesn't realize —" I hesitated. "Maybe he thinks he's being funny."

She reached over and pulled Nimble into her lap, hugging my dog against her like a shield. Nimble, who loves pets and pats and all sweet words, verbal or otherwise, will-

57

ingly cuddled close and licked Neva's chin. If I hadn't known the girl needed the solace, I'd have been a little jealous.

"No." Seeming to take heart, she looked me in the eye. "He knows I hate it. I wish I could hide my feelings from him, but he can always tell what I'm thinking. He, and my mother, are why I'm here. I heard her talking to Mr. Howe last night, lying to him, and I thought . . . well, he . . . Mr. Howe, said —" She stumbled to a stop.

"Who is your grandfather?" I asked.

"Louis Duchene. My mother is Hazel O'Dell."

"Oh, so you are talking about the . . . the tragedy at the races yesterday?" I stumbled a bit myself, but figured I was on the right track.

"Tragedy? I'm talking about my brother, Robbie. He got killed." Her breath caught on a sob. "And Mercury lamed. Sneaking, slimy snakes in the grass, both of them!"

Goodness gracious. Neva was certainly an intense young person.

"Who are sneaking snakes in the grass, Neva?" I understood the alliterative to refer to her grandfather, but . . . her? Grat had spoken of the mother saying something strange. Was it she who Neva meant?

58

A second later, she confirmed my suspicion.

"Granddad. And my mother. They got paid to run up the odds on Mercury. So Robbie was supposed to pull him up at the pole, but he said 'no' so something bad happened and then he got killed. And it's their fault."

Appalled, I leaned forward. "You're making a pretty strong accusation. Are you sure?"

"I'm sure." Her jaw set. Oh, yes. She was sure, all right.

"But why would they do something like that? Don't they want their own horse to win?"

"Yes, well, sometimes." Her chewed-upon lip curled in revulsion. "But only when the price is right, like on derby day. Not yesterday. I told you. They got paid to make sure Mercury lost. Well, he lost all right. And so did Robbie." Another sob punctuated her claim.

Her explanation sounded remarkably like the kind of scam Jimsy Woodsmith would cook up. Illegal and immoral. But what she described was not only about money. It was also about a dead boy. A name. I needed a name. "Who paid them, Neva?"

Her shoulders sagged. "I don't know. I'd

never seen him before. But I heard him and Granddad and my mother talking. They didn't know I was there."

"Where were you?"

"In the racetrack stables, in the tack room beside Mercury's stall. It was the day before yesterday." The sentence ended with a gulp, but she gathered herself and went on. "I wasn't supposed to be there, but after supper I wanted to make sure the dray team had enough food and water. They're staked out in an area next to the track. Granddad tends to forget everything with a race coming up — win or lose — and I went out to check if they were all right."

She stroked Nimble's head. "The grass is pretty well grazed out, so I was in the barn fetching them a handful of grain from Mercury's sack when I saw my mother and Granddad and another man coming. My mother had told me I had to stay in the wagon and guard our camp, you see, while they went off to meet somebody."

Her voice faltered. "Although, I don't see why anyone would want to steal our stuff. I think they just didn't want me around. So when I saw them coming toward the stable, I hid. I didn't want another beating."

A beating? Was her family — her mother — an ogre, then, to make Neva so frightened of disobeying her? I noticed the girl never referred to the woman as Mom or Mama, or even Mother, but always said "my mother" in the same tone of voice I used to speak of my own stepmother, who is not my favorite person.

"Oh dear," I said, and although I wanted to ask if she were truly afraid of them, refrained in view of the girl's stony expression. "What happened next?"

"When the stranger said he wanted to see the horse, Granddad opened the gate into Mercury's stall and they went in. He, the stranger, told my mother to keep watch and tell them if anybody came poking around, so she stayed outside. Didn't even argue. They were acting queer and secretive, all of them, which really scared me. The partitions have big gaps and I thought for sure I'd be caught. So I kept still. Didn't hardly breathe or move, even when a mouse ran over my hand. I was afraid I'd faint."

I had a notion Neva was a strong-minded girl not inclined to fainting spells. Much like me.

"What did they talk about?" I asked.

"Money. About rigging the race. About how much he — the man — was paying Granddad to pull Mercury. I think it was a lot of money." She gulped and glanced up

61

at me. "You won't tell Granddad what I said, will you, Miss Bohannon? They . . . I don't know what they'd do to me if they knew I told anyone."

Melodrama or a genuine fear? Either way, it seemed she'd finished her story. I waited for her to say more, but she just sat in the chair and petted Nimble.

After a while, I said, "Why did you come here, Neva?"

"Because of Robbie getting killed." She sounded surprised I had to ask. "And because Mercury pulled up lame."

"I'm sympathetic. And so sorry about Robbie. But why here? Why tell me?"

Another drop of blood formed on her abused lip. "Granddad and my mother plan on racing Mercury anyway. Use the whip, my mother said. Lay into him good and he'll run." She sounded bitter, as if she, too, might know the taste of a whip. "He will, too, even if it hurts. He's born to run."

I was appalled. I am horsewoman enough to know a lame animal may be ruined for life and never race again. And yet, as long as her people owned the horse, they could do as they liked with him. Throwing the race, however, was something else.

"Please, ma'am." Tears formed in her great dark eyes. "I want you to stop them. I want you to prove Robbie was hurt . . . killed . . . on purpose. I want you to put Granddad and my mother in jail right alongside the man who paid them to pull Mercury."

Her vehemence was more than a little shocking. What kind of existence did this girl lead to make her so bitter, even when accounting for her brother's death?

"I'm sorry," I began, feeling like the lowest worm as I said it. "I don't think there's anything I can do to stop them from running Mercury. And . . . are you certain your brother was murdered? Because if he was, you're diving into some deep water. Stop and think, Neva. Would your grandfather or your mother really intend such an awful thing?"

Her lips formed the word *murder,* tasting and testing it. Her hands trembled as they rested against Nimble's curly gray fur. The sunlit room dimmed as a couple paused outside the window, casting a shadow across the desk. Neva jumped to her feet, tumbling Nimble, who yipped sharply, to the floor.

"Who's that?" she croaked.

The shadow disappeared as abruptly as it had appeared when the couple resumed their walk. I got up and went to the door. Peeking outside, I caught a glimpse of them from the back. One was a tall man wearing a big farmer-style hat; the other an immensely fat woman with a pronounced waddle. They seemed innocuous enough.

"It's no one." I turned back to Neva. "Passersby, is all. See, they're gone now."

"Did they look in at us?" Neva's feet did a little dance, as though she wanted to flee.

"I don't know. Maybe. People sometimes do." One of the problems with our ground-level office was its proximity to the sidewalk. The sunshine and light pouring in had been nice as I worked by myself. I'd neglected to pull the window shade this morning when Neva entered, which I often did to help protect our clients' privacy. "I'm sure it's all right."

I tried not to show her nervousness had infected me, but it had.

"Is your mother a large woman?" I asked. "And your grandfather tall?"

She shook her head. "No. My grandfather is short for a man. Years ago, he was a jockey. And my mother is little, too, like me. And like Robbie." Her breath caught. "It runs in the family."

"No resemblance to those people just now," I assured her.

She seemed to relax, if only a little. She didn't sit again, but remained standing by

64

my desk, her hands gripping the edge as she leaned toward me.

"Will you do it?" she said. "Please?"

I sighed. Time to rain on her parade. "Put your people in jail, you mean? And the other man?"

"Yes. Yes. I want them to pay for what they did to Robbie. And to Mercury."

I suspected she cared almost as much for the horse as she had for her brother. Sitting down, I got a pad of paper from my desk drawer and poised the pencil over it. "Do you have, or can you get proof of bribery?"

"I told you. I heard them talking. I saw the money."

"What did your granddad do with the money?"

She frowned. "He put it in his pocket. Why?"

"Your word against theirs about the bribe." I tapped the pad. "And you're a child."

Her eyes flashed. "I'm not a child. I'm almost fifteen."

I leaned forward, the better to study her face. "Proof, Neva. First of all, you need to go to the police. To bring charges, they'll need something tangible. A note in the culprit's handwriting. Marked money. Witnesses. Confessions."

65

"But my brother is dead!"

I had to be brutal. "I know. I'm so sorry, my dear. But was he shot? Stabbed? Poisoned? Beat up?" I stopped short of saying "beaten to death."

Her face puckered. Tears welled as she pounded a small fist on her knee. "You know he wasn't. He was crushed and trampled."

"Which is why it's going to be hard to prove he died by any means other than an unfortunate accident. If he did."

"Oh, he did," she said grimly. "He told me. Yesterday morning, before the race. He told me, and he was madder than heck."

"Told you what?" My heart took a little leap. Start with a name and, if she was right, perhaps I could discover the rest. Maybe this wasn't a lost cause after all.

"Robbie said he was going to tell them all to go to Hades. He was going to run Mercury like he's meant to run. And he knew he'd be in trouble. But he figured he'd have to take a whipping, not be killed." Her words ended on a wail.

I let the part about a whipping instead of death slide past. "Tell who to go to Hades?"

Her face fell. "I don't know. Granddad and my mother, for starters. The man Granddad was dealing with. See, I didn't

66

know the man in Mercury's stall, but when I told Robbie what he looked like, Robbie knew him." Her breath caught. "He wouldn't tell me his name. He said it was too dangerous."

Yes, I'd known Robbie had to have been part of the conspiracy, something I didn't think Neva had realized as yet.

"For him, too," I said. She'd pretty much convinced me.

Her dark eyes rose to meet mine. "Yes."

I guess it never occurred to her it might be dangerous for me, as well. To tell the truth, I didn't think of it either. Until later.

CHAPTER 5

Patting Nimble's boney little head in fare-well, Neva went on her way with a great deal less dillydallying than when she'd ar-rived. Hunched like an old frail woman, she slouched down the sidewalk glancing over her shoulder every few steps as if she expected a bullet in the back. Wishing herself invisible, I expect.

I watched over her for a block or so, scan-ning pedestrians, horseback riders, and loiterers for any who might show untoward interest. No one took the slightest notice of her as far as I could tell.

"Come inside, Nimble." Feeling her mus-cles tense, I hooked a finger in the dog's collar an instant before she could run into the street to procure a fresh horse apple, and we retreated to the office.

"You liked her, didn't you?" I asked the dog once I settled at my desk again.

Nimble, with a deep, put-upon sigh,

flopped down on the floor and stretched out on her tummy, basking in a shaft of sunlight. She gave a quick wag of the tail.

"You don't think she's imagining things, do you?"

The Bedlington cocked her wedge-shaped head as if questioning the theory.

"Yes, I agree. Me neither. But would her grandfather and her mother really be complicit in her brother's death? The very idea makes me sick for the poor girl. Perhaps we should discuss the question with Uncle Monk, or Gratton." I hesitated. "Hmm, I think Monk is the better choice."

I didn't know what to make of Neva's story. Her account of witnessing a payoff seemed convincing enough, if we ever reached the point of testifying before a judge and jury. But murder? A fourteen-year-old pitting herself against her elders? Her word against theirs? Her reluctance to go to the police made sense. I doubted she'd be taken seriously. As for me? I believed her. Mostly. I just didn't know what to do in order to help her. Aside from talking with Monk about what she'd said, I mean. With the men already working the case, even if from a different perspective, it only made sense for me to share this new piece of information. I'd bet the racing commission would be happy to expand the parameters of the investigation.

I felt a little reluctant to involve myself in the business. First, because my uncle and his partner don't always appreciate my involvement and second, because this showed signs of becoming another case of pro bono work. At least the part of it I took on and, though they may fret at managing the books, pro bono is payment they frown over. I do too, most of the time. The difference is, they only object when I'm the one giving services away. They can be careless about keeping records and time charts and getting bills out, let alone seeing said bills are paid on time. Apparently, they think it's the way to conduct business. Hence the fact they were almost broke before I took over the bookkeeping. If I do upon occasion let a few things slide, like charging women and children a fee, I don't see their beef. But still —

I ruined two sheets of paper, rolling them into balls and tossing them for Nimble to chase, before I managed a clean copy of a bill to an insurance company for whom Monk had proved a fraud case. I got it in the outgoing mail mere seconds before the postman arrived.

The telephone rang twice during the next

two hours. One call was from Mavis, wanting to speak to Uncle Monk. She sounded disappointed when I said he was out. I expect she wanted to arrange an assignation with him for tomorrow.

The second call, going by the background tinkle of a honky-tonk piano coming over the wire, was for Grat. I had to hold the receiver away from my ear as the man on the other end shouted imprecations at or about someone or another. He did apologize once he figured out it wasn't Grat on the line. Confession time — I never did understand what he wanted even though, in order to be rid of him, I promised to pass on his message.

The morning passed. Noon found me feeling as if I were aboard a ship stuck in the doldrums. I couldn't stand the lack of activity. Nimble needed a walk, I decided, and so did I. A visit to the stables at Corbin Park sounded just the thing to work off our energy.

With the closed sign propped in the window and a sign on the door telling clients to either call back later or to push a note under the door, we set off. First on the streetcar (dogs ride free on their owner's nickel), and then by foot.

Mind you, I planned on purchasing a

bicycle as soon as I saved up enough money for either a Columbia Safety or a Victor Pneumatic Safety. With a wheeled vehicle I'd have freedom to go where I willed without having to rely on streetcars or hansom cabs or shank's mare. And Nimble could run alongside the bicycle, getting her exercise.

I couldn't wait. Think of it! No more enduring obnoxious people like the man on the streetcar who seemed determined to crowd in beside me — practically in my lap — until Nimble ran him off with a fierce growl. What a good dog. Even the conductor smiled.

The first race of the afternoon was being announced as we entered the fairgrounds. The race caller, his voice loud but tinny, was declaring the competing horses' names through a megaphone. "In position number three, Benjamin's Folly. In the number four slot is Winter Sun, followed by number five, General Grant."

I lost track of the others because I spied Uncle Monk standing outside the saddling enclosure talking to a dark-haired woman. She wore a drab blue skirt splotched with stains of some kind, and a man's red-plaid shirt. Since she bore a distinct resemblance to Neva, in attire — except Neva wore

72

britches — as well as looks, I had no doubt it was the girl's dreaded "my mother."

Nimble, spotting Monk, jerked on the leash. I allowed her to drag me forward. Of Gratton there was no sign — probably just as well.

Monk saw us coming. "China," he said, woolly eyebrows arching in surprise. "What are you doing here?"

Deciding to playing it cagey, I smiled and said, "Good afternoon, Uncle. It's such a nice day, I decided to visit the fair. I hope you don't mind, but I closed the office."

"Not at all. I expect you can use some fresh air," he said.

His reply was nearly drowned out as the woman inserted herself into the conversation. "The fruits and flowers are on the other side of the fairgrounds," she snapped as though I'd interrupted a discussion of some importance. "This area is reserved for men and horses."

"Oh." I kept my voice sweet as sugar while gazing pointedly at several well-dressed women clinging to the arms of their male escorts. "You mean all these women are in violation of some law? How odd." My stare, when it settled on Neva's relative, spoke volumes. I meant it to. "Fascinating. But what about you? Have you, personally, suffered persecution?"

"Me? No. I belong here," she retorted.

I almost laughed. If only she could hear herself.

I sniffed, as if I detected an odor not three feet from me. "Yes. I'm sure you do."

Her dark eyes glittered and I knew she wanted to say something spiteful in return. I suspected the only thing stopping her was fear of antagonizing my uncle.

My uncle's lips twitched beneath his mustache, but I know he was puzzled by the instant antagonism between the woman and me. I'm often blunt, but not usually downright rude. Especially to one who has just suffered a death in the family. But then, I wasn't supposed to know this one had lost a son — at this point, at least. Or even that she possessed a daughter.

With an effort, I reined myself in. "Aren't you going to introduce us, Uncle Monk?"

I do believe he had to think about it. "Mrs. O'Dell, my niece, Miss Bohannon."

Oh, yes. He'd had to overcome reluctance.

"How do you do," I said. Her head, heavy with a large, untidy bun on the nape of her neck, dipped the barest inch in return.

"I gotta be going." She edged away from my uncle as though eager to escape. Those hunched shoulders were something else she had in common with Neva. And speaking of Neva — Mrs. O'Dell hastened to make an excuse. "I gotta make sure the stock is fed and the stalls cleaned. My lazy daughter probably ain't done with her chores yet and now she's got her brother's to do as well."

My uncle nodded. "Let me know if you see or hear anything amiss," he said. "There'll be a few dollars in it if you do."

"Yessir. I will. Right now we ain't even got the money to bury my son. He's still at the morgue until we can raise enough cash for a casket and a burial plot. But like I told you already, I haven't seen anything going on like you described. Just people and their horses, and now I got a racehorse turned up lame with only four days before the derby." She backed up as she spoke, her dark eyes shifting from my uncle to me with at least one quick scan of the people around us.

And then she was gone, darting through the crowd toward one of the stables.

"What a peculiar woman," I said when certain she was beyond hearing. "And a liar to boot."

My uncle stared after her before withdrawing his hand from his inner jacket pocket. I had no doubt he'd been reaching for his wallet to contribute to the O'Dell boy's burial fund. Unless he'd been guarding against pickpocket activity, a wise idea.

"Liar? Dunno about her being a liar but she is uncommon nervous," he said. "She's hiding something. Wish I could get her to tell me what it is."

I smiled. Well, my uncle calls this particular expression an evil grin. I'm never evil, even if I am a bit . . . evasive at times. This wasn't one of them. "I believe I can enlighten you, Uncle."

My words received a satisfactory reaction.

"You can?" His eyes bugged. He and Grat had deliberately left me ignorant of what this job entailed, so I guessed he must be gnashing his teeth, metaphorically speaking. He shook his head. "Lambie, I don't know how you do it. So go ahead. Enlighten me."

"Well, for starters, I can fairly well assure you Mrs. O'Dell will not be carrying tales to you of rigged races."

Monk sighed and pushed back his hat. "She won't?"

"Not anything true, at least." Unless, of course, she was able to place any blame going around on someone else.

"Why not?" my uncle demanded.

I gathered Nimble's leash closer as there was a sudden rush of the crowd to the rail delineating the racetrack. The voice on the megaphone boomed out. I heard — more, I felt — the earth shake beneath the pounding of hooves.

"Because I'm afraid the blame might strike a little close to home for her. And for her father."

Monk turned his back on the track as dust rose up in a cloud and a half dozen horses running flat out sped past us. Encouraging screams and shouts rose to a frenzy. We seemed to be the only ones not paying attention to the race.

In fact, my uncle took my arm and led me a few yards away, until the noise eased and we could hear one another without shouting. Not all his attention was on me and what I had to say. Monk's gaze scanned the crowd, watchful and alert. After all, he was on the job.

"Explain," he said.

"Simply put, because those people are part of the problem. I'm told on good authority they ordered the boy who died to pull the horse up at the halfway pole and make certain he didn't win." I paused. "He refused. Although with his death he ended up doing what they wanted after all. Someone made sure of that."

"How do you know? Or rather, what makes you think so?" He looked quite intense. "Who have you been talking to, China?"

"The daughter." I lifted my chin. "Neva Sue O'Dell."

"Daughter?" Monk blinked.

"Yes. Who is much more broken up about her brother's death than the mother seems to be." I couldn't help the acerbic way those words came out of my mouth.

My uncle shook his head at me. "Don't be too quick to judge, lambie. She'd been weepy enough about her son a minute before you showed up."

Funny. She hadn't displayed any signs of sorrow I could see, but I was willing to change my opinion if Monk said so. Although he was the kind of man who generally believed the best about women. Grat did too, surprisingly enough.

Me? I knew better. Every major case the agency had handled during the time I'd been in Spokane had revolved around a woman. A bad woman. A woman hard as nails and twice as tough.

"Harrumph," I said, which drew Nimble's attention to me. She probably thought I was growling, and I guess I was.

My uncle sighed. "Where did you meet this O'Dell daughter? You didn't go poking into this business, did you?"

"No, I didn't." I pretended affront. "I met Neva this morning when she came around to the office. She told me she overheard you talking to her mother and grandfather last night and thought you looked kind. She wanted to speak with you."

Monk's mustache twitched as he stared down at me. "Are you sure she's Mrs. O'Dell's daughter? I was under the impression —"

"She resembles her mother to a marked degree. Although prettier." And then, just because I felt like it, I added, "And when she spoke of her brother, the tears running down her cheeks were real."

He stood there, not saying anything as the race caller proclaimed the winner of the race. Winter Sun, I believe he said. When the crowd's huzzahs — and some boos, too — had faded, I found more to add.

"Neva, who prefers to drop the Sue from her name for valid reasons, probably never would have approached us if it had only been because of throwing the race. Not a major crime, in her world, although I dare say she disapproves. She wants her horse to win every time."

I had my uncle's full attention now.

"Why did she approach?"

"She says her brother was murdered. She

79

wants us" — I pointed toward my chest to include myself — "to find the killer. Or rather, to find the man who paid to have him killed."

He drew a big gulp of air in through his nose. His eyebrows twitched. "So she's making accusations. Has she anything to go on? Any proof?"

Hah. The exact question I'd asked Neva. I was catching onto this detective business quickly under Grat's and my uncle's tutelage.

I shrugged.

"But I see she's managed to convince you," he added before I could explain. "Do I have your correct read of the situation?"

"Yes. Well, mostly. Not entirely."

"What part have I got wrong?" Definite challenge colored Monk's voice.

"The part about nothing to go on."

CHAPTER 6

Over at the finish line, a shout went up. Horses sweating, some lathered, and all excited by the press and roar of people, crow hopped and tossed their heads as they were led away toward the stables. My uncle turned to look, took a step and stopped. He turned toward me again. "What haven't you told me?" he asked.

"Robbie knew whoever killed him — or had him killed." I talked quickly over the noise. "He told Neva as much. He also told her he only expected a beating for refusing to cooperate. I don't know, maybe his death truly was an accident. Neva doesn't think so, because Robbie threatened to tell the authorities about rigging the races."

"Who, China? Name a name." The finish-line shouting grew louder, Monk more distracted.

I couldn't see what was going on, but with the horses exiting the track, nothing seemed to account for the excitement.

"There lies the problem," I said, "but I think with a little digging —"

Propelled by a punch, a man stumbled out of the crowd and landed on his behind in the dirt. A man in a black-and-white houndstooth suit followed him, standing tall and dusting his hands as if finished with a job well done.

"Lying hound," the man on the ground bellowed, carrying on a detailed tirade that made me want to cover my ears.

Monk shook his head as though disgusted and shot me a stern glance. "The O'Dell boy will hold until I get home this evening. I can't stop now." He headed off toward what had become a wrestling match as the man on the ground had tackled the snappy dresser at the knees and pulled him down. They pummeled each other with fierce determination, neither, in my opinion, very successfully.

My uncle turned back and wagged a forefinger at me. "Don't you mix in this business, China. You know what happens when you start poking in the anthill. I'll talk to the girl."

I nearly strangled in holding back a retort along the lines of "there'd be no anthill if you and Grat would keep me informed and treat me like an intelligent human being."

"When?" I asked instead.

"Tonight, if I'm not too tired."

My mouth opened and closed as he jogged away. I tightened my hold on Nimble's leash as she gave a determined jerk. She wanted to go with Monk and join the fun.

Tonight, my uncle had said. Qualified by an excuse I was positive would come into play. His excuse might be real, a fact I had to acknowledge. He'd been badly wounded a while back. Perhaps he wasn't fully recovered.

Perhaps.

"Come along, Nimble." Making certain my uncle was fully occupied in quelling what would be reported in the newspaper the next day as "a minor riot," I drew the dog to my side. We went opposite the direction taken by my uncle. And not toward either the fairground gates or the fruit and flower displays as Mrs. O'Dell had declared were appropriate for one of my station. The stables interested me more. Nimble, too, as her flaring nostrils indicated.

A few minutes later we were walking between white-painted stables with me gawking about with as much interest as Nimble. The barns were a hub of activity, odors, and loud talk. Several diminutive young men strutted about attired in gaudy shirts, the colors identifying which horse they'd been hired to ride. Older men, still short but not so slim, led thoroughbreds — along with a few animals of more plebeian origin — around in circles; some in a warm-up area, some in a cool-down section. The horses waiting for their competition shone with health and good grooming. Remains of dust and sweat dulled the hides of those who'd already run their race.

Some stall doors hung open, the stall itself empty; others contained a curious horse, its head hanging over the gate watching the activity. Which one of these, I wondered, was the O'Dell's derby favorite, Mercury?

Keeping my eyes open for Mrs. O'Dell — with the intent of avoiding a meeting with her — Nimble and I ambled into the first of two barns. Neva had said she'd gotten trapped last night in an empty stall given over to tack and feed, which was located right next to Mercury. Such a stall sat at each end of the stable, along with another in the middle. It shouldn't be too onerous to find Mercury and, through him, Neva.

The stable was set up like a lean-to, with a wide overhang sheltering the stalls and providing a place out of the elements for people to stop and chat. One of the wizened little men who'd gained a pound or ten, sat in a chair tilted against the wall. He looked me over as I approached. His lips puckered and he blew out a whistle. "Well, howdy, little lady," he said, grinning with a show of four buckteeth. "You here all by your lonesome? How about I show you around? We'll have a good time."

My face turned hot. "Certainly not, sir," I said coldly before I remembered honey caught more flies than vinegar. "Although if you could tell me where to find a horse called Mercury, I'd be grateful."

"How grateful?" The chair legs slammed down to earth.

I felt in my pocket. "Twenty-five cents' worth."

"I guess it'll buy me a beer." His thumb jerked back the way I'd come before the palm flattened into a receiving platform. "Other barn. Last stall, north end."

I paid up and, snugging Nimble close to my side — she wanted to personally greet every horse with its head hanging over the aisle — we quickened our pace. The north end of the barn the bucktoothed man had indicated showed an open area just beyond the wide double doors. Along with a couple dirty white tents, several wagons were parked under some sugar maple trees whose leaves were in an awkward stage between green and gold. Just as Neva had said, the dray animals required to pull the wagons were staked in a small grazing space. The grass had already been chewed down to the ground.

Mercury was easy to find. A beautifully made wooden plaque with his name wood-burned into it hung on a nail outside the last stall. The tall bay inside the stall stood calmly watching the world go by. I held back a few moments in the shadow, also watching. Lord knows I didn't want to come face-to-face with Mrs. O'Dell.

When the way seemed clear, I went to peek in at the horse. He was lovely, his bright coat shining clean, his mane braided with bits of green ribbon. A spotless white bandage guarded his left front shin.

I'd be willing to wager the green ribbon was Neva's doing, and probably the bandage, too.

Nimble showed signs of wanting to make Mercury her new best friend, butting the horse's lowered head with her nose. Until the horse snorted a gust of air at her, at which she shied away.

"Serves you right," I told her.

The stall had been freshly done up with clean bedding. It smelled of summer and alfalfa fields. A water pail filled to the brim hung on a peg in the corner. It appeared Mrs. O'Dell had unjustly accused her daughter of slacking off. But where was Neva now? I really didn't want to approach those campsites and risk running into her mother.

Just as I was about to abandon my quest, Neva appeared from between two of the wagons. The poor girl carried a galvanized bucket of water in each hand. Water slopped over the sides as she headed toward a couple of brown dray horses. The buckets looked heavy, as if to pull her thin arms from their sockets.

I went out to meet her. She was concentrating so hard on not spilling the water, she didn't notice me until I took one of the buckets from her. "Let me help."

"Oh." Alarm darkened her face before she recognized me. "Oh, Miss Bohannon, what are you doing here? Go away. Please, I don't want my mother to see me with you."

"I agree. I met your mother already and frankly, I'd as soon not meet her again. I don't believe I charmed her." I was sorry to see the worried look on her face grow and hastened to relieve her anxiety. "Don't get in a flap. I didn't mention meeting you. She was talking to my uncle when I arrived at the fairgrounds and he introduced us." I forced a carefree smile. "She tried to shoo me away."

The girl took a moment to decipher the last comment. "My mother doesn't care much for women. She'd rather be with men."

We'd reached the horses and set down our burdens, one for each. My animal snuffled my arm in a friendly way before plunging his muzzle into the water. In less than a minute the bucket was sucked dry.

"Do we need to fetch more?" I asked.

"Not right now." She picked up the pails and with a quick glance around, scurried toward the wagon. Nimble and I followed.

"Have you changed your mind about —"

She whipped around, eyebrows drawing together as she interrupted. "Shh. Don't say another word. I can't talk here."

I spun in a circle, scanning the area. "Why? There's not another soul in sight."

"But we can be seen from the stable, or the trees, or from the next wagon over. The man who owns it is trying to cozy up to my mother. If he sees you, he'll tell on me. Please, go away. I told you all I know this morning."

"I don't think so, Neva. Most people notice things without realizing they do. For instance, I'm sure we can use the information you have stored in your brain. We just have to dig it out."

"I do? Really? But what if . . ."

Her nervousness was catching. "Do you want to meet me somewhere else?" I asked. "Is there a place we can talk in private?"

"No. Yes. I don't know."

Nimble, sensing the girl's distress, leaned against her knee. This time the dog's presence failed to calm her.

"Have you changed your mind about your grandfather and your mother's involvement? Do you now believe your brother's death was accidental?" I asked.

Unless her story from this morning was a total fabrication, Neva could hardly deny the race-fixing charge. As for the rest? Who knew?

But she was made of sterner stuff. Slowly, she shook her head.

"Please, Miss Bohannon, go over to the flower barn. I'll meet you as soon as I'm free. My mother won't go round there." Her fingers crossed.

"She doesn't like flowers?"

Neva's lips twisted. "Oh, probably, if some man gave them to her. Except they make her sneeze. But mostly she doesn't want anyone to think she's weak."

"She believes liking flowers or sneezing makes her weak?" I gave a snort almost equal to the one Mercury had showered upon Nimble. "Harrumph. Guess she doesn't know most flowers are propagated by men."

She replied with a blank stare, and rightfully so. Propagation had nothing to do with the present circumstance.

"Neva," a man's voice boomed out. "Neva Sue, where are you, girl?"

The poor girl jumped a foot and let out a little moan. Even Nimble turned to look toward the barn.

I took a guess. "Your grandfather?"

"Yes. Please . . . I've got to go. Hide until I draw him away. I'll meet you later."

She suited action to words, dashing away before I could say anything more. Either Neva's planning or pure good luck had put us on the off side of the wagon, out of sight from the stable. I peeked around the corner to see a man in a black hat with hands cupped around his mouth yelling, "Neva Sue-ee," even though she was in plain sight and running full tilt toward him. Her arrival at his side earned her a cuff on the cheek.

Beast. Any doubt I might have felt about pursuing the case faded.

■ ■ ■ ■

Curiously enough, I did spot Mrs. O'Dell as Nimble and I made our way towards the fair's agricultural displays. We had stopped to watch a juggler and, purely by accident, managed to embroil ourselves in a purse snatching. Nimble started our involvement by darting in front of the thief — just a young boy, really — when he sped off with the purse and excited cries ensued. Between the two of us, we managed to trip him in the second before the leash jerked from my hand. The boy sprang up in a flash, dropping the woman's bag as he fled. He raced away as though the hounds of Hades were after him instead of one small Bedlington terrier.

"Nimble, come," I called, which didn't do a particle of good since she was having so much fun playing tag. Unfortunately, I had to stop and return the purse.

"Oh, thank you, thank you. I'm so grateful," the victim cried, her voice soft and almost childlike. Overdressed for a fair, she wore a slubbed-silk afternoon gown and smelled like a whole field of flowers. She extended a hand, clad in a lace half mitt, for me to shake.

I touched her fingers. "I'm happy to help," I said.

"Why," she went on, "the little imp almost stole my entire week's pin money! My husband would be so upset if he had."

"Anyone would be upset." I peered around, looking for Nimble.

In a worry about my dog running onto the racetrack or some other dangerous adventure, I tried edging away, barely listening to the lady's effusive thanks. Nothing would do but we rehash the adventure and exchange our names, after which I sped after the dog. I turned the corner around one of the displays and found her ensnared, struggling against a gentleman's boot-clad foot standing firmly on the end of her fancy red leather leash. He and Mrs. O'Dell stood elbow-to-elbow, only her hands were on her hips in an argumentative kind of pose.

She stood sideways to me and there was no mistaking the woman's wealth of messy hair or the splotchy skirt and man's shirt. And although I didn't actually see her speak to the man holding Nimble prisoner, I had the feeling I'd interrupted a conversation. A flip of her hand, as though she were hushing him, seemed to confirm my hypothesis as, after spotting me, she hurried away.

She could've been telling him I owned the dog.

Or discussing almost anything.

The gentleman turned. If there'd been any doubt as to Nimble's mistress, my set lips must've been a confession.

He bent and picked up the leash. "Yours?" he said.

"Yes. Thank you." I held out my hand for the leash. He jerked Nimble's head up, surprising a cry from her before handing the end over to me.

I stiffened, ready to lay into him.

A stern look deepened the lines from the corners of his long, thin nose all the way to his chin. Other than that, his features were well put together, his physique straight and muscular.

"I'll thank you to keep a tighter hold on your dog — which I'm about to declare a public nuisance," he said. "You would've been in serious trouble if he'd knocked down or bitten the child he was chasing. The lad was frightened."

His attitude not only rubbed me the wrong way, it caused my temper to soar. Enough so I didn't mince words. "Of course the lad was frightened. Frightened he'd be caught! He's a purse snatcher and because of you, he's gotten away."

His eyes, an odd shade of pale green, hardened. "Young woman, I don't like your tone. Do you know who you're talking to?"

"I don't believe we've been introduced. What of it? Unless you're the chief of police and need details of the purse snatching." I knew very well he wasn't.

If I thought he looked stern before, it was nothing to what he looked like now.

"I am Mr. Warren Poole, head of the fair board," he said through gritted teeth. "I have the power to eject you from this facility, which I am about to do right now. I don't believe your fanciful story of a purse snatching. I do believe you're some little shopgirl trying to avoid trouble and a fine you can't afford to pay."

A rude, and rather uncouth retort hovered on my lips, fighting for release. My better self fought the good fight and won — more or less.

Arrogant toady. As if I hadn't met the wife of one of the other members only moments ago!

"Well, Mr. Warren Poole," I said, staring him in the eye, "I, on the other hand, believe that while you are one of the *four* fair board members, and that you have the power to eject my dog and me, you're on the wrong track. Your other two conclusions are quite erroneous."

He seized my upper arm in a strong grip, crushing the full sleeve of my shirtwaist into the flesh beneath it, and began towing me along.

"Ouch! You're hurting me." I glared at him. Nimble growled with a show of fierce white teeth, earning herself a kick, which she easily dodged.

"Yoohoo! Miss Bohannon." A woman's cry broke into a pained reflection of the bruises I'd soon have. "Miss Bohannon, please wait up."

Recognizing her voice, I stopped in my tracks. Trying to ignore the ache in my arm, I turned to face Mrs. Lloyd Branston, the purse-snatching victim. To tell the truth, I was happy to see her, if only because Poole's grip noticeably slackened.

"Dear Miss Bohannon," Mrs. Branston said breathlessly as she approached, "I don't know where my manners are this afternoon. Please, won't you allow me to reward you and your dear little doggie for saving me from that horrible young person?"

She stood out like a Christmas cupcake in a basket of biscuits as simpering, she twinkled up at Poole. "Good day, Mr. Poole. You're a member of the fair board, are you not? I recognize you from a meeting you had with my husband a few weeks ago. I am Mrs. L. L. Branston."

He bowed. "Warren Poole, madam, at your service."

"Oh, just the person I need to see, then." She laughed. "Although it's not my service, but Miss Bohannon's with which you should be concerned. Did she tell you she saved my purse from a boy who stole it right out of my hand? And her little doggie gave chase. I owe her such a debt, and I dare say the fair board does as well. We certainly don't want word to get around about boys at our fair who grab purses right out of one's hands!"

"No, indeed we don't, Mrs. Branston." Red mottled Poole's face. He avoided even glancing at me.

Mrs. Branston didn't seem to notice his discomfiture as she rushed on. "I know my husband would want me personally to reward you as well, Miss Bohannon. He keeps telling me I shouldn't carry so much cash."

I couldn't help myself. I grinned at Poole — or maybe my expression was more of a smirk. At any rate, I went on to thank Mrs. Branston for thanking me (it all became a bit confusing) and to turn down the reward she offered. I hadn't, after all, nor had

Nimble, succeeded in capturing the thief. We agreed to hope he'd been frightened away from a life of crime by Nimble's and my efforts.

Or so I told Mrs. Branston. I didn't believe it for a second. Neither did Poole, and by the flash of his green grape eyes, I could tell he'd still rather have collared me. Alas for him.

And alas for me, too. While I hadn't made any progress on discovering Robbie O'Dell's killer, I'd found a surefire way to make enemies in high places.

CHAPTER 7

My impatience like a rash I'd best not
scratch, I'd almost given up on meeting with
Neva when finally I spotted her slinking
around the door to the gardening section.
Once inside, she quickly melded into the
shadows. The girl was an expert at hiding in
plain sight, a knack I promised myself to
emulate.

Nimble and I had observed every vase of
flowers, some of which almost made me
want to try my hand at their cultivation.
We'd admired every tray of vegetables,
which included onions and beets and foot-
long carrots, along with every pile of glori-
ously scented melons. Twice. Nevertheless,
just how much attention can one shower
upon such items when they're not even
available to purchase? They just made me
hungry.

I went to join Neva in a secluded area near
the door where giant sunflowers and dried

corn stalks made a bower over our heads. She appeared relieved to see me.

"At last," I breathed. "I'd begun to think your grandfather was holding you hostage." Actually, I'd wondered if, for all Neva's bold words of retribution involving her relatives, consideration of what they would do to punish her had frightened her into staying away.

"Granddad, he kept finding things for me to do. Please, I can't stay long." She pushed a lock of sweaty hair from her forehead and took a deep, shaky breath. "What do you need from me?"

Cooperation, for starters, I thought, but said, "I need a description of the man who paid off your grandfather." I smiled, trying to put her at ease.

"A description?"

It was as if she'd never heard the word before. "Yes. I need to know what he looks like."

Her dark eyes went wide and panicky. "Oh, Miss Bohannon, I don't know. When I saw Granddad and my mother and the stranger coming, I hid. It was awfully dark in the stable and I didn't want to look. I thought if I did they'd somehow know and catch me. And then my granddad would slap me. Or my mother would, or make me fast for a day."

"Fast?"

"Yes."

The situation struck me as a scene copied from a Charles Dickens novel. David Copperfield came to mind. Was any of it even real?

Yes. At least one fact remained, Gratton and Monk were working the race meet to prevent the kind of thing that had led to Robbie O'Dell's death. Or murder, according to his sister. If this wasn't just some kind of act. And I didn't believe it was.

A perambulator containing one of the ugliest children I'd ever seen mashed into my legs. "We can't stand here." I clutched a sturdy-looking cornstalk to help me remain upright, its dry leaves crumpling to powder in my hand. I rubbed the dust onto my skirt and guiltily looked around. "We're right on the path to the public toilets. Not a good place if one wants to remain unobserved."

So, although I'd already practically admired the petals off the blooms, we traversed the flower section once again. Blending, I hoped, with the crowd. It was easy to pretend we were discussing the displays as many others were doing.

"Now, for a description. What was the man wearing?" I asked Neva.

Her eyes widened. "Wearing? I don't

know. What difference does it make? Anyway, he may have changed his clothes by now."

"A distinct possibility, but the clothing he had on last night may give clues to his profession. For instance, see the gentleman with the white hair and bushy mustache over there?" I pointed at the back of a man walking a few steps ahead of us. "Do you suppose he's a banker? Or maybe a baker?"

She gawked, then shifted her scornful gaze to me. "No. Neither."

"What makes you think not?"

"Look at him. He's one of those sawmill men, for sure. There's even sawdust in the cuff of his pants. Besides, those men always wear heavy plaid shirts and suspenders, just like he is. Funny to see him viewing all these flowers, though."

"So, you agree you can tell something about people by the clothing they wear?"

"I guess so." Her eyes glazed over as she stared at a mason jar full of pink and yellow gladiola blooms. They had probably been beautiful yesterday. "He dressed like a banker." She sounded surprised. "Real natty, and he wore shiny shoes. I guess I noticed because he went out of his way to avoid a pile of droppings in the barn aisle."

"Good, Neva, excellent." I patted her

shoulder. "What else? Did he wear a hat?"

"Yes. One with a narrow brim, as if he didn't need it to keep the sun off his head." She paused and looked thoughtful. "There was a red feather in the band."

We strolled over to where some spiky, many-petaled purple blooms drooped in their vase. I touched one and found, to my surprise, the flower soft. "Was he tall, short, stocky, thin? Was he stooped or did he limp?"

My questioning had become like a game to her. Neva's enthusiasm grew. "Fairly tall. When he stood beside Granddad, he was a lot taller. He's not fat, but not thin, either."

"And his walk?"

This brought on a frown. "Well, he wasn't stooped and he didn't limp. He just walked like everybody else."

"Really?" I indicated a down-at-the-heels young man shuffling toward the toilets. "Like him?"

"Oh." Neva seemed surprised. "No. Not at all. Head held high, and my mother and Granddad had to trot to keep up with him."

We soon established the man who'd paid off her grandfather was well-spoken, with something of an accent. "Upper-class," Neva said, as if she'd been discriminating between such attributes all her life. "Like

102

rich men talk."

She glanced around the cavernous room. Watching for her mother, I suspected, although the noisy, shifting crowd made it difficult to separate out a person from more than a few feet away. And certainly difficult to hear any individual conversation.

Her nervousness was catching. I sensed how badly she wanted to get away, but I needed more from her.

"Very good, Neva. You've given me something to go on. If, by chance, you learn his name, I need you to drop everything and come tell me." As a matter of fact, I had a name forming in my mind right now. Had I not just observed Mrs. O'Dell meeting with Poole? He certainly fit the bill Neva had presented.

"Yes, ma'am. I will." She was getting a little twitchy. "Please, I need to go now, before Granddad misses me. But" — she paused to chew her lip — "there is one thing I want to ask."

"What is it?"

"Robbie . . . my brother . . . I want to see him. Please, will you go with me?"

"At the undertakers? Oh, honey, are you sure?" How badly had the boy been damaged in the fall? Badly enough to give her nightmares? "In any case, you must ask your

103

mother. I don't know where his bod . . .
where they have taken him."

"I know. And I know Granddad says
there's no money for a proper funeral.
Anyway, he says, Robbie wouldn't care.
Plant him anywhere. One place is as good
as another." Her face reddened and her eyes
blinked rapidly in an effort to hold back
tears. "But I care. Just like Robbie would if
it were me dead and laid out on a slab. I
want to tell him good-bye by myself, without
them." Her voice broke.

"Surely your mother . . . ," I began, but
she cut me off.

"She told me I had no business looking at
his dead body. She said I should remember
him as he was."

My heart ached for the girl. I'd been told
the very same thing when my father died.
My stepmother hadn't wanted to deal with
my feelings, only her own. I suspected Mrs.
O'Dell was cut from the same cloth. And
yet, if the boy had been badly torn up,
perhaps she was right. Perhaps seeing Robbie's body would only hurt Neva more.

"Why don't you give it a day or two," I
suggested. "Then, when the undertaker has
finished his . . ."

She interrupted again. "I told you! There's
not going to be an undertaker or even a

service. I heard Granddad say. The county will put . . . they'll dump . . . Robbie's body into an unmarked grave and that'll be the end of it." She waved her hands, nearly knocking over a vase of dark-red flowers in her agitation.

I'd never heard of such callous people. In my time at Doyle & Howe Detective Agency I'd met up with some evil, wicked criminals, but even they had shown care for their families.

"Say you'll go with me," she begged. "Please. They might even bury him tomorrow, as soon as the police say they're done with their investigation."

A dull ache pounded behind my eyes. Investigation? I had some experience with the way the police handle the death of a poor young person in this city, and I was not impressed. A couple patrolmen would probably talk it over and decide on the easiest course of action. Upon which they would, of course, declare Robbie's death an accident.

And maybe it was. Who could know for certain if no one looked into it?

Regardless, Neva deserved . . . needed . . . to say good-bye despite bad dreams.

I gave in. "All right. If you're sure. When do you want to go?"

Her face slackened with a release of tension. "After supper. Granddad always goes off to play poker with some other men, and my mother just disappears. I don't know where. She doesn't usually come back until late."

Interesting information. I wondered if it would be of some use. "All right," I said again. I doubted if Uncle Monk would be home until late, either, as the fair gates didn't close until eight, so I would be free as a cricket. "Where did they take his . . . take Robbie?"

One of the smaller, less expensive mortuaries, I expected, if the family truly couldn't manage a more elaborate funeral.

"The city morgue," Neva said. She touched one of the blooms in front of her with a gentle forefinger. The petals dropped, leaving the center bald.

"The city morgue," I repeated. My heart thudded. Gratton had told me about the place, about the gruesome doings that went on there. I didn't actually want to see it for myself.

CHAPTER 8

When my father died, I, like Neva, had ignored the advice about remembering our loved ones as they were. I'd seen his body before the undertaker got to him and, although the memory still made my breath catch, in a perverse sort of way I was glad. He'd looked quiet, at peace, even though he hadn't, as some folks tried to tell me, appeared as though he were asleep. In plain truth, he looked dead. I've always thought it made acceptance of his loss easier — or at least faster.

Now, although my mind said supporting Neva's expedition was harebrained in the extreme, I'd agreed to meet her on the corner outside the police station at seven o'clock. I knew the morgue occupied a room in the station basement. And, since I'd really rather nobody saw me there, accessing it without being seen made me a bit nervous.

We had one thing in our favor. At this time of the day the place should be as deserted as it ever got. Except for the dead, of course.

The evening, clear enough to see all they way to Mica Peak, with stars and a rising quarter moon shining overhead, was warm for late September. I wore a sweater and needed a coat. I'd left Nimble sleeping on my bed at home, and found myself wishing for the comfort of her presence as I waited for Neva.

Having arrived before Neva, I bounced on my toes in an effort to stay warm. Thankfully, after only a few moments, I spotted her hurrying along the sidewalk in the oddly hunched stance she assumed. She wore the same trousers and shirt as this afternoon, although the shirt's sleeves were rolled down over her arms. A small defense against the almost-frosty night. Or was she covering up new bruises?

"There you are," I said as she approached. "I wondered if you'd actually show up."

And if she hadn't, I knew she had an excuse. Even in the poor light the hand-shaped mark on her cheek glowed red. Judging by the hand's size, I guessed she'd somehow displeased her mother.

"Sorry." Her voice sounded an octave lower than usual, as if she'd been crying —

or screaming. "Have you been waiting long?" She avoided looking me in the eye.

"No, no. You're fine. We agreed to meet after dark." I gestured at the sky where a tiny streak of pink light lingered. "And we're not quite there yet."

Isn't it true some people think ten minutes late is right on time?

"Oh. It seemed like it took forever for me to get here. Your uncle came. He talked to me. I don't think he believed anything I said."

"No?" That didn't sound like my uncle.

She shook her head. "And my mother slapped me for talking out of turn."

I'd be willing to bet Neva hadn't said enough.

The girl's teeth chattered, although I don't think it was from the cold. If the run-in with her mother was not to blame, I suspected she might be rethinking her decision to view her brother.

"We can call this off, you know," I said. "We don't have to go in."

Neva was nothing if not steadfast. "We're here now, and I want to see Robbie."

I confess I didn't, but I'd promised. Rash of me, and a little late to go back on my word when we stood on the morgue's doorstep.

Considering Gratton and Monk's reluctance to include me in any dealings with the police department, I made the decision to be ultra circumspect. "Before we go barging in, let me scout the area. It would probably be best if no one spots us."

She looked at me with a puzzled expression. "Why? I don't care whether they do or whether they don't." She paused. "Unless they try to prevent me from seeing Robbie."

"They might try. You're so young."

Her eyes were huge in her drawn face. "I'm not so young," she said, and in this moment, I could believe it.

I asked her to stand beside a horse and buggy tied at the hitching rack and act as though waiting for someone. She could see my wave indicating when the coast was clear from there. Scampering up the entry steps, I peered into the station lobby.

I'd heard seven was a sort of dead hour in the police department, which had been part of my plan. It struck at a time after supper, but before men had gotten too liquored up and the patrolmen busied themselves bringing in drunks. My uncle thought I didn't — or shouldn't — know about such things. Gratton was a bit more forthcoming. And a very good thing, too.

I spied the blue-clad back of the desk officer as he headed off down the corridor toward the rear of the building. The cells were there, as well as the latrine, which I hoped was his destination. If so, Neva and I had a couple minutes to gain our objective.

The basement entrance was located a few steps to the right of the station door. Once in the main room, I glanced around. Coast clear, I waved Neva inside. With her eyes wide and her face pale, she looked guilty as sin. Together, we dashed for the stairway.

Halfway down the stone steps, a stench rose to greet us. I gagged. Neva's throat worked and she seemed to have trouble swallowing.

"What is that awful smell?" she whispered.

I shook my head. I suspected it was the odor of death, a combination of feces, blood, and rot. I didn't know how to explain the source to her. I didn't like to think of it myself.

"Try to ignore the stink," I said. "You'll get used to it." Or so Gratton had once told me.

Her cold little hand reached for mine and gripped hard. We crept the final five treads to the bottom, reaching a rough cement hallway — a very dark hallway — with four doors opening off it. One, I knew, was a cell reserved for those accused of the most heinous crimes, who, reluctant to confess, were brought to reconsider. Helpfully, one of the doors bore a sign saying "coroner's office." One, opened by mistake, led to a collection of musty mops and buckets and assorted supplies. It seemed obvious we wanted the last room.

Well, not wanted, exactly.

About the time Neva finished squeezing all the blood from my fingers, we heard footsteps pounding overhead and, in a bit of a panic, we ducked inside.

The door closed with a soft *snick* behind us. I reached for the chain dangling overhead and gave it a yank, tripping the electric light. Slowly, the bulb warmed. The light grew.

The morgue's chill raised goose bumps on my arms. I have no idea how such an icy temperature was accomplished, except for it being an underground facility. Perhaps the ice deliveryman made more than weekly visits.

A table of the kind one would expect to find in a hospital stood in the middle of the room. On it lay the body of an old man covered to the neck by a bloodstained sheet. A foul-smelling drain lay directly below. A stone sink sat in the middle of a metal counter with bottles and tubes, syringes and knives, neatly arranged on either side. A microscope reserved pride of place.

I glanced at Neva. Her dead-white face appeared frozen, and when she spoke, her lips barely moved.

"Where's Robbie?" she asked, as if I should know. Her eyes flicked to the old man and as quickly away.

The memory of a drawing I'd seen in the *Spokesman-Review* a while back floated to the fore. The subject had been this very room. The reporter had been lauding its modernity.

"Here, I think." I trod heavily, my feet feeling as if each weighed a ton, to where handles stuck out the front of what appeared to be large dresser drawers.

I pulled the nearest and the drawer slid out on silent runners.

Empty.

Pushing it closed, I yanked on the second.

Success.

My indrawn breath must've warned Neva because, her dark eyes seeming as large as bread plates and her feet dragging, she came to join me.

Even without Neva's choked sob I knew this was Robbie because the slight young man lying there wore riding silks sewn from some tawdry green and purple fabrics. He'd been a handsome boy, but Robbie's face, washed now in a gray pallor, bore the evidence of his lethal injuries. A wound the exact size and shape of a horse's hoof dented one side of his skull. Blood and pinkish brain matter oozed from the injury. So far, no one had bothered to clean him up. His eyes, once as dark as his sister's, opened a mere slit. Enough to see they bore the awful milky glaze of the dead. His face, so young he barely had a trace of peach fuzz on his chin, was otherwise unmarked, a small mercy.

Tears ran down Neva's cheeks and dripped to the floor. I put my arm around her waist. "Do you want me to leave you alone while you say good-bye?" I asked.

She looked helplessly at me, shook her head no, then nodded. Poor girl.

"I'll be right over here," I said and went to stand by the sink, far enough to give her some privacy, but near enough, I hoped, to catch her if she fainted. Proximity to the sink seemed a good plan for myself as well, in case my supper came up as it threatened to do.

Trying not to overhear her actual words, I was aware of her talking to him. She said something about Mercury. Something about their grandfather and their mother. How she missed him. That she loved him.

I felt like a voyeur and looked away. A clipboard lying farther along the counter caught my attention. I inched along until I was able to read the attached document. It was the coroner's report on the old man lying on the table, one Otto Pearson by name. Age sixty-two. Deceased on September 10th, 1896. The date of his death seemed to explain the potency of the smell.

I was more interested in the document clipped behind the current work in progress. The one on Robert Duchene O'Dell, age sixteen, date of death, yesterday. There'd been no autopsy. The document was a simple, uncontested death certificate. Cause of death: accidental, kicked by horse.

So. Neva had been right. No mention of murder. And no real surprise. Nevertheless, it made any investigation more difficult.

"Miss Bohannon?"

Neva's soft call finally reached me and I realized it wasn't the first time she'd spoken.

Laying the clipboard back in the exact position I'd found it, I turned to her. "Are you ready to go?"

She chewed viciously on her chapped lips. "Will you come look at something? If you can, please." Her right hand rested on the boy's chest as though trying to feel a beating heart.

"Look at something?" I repeated.

Her throat moved as she swallowed. "Yes. On Robbie."

"Ahh —" I really wanted to say no. But, I reminded myself, her brother was not the first dead body I'd been close to, not even the only one with awful injuries, and anyway, the dead can do us no harm.

My head knew as much, even if my heart didn't.

I took in a breath of tainted air and rejoined her. "What is it?"

Her hands shook as she tilted up her brother's chin. "See this? What do you think it means? Why —"

She must've put her head on his chest. Otherwise, I don't see how she could've found it — it being the welt across the underside of his throat.

I leaned closer. Not a welt as though he'd been hanged, but more like he'd run into a thin, whippy object. Or it had run into him. The skin was broken and had seeped blood in spots. What's more, from where I stood now, I could see his neck lay at an unnatural angle. I wondered if Neva had noticed.

Apparently the coroner wasn't the most observant of fellows either because considering the manner of his death, Robbie's injury should've raised questions in his mind. Unless he was paid to be blind as well as incurious.

I met her eyes and answered her question with one of my own. "What do you think happened?"

She wasn't crying now, although she looked shocked. And angry. "Have you ever seen somebody who's been whipped, Miss Bohannon? You know, where a quirt is used? Well, this looks just like those welts do." Her voice, a little hysterical, grew louder. "Another horse and rider were in the wreck, too, you know. A horse was killed. The rider, the horse's jockey, was Billy Banks. He's . . . he's like a sneaky coyote. He hated Robbie 'cause Robbie always beat him. He'd do it. He'd hurt Robbie if somebody paid him. He did. I know he did."

Her dark eyes glittered. "Billy, all he got was a broken arm." Her voice lowered. "I wish it had been his neck."

I thought a moment, trying to visualize the scene. Neva's description made as much sense as anything else. The mark on Robbie's throat was an odd one, for certain. I couldn't see how being trampled by a horse could cause such an injury.

And yet, what could I do?

Taking a final look, I straightened and

went back to the counter where the clip-board sat. I dug in my pocketbook until I found a blank scrap of paper. Using a wayward stub of pencil, I wrote a small note and put it under the clamp.

Neva watched over my shoulder. "What are you writing?"

"Read for yourself."

"Check laceration on Robert O'Dell's throat," she read out loud. "Speculate. Report on status of victim's neck. Neck?" She frowned, fresh worry on her face. "What do you mean?"

I blew out a breath. "I hope it means the coroner is an honest man with a lively sense of curiosity. One that will cause him to delve deeper into Robbie's death. And then report his findings to the police, who will, I trust, see Billy Banks gets his comeuppance."

"My mother says —" Neva stopped. "Will any of this do any good?"

"I don't know. We can only try."

She looked at my note again. "You didn't sign this."

The comment drew a snort from me. "No. I most certainly didn't." Shudders! If Monk or Grat, or even worse, Lars, knew I'd been here, I'd be in the soup yet again.

"Your note . . ." Neva hesitated. "It

doesn't mean you'll stop investigating, does it?"

"If the police take over, I won't have to."

As though on cue, the heavy tread of footsteps resounded on the floor outside. They stopped at the morgue door. I tossed the clipboard back on the counter and stepped away. Then, before Neva or I had time to do more than exchange a wide-eyed look — panic-stricken on her part, less so, I'm almost certain, on mine — the door crashed open. A tall man in blue stood there, his baton held in a defensive position. The officer from the desk lurked in his shadow.

"See," the desk officer said triumphantly. "Told you I seen light under the door and heard someone down here. I knew it wasn't the doc. He went home an hour ago."

"Well, well, if it isn't Miss China Bohannon," Lars Hansen said, fulfilling a third of my fears. "If somebody'd given me a half dozen guesses, I'd probably have got it in two, three at the most. What are you doing here? And who is this?"

His severe gaze fell on poor Neva, who seemed to shrivel under his glare. "Leading this young lady into trouble, are you?" He shook his baton at me. "What's Monk going to say?"

CHAPTER 9

"But Uncle Monk," I said, "the girl, Neva O'Dell, asked for my help and she looked so desperate I hated to say no."

My uncle snorted. "Try your puny excuses on somebody else, China. You didn't want to tell her no."

"Oh, but really, that isn't how it happened at all." My words tumbled over each other as I rushed through my denial yet again. The conversation had become repetitious. We'd already been over it twice.

We sat across from each other at the scarred oak kitchen table in the apartment a floor above the office. Monk was in the process of buying the building and since I'd arrived and begun keeping the books and running the office — which included billing and the handling of expenses — the bank payments were now up to date.

Did I get any credit for this? Not much. Just a notation on a sign outside with the words *Miss China Bohannon, Office Manager* in small — very small — print beneath Monk and Grat's names.

My uncle shook his head. He knows me very well considering I've only lived here with him since June. I daresay we've packed a lot of living into these few months, more than most families see in a dozen years, if ever. He says I'm no mystery; I'm just as headstrong and impulsive as my mother — his sister — was. I take it for a compliment.

Still, no matter how many times or ways I repeated how I got involved, he wouldn't be convinced.

Monk brushed crumbs from his mustache. He'd enjoyed a hearty breakfast of ham and eggs, while I nibbled on a piece of slightly burned toast. My appetite failed as I steeled myself to sit through more of his lecture on deportment, responsibility, procedure, sneaking behind his and Gratton's backs, and just about every other fault one can conjecture. He did have a tendency to go on and on.

The lowering part? He was correct when he said I hadn't wanted to tell Neva I wouldn't take her case. My curiosity had been whetted from the moment I learned of the young jockey's death, and after Neva's and my discoveries last night, I wasn't about

121

to let it go. As a matter of fact, although I pretended attentiveness to my uncle's diatribe, I was actually wondering if the coroner had read my note. And if he had read it, had he acted on the information?

Somewhere in the background, my uncle's voice finally went silent. Then . . . "China, are you listening to me?"

I almost missed those softly spoken words. "I hear you, Uncle."

"Yes," he said, "but are you listening to me? Don't forget Grat and I have contracted security with the racing commission for this meet. We don't need an amateur, namely you, horning in on the business. And no matter if you have been on the mark with a couple cases, it doesn't mean you're a professional."

"I know." I dabbed my toast in the puddle of jam on my plate. "As you both take every opportunity to remind me."

I should've filled my mouth with toast instead of a rebuttal.

"You listen here, young lady. We had a deal. Grat and I investigate, your job is to mind the office. Answer the telephone, keep the books, smile . . ."

"Yes, yes. Smile pretty for the clients." I could no more have prevented the scowl on my face than I could've stood on the tracks

122

and stopped a train.

"Right." His mustache waggled. "Looks like you need a little practice, lambie."

I harrumphed. "But why should it bother anyone if I help Neva? Especially so small a thing as accompanying her to the morgue last night. The poor girl simply wanted to say good-bye to her brother. She was afraid they'd take him away and bury him and she'd never get the chance if she didn't go right then."

"Her mother —" Monk began.

"Her mother refused to even tell her where Robbie's body had been taken. Neva found out by chance."

"Mrs. O'Dell probably figured her daughter too young."

"Mrs. O'Dell is not a nice woman. Haven't you seen for yourself how she is? I doubt her daughter's feelings enter into any decision she makes. Personally, I consider the woman's actions quite despicable."

"It ain't up to you." My uncle's exasperation grew as he took a giant slurp of scalding coffee, burned his tongue and broke out in strangled coughing mixed with a mild curse word or three.

I waited until he stopped. "No, it isn't. But it is up to Neva and I support her."

"Could be a conflict of interest for the

agency," Monk said, "and our job comes first."

I blew a raspberry. "Pooh. I don't see any conflict of interest. You're doing one job, I'm doing another. Trying to do another. That they're taking place in the same location is coincidental."

He stared at me. "Is it?"

"Isn't it?"

"Doubtful," he said.

So. He, and I expect Gratton as well, were willing to ignore those doubts in order to keep to the letter of the agency's employment. Maybe Neva had done more convincing than she thought when she spoke with Monk last evening. This was the first time my uncle had admitted he wasn't satisfied with the official word on Robbie's death.

Robbie's murder, rather. I didn't think I'd wave the murder word in front of him so early this morning. He was aggravated enough without me setting match to the wick.

"You talked with Neva last night," I finally said. "Doesn't her story ring true to you? It does to me."

"I'm betting she doesn't know as much as you think she does. She's young. Imaginative." He eyed me. "Female."

I glared back at him. "She didn't imagine

her brother's death. And I didn't imagine the slap marks on her face. I'm convinced she didn't invent the man she saw meet with her grandfather, either."

His jaw tightened. Oho. He was convinced as well.

We might have gone on bandying words all morning if someone hadn't rattled the office door downstairs just then. An impatient banging arose. A client? Whoever it was sounded quite desperate.

Glad of the interruption, I jumped to my feet. "I'll get it."

Monk, whose knees protest climbing the flight of stairs more than a half dozen times a day, waved me on.

I flung open the door to a gentleman wearing a brown suit, well-tailored to hide a few pounds of extraneous weight, with a gorgeous vest of gold and brown brocade atop a crisp white shirt. His sandy-colored hair and beard were neatly trimmed. His demeanor shouted wealth and power. As though to amplify this impression, I glimpsed a closed carriage drawn by two white horses parked outside our door. A hulking man wearing a uniform-like suit waited at the horses' heads.

A coachman, no less. I almost giggled.

"I need to speak with Mr. Howe or Mr.

Doyle immediately," he said as if I were below his notice. Pale-blue eyes seemed to stare right through me. "Hurry and fetch one of the detectives."

Hoity-toity. "Who should I say is calling?" I stood in the doorway barring entry even though I recognized his fruity voice.

"I'm Mr. L. L. Branston," he said, his intonation indicating he was an important man and I should've immediately known as important a personage as he.

In other words, jump, little froggie.

"Come in." Gritting my teeth, I stood aside and made a sweeping gesture with my hand. "Wait here, please. Be seated while I tell my uncle you're here. I'm sure he'll be with you shortly."

"Your uncle?"

"Yes. Mr. Howe is my uncle."

He removed his bowler hat as if I'd risen the smallest of notches in the social strata.

"Ah," he said. "I've heard about you. Pardon me for arriving before office hours, but I have an important appointment in a few minutes and I must speak to Mr. Howe first." He paused. "Quickly, if you please, young lady."

His insincere smile failed to move me. What had he heard? I wondered. And from whom? His wife, whom I'd met yesterday?

But she hadn't known I was connected to the detective agency.

Wondering how such a nice lady had come to marry an arrogant fellow like Mr. L. L. Branston, I went upstairs to let Monk know he had the racing commission bigwig waiting for him. I found him finishing the last of his coffee, the newspaper strewn across the table as he always left it.

"Branston here?" He looked thoughtful. "He say what he wanted?"

"Not to me." But I daresay I planned on finding out. "He said he's in a hurry. So . . . chop, chop, Mr. Howe. He demands your presence immediately, if not sooner!"

"He does, does he?" Without any particular haste, Monk shook a handkerchief out of his pocket. He wiped his mustache and brushed a few stray crumbs from his shirt front before rising from the chair. Winking at me, he started down the stairway. "Don't let him catch you listening, lambie. He's a queer duck. Might take your . . . interest . . . the wrong way."

I waited at the top of the stairs until I heard voices in the office below. One of them, to my surprise, belonged to Gratton. I hadn't heard him come in. What brought him here so early?

Two probable choices. My peccadillo from

the previous evening, or the lordly Mr. Branston had called him earlier. I sighed. Only one way to find out.

I crept down the stairs, staying to the inside wall to prevent the treads from creaking.

". . . a message last night saying someone from this office was poking around in the morgue, most particularly, around the O'Dell boy's body," Branston was saying.

Drat. My peccadillo.

Lars. He must've sent Mr. Branston the same information as he had Monk. But why?

I hadn't expected this. Ears straining, I held my breath.

Curiously enough, Grat answered instead of Monk. With a question, one of his investigative techniques I find handy myself.

"Is there a problem?" he asked.

I tensed.

"No, no. I'm sure not," Branston said. "However, I don't like it. We — I'm referring to the racing commission — have decided we'd be better off if no undue attention is paid to the boy's death."

Undue attention indeed!

"Any accident is newsworthy, of course," he went on, "but the less notoriety connected with the incident, the better. We don't want to discourage paying customers from attending the fair. This race meet needs to be a success if we plan to remunerate Corbin for the continued use of his track."

"Did your message mention who from this office was involved?" Grat spoke again. "Or why?"

"No." Branston's answer came almost too fast and sounded snappish indeed. "I expected both of you to know better. My only concern is keeping the public safe and avoiding bad publicity. We hired your firm to make it so. The only reason we hired your firm. Anything else is up to the police."

By which he meant keeping a lid on any criminal doings. And the police, according to their reputation, would be only too happy to oblige the power brokers of the city.

For a hefty fee, no doubt.

My uncle said, his voice cool, "The visit to the morgue was personal, nothing to do with either the police or the racing commission."

I sagged with relief, even though his support was no more than I expected. Being family, we looked after each other, even if we disagreed with certain positions. A wholly different situation than the one between poor Neva and her relatives.

"I wonder why Hansen thought to tell you

anything," Gratton said, and I fancied I heard wariness when he added, "Is something going on the agency needs to know about?"

"You know what you've been hired to do." Branston's words and the tone of voice in which he delivered them struck me as vaguely menacing. "No more, no less. I won't have you or anyone from your office stepping outside your contract obligations. Period."

Was I the only one who heard a peculiar emphasis on a few of those words?

"Do as you're told," he finished crisply.

I could very well imagine the stifled retorts and clenched jaws this statement caused Monk and Grat. Neither man takes to condescension — not from anybody. I figured Mr. Branston had just used up his one pass.

A charged silence fell among the men. Nimble provided a welcome break as she ran past me down the stairs, bursting into the office with a yelp of joy at spying Grat. Have I mentioned he's her favorite person after me?

With enough noise to serve as warning, I followed her and entered the office. All three men stood in stiff postures. Monk's face was so red I feared an apoplexy. Grat's expression had gone stone cold. He unbent enough to pat Nimble on her bony little head.

"Sorry," I said, assuming an innocent expression. I smiled. "Are we interrupting?"

I think Grat and Monk both were a bit relieved at my intrusion. Gratton caught my eye and made a preemptory gesture which meant *see me in private.*

No choice. I nodded.

"Excuse us. I'm expecting word on a case, and have instructions for Miss Bohannon," he told Branston, lying so smoothly I almost believed him myself.

Until, with Nimble bursting through the door ahead of me, we got outside.

CHAPTER 10

"Tell me, sweetheart," Grat said in a tone I knew meant he'd rather be calling me some other name, "what in the . . . what were you doing at the morgue last night? Besides getting yourself in trouble."

The best way to handle this kind of question — the ask-and-answer-oneself kind, I mean — was to start out firm and not take any guff. As I've learned from previous experience.

"Trouble? Why on earth do you think I'm in trouble? All I did was accompany a young friend on a sad errand." Head up, voice crisp, I looked him right in the eyes. I loved his eyes, a mysterious deep warm gray. Except when they turned cold, of course, which they hadn't. Yet.

"A friend?" He folded his arms across his chest. "Or one of your so-called clients?"

I took a deep breath. "Both." No point in ducking the issue. All he had to do was speak to Monk.

"Doggone it, China," he began, but stopped when I took aim and poked him in the chest with my forefinger.

"I am not interfering with your job for the racing commission," I said. "I heard Mr. Branston restating your task and Miss Neva Sue O'Dell's request of me is different. Connected I suppose, in a way, but different." Sometimes one had to drive the point home, so I poked him again.

"Don't." He captured my hand and held it. "How different?"

I could see no advantage in withholding the facts of Neva's case. Once he considered the evidence, he might be more open to her argument than my uncle had proven himself to be. Besides, it never hurt to let someone know what I was working on. I had gained a healthy sense of self-preservation in these last few months. Caution is now my watchword.

His lips tightened as he heard me out. "Doesn't sound like much to go on. What are the facts? That her mother and grandpa took money to throw a race? We already pretty well knew they had, although proving it might be difficult. Not unless —" He stopped what he'd started to say and, perhaps involuntarily, gave my hand a little squeeze.

Not unless what? I wondered.

Gratton quickly shifted tactics. "So the girl thinks she saw a man giving her grandpa some money. Can she even identify the man?"

"Knows she saw the man give her grandpa money. And no. She can't identify him." I snatched my hand away. "Not yet. But here's one undeniable fact. Her brother is lying dead in the Spokane morgue."

"Accidents happen. You know they do."

"Yes. And I know murder can be made to look like one of those accidents."

Grat frowned. "People get killed riding horseback every day. All it takes is a stumble, the horse to shy, or a rider not paying enough attention to his surroundings. And when racing at top speed in a crowd of other horses and riders, it's bound to happen on occasion."

"You don't find it suspicious when a boy's death is swept under the rug by his own mother and grandfather? And it's not so common to find the boy's throat marked up with welts and bleeding cuts, either. Especially considering he had gotten threats."

"Welts? Cuts? Threats?" Grat's voice rose. "China, what are you talking about? You sure you didn't leave a thing or two out of

134

this talk?"

"Shh. Not so loud." Our backyard was empty, the ground as dusty and dry as summer, but sound carried well out here, bouncing off the brick walls of neighboring buildings as though in a canyon. I glanced toward the door where I heard Uncle Monk and Mr. Branston still speaking, their conversation indistinct and perhaps a little friendlier now. "Yes, threats. I'm trying to tell you."

In a happy interruption, Monk stuck his head out and said, "Grat, Branston needs a word with both of us before he goes."

Grat nodded, and with what I suppose he thought was a scowl threatening enough to quell any errant detecting aspirations on my part, strode inside to glad-hand Mr. Branston.

Calling Nimble to come inside with me, I escaped upstairs to the apartment, the dog on my heels. Soon my uncle called to me, "China, we're leaving. You're in charge of the office. Don't" — there was a wealth of meaning in such a short word — "go off on any harebrained schemes of your own. I'll talk to you tonight. Understand?"

"I understand, Uncle. I'll be happy to talk with you tonight," I said. Harebrained schemes indeed!

I heard the rumble of the men's voices as they left, upon which I deemed it safe enough to get to work opening the office and taking care of a few minor billings. I anticipated a day of tedium stretching in front of me.

As it turned out, I couldn't have been more wrong about the tedium. The morning, which had started off badly, soon grew downright awful. Although, eventually, the day turned into what was almost a family reunion, only without the family. Just friends. But first, I had to get through a visit from Sergeant Lars Hansen of the Spokane Police Department.

Oh happy day.

Sunshine blazed through the office window. Remember? I don't like to close the shades. Nimble lay sprawled on the floor snoozing in a puddle of light. She lifted her head as the door banged open and Lars Hansen bulled his way in. All signs of drowsiness disappearing, the little dog jumped to her feet, pushed in between my legs, and hid in the kneehole aperture of my desk.

In league with Monk and Gratton, she doesn't care much for Lars. Sometimes I don't either. Sometimes I'm merely ambivalent on the subject.

We started off with this being one of those ambivalent times, until we got to the events of yesterday evening.

"China," Lars said in his deep booming voice, "here you are, pretty as ever after your . . . uh . . . adventure last night."

Taking my fingers from the keys of my typewriter where I'd been filling out a billing requisition, I rested my hands in my lap. Easy to guess this meeting would not go well, not with such an inauspicious beginning.

"I'm busy, Officer Hansen. What do you want?" I asked. He only talks like this when he wants to get around me somehow. Besides, this wasn't a good time for false geniality. I knew I looked quite haggard. And why not, considering the hours of sleep I'd missed? Viewing dead bodies is not conducive to a restful night.

He sat on the corner of my desk and swung his leg in a casual way. "Want? No, no. You've got me all wrong. That isn't my intention. In fact, in a manner of speaking, I'm looking out for your welfare. I want to make sure you understand the privacy laws in this city. I don't want the office manager of this fine establishment" — he was being sarcastic — "landing in a pile of trouble, now do I?"

"I don't know, do you?" Then, a tick later, "What privacy laws?"

His leg kept up its rhythmic swing, moving perhaps a trifle faster. "The ones preventing young ladies from sneaking into the morgue to view the remains of an unrelated person."

Hah! How long had it taken him to make up that particular law?

"I was with a related person at her request," I said.

"You were with a young girl who could've been anybody."

"Nonsense." I was getting a queasy feeling in the pit of my stomach. This was on the edge of indecency even for Lars. "She's the boy's sister, as we all very well know. I went to the morgue with her out of consideration of her feelings. She needed to see her brother one last time."

Who had sent him on this ridiculous mission? Mrs. O'Dell? The grandfather, perchance? I didn't even know the grandfather's name. Surely not my uncle Monk. No, I answered myself. Never Monk or Gratton, even if they did disapprove of my quest. They preferred I never speak to Hansen for any reason. So who?

An answer occurred. Actually, a choice of two.

My queasy feeling grew stronger.

"Who is inconsequential," Lars said, stumbling over the word. Clearly he hadn't come up with it on his own. I doubted his mission was at Mrs. O'Dell's instigation, either. She didn't seem the type to bandy around a word like inconsequential.

I must have made some sort of sound. Most probably one that didn't strike him as complimentary.

Lars gave me a sideways glance. "Her mother didn't want the girl seeing her brother all bashed in like he is. She's afraid the girl will be permanently disturbed by the shock. I figure you're gonna be in deep trouble for smuggling her in there."

His last sentence was the only one I figured stood a chance of being true.

"I didn't smuggle anybody anywhere. I went with Miss O'Dell at her request and we walked right in. Openly. Is it my fault if your desk officer left his post unattended?"

"Yeah, convenient for you, wasn't it?"

I smiled sweetly. "It was. I should send him a thank-you note."

"Don't be flippant, China." His face grew hard and this time I knew he meant to intimidate me. "It don't become you."

I felt Nimble, safe in her out-of-the-way hidey-hole, burrowing in close against my knees as she sensed trouble. Not a shouting match, I vowed. She turns into a quivering mass of jelly when people shout.

"And it doesn't become you to use hostile tactics against me." Pushing my chair back, I rose to my feet and said, keeping my voice quiet, "It only makes me wonder why you've come to the office when you know Monk or Grat aren't here. It makes me wonder who you told about seeing Neva O'Dell and me at the morgue last night."

"Monk," he said. "I told Monk. And Grat."

Yes. And took great pleasure in the telling, too. I waved his interruption aside. "So I've been informed. But you told — no — reported to others, too. Who?"

How many others, for goodness sake? Would he admit to reporting to Mr. L. L. Branston, as well? No. He wouldn't.

Lars stood and pointed his finger at me. "It's none of your business, missy, and you need to remember I told you so."

The murderer. Had he told whoever caused Robbie O'Dell's death?

"Are you threatening me?" I gripped the edge of my desk, trying to still the trembling of my hands. Then, and I can't explain what came over me, I spoke the most unwise words of my life. More appalling even than the challenge I'd once thrown at a kidnapper who planned to kill me during my first case with the Doyle & Howe Detective Agency.

What I said was, "Are you openly in league with murderers now?"

He slapped me.

Hard.

Hard enough to rattle my brains. I reeled backward and stumbled over my chair, falling into it only by lucky chance as my legs collapsed. Pure shock kept me from crying out.

He looked at his hand as though in wonder. His fingers curled. "You don't want to say things like that, China, not even in fun."

Fun? Blood trickled from my cut lip. My cheekbone blazed with pain.

"I don't take such accusations from anybody. I'm fond of you, China, but you want to watch your mouth. Things happen to people who talk too much. And sometimes things happen to the people you repeat it to." It seemed as though his voice thundered.

Another threat made. Against Monk? Grat? Neva?

Nimble crept out from her cave under the desk. She was growling, her little white teeth showing in a full blown snarl, her hackles

141

raised, every combative instinct of her terrier breed at the fore. Too bad she wasn't the size of a Shetland pony.

"Shut your dog up if you don't want her dead." He touched his holstered pistol suggestively.

Put her on the list of those threatened. I understood the hint.

Bending down, I gripped Nimble by the collar with one hand. With the other, out of Lars's sight, I slid open the top drawer of the desk.

"Do you understand me, China?"

His face changed. Smiling a little, Lars leaned toward me with his hand out as though to caress my smarting cheek.

He stopped, smile fading as I jerked erect. I came up holding the Smith & Wesson .32-caliber D.A. pocket pistol Grat insisted I keep in my desk drawer. The click as I thumbed back the hammer sounded loud.

"Leave," I said, barely able to move my mouth. I was no longer shaking. "Now."

"I'm sorry, China. I don't know what came over me. I didn't mean to hurt you." He pasted a rueful look on his face. "Please, forgive me. See, this is what happens when a Norwegian loses his temper."

"Leave," I repeated.

He raised his hands as though in surrender and backed away. "Irish girls are known for their tempers, too. And their waggery. You forget this happened and I will, too. Deal?"

Waggery? Was he insane?

"Go. Don't ever come round me again."

Oh, he could see I meant it, all right. He could see I was one jiggle away from shooting him.

"I'm going, China. I apologize. I'm truly sorry." Hand on the doorknob, he had one last thing to say. "But for your own protection, don't forget what I told you. It doesn't do to be too curious." He sidled out the door so the last few words were almost lost.

When he walked away he was whistling as though this had all been some kind of joke.

Maybe he'd meant me to think the slap a freakish mistake, but he hadn't been able to hide his eyes. I'd made an enemy. A bad enemy. And not just for myself.

I guessed any chance of a romance between us had just gone south.

CHAPTER 11

Nimble jumped onto my lap as soon as Lars — and his obnoxious whistle — was out of sight. Even after the sound faded, she didn't stop shivering for a full five minutes. It took me longer to regain my composure. I was still holding the cocked pistol when my next visitor barged exuberantly into the office. He took one look at the gun and threw up his hands.

"Whoa, angel, don't shoot." My friend Porter Anderson grinned as though certain the gun pointed at him was some kind of joke.

Porter calls me angel when he wants to tease. The name is an unfortunate — or fortunate, depending on how you look at it — reference to our first meeting. I'd been thrown off a steamboat into the middle of Coeur d'Alene Lake and Porter and his logging crew fished me out. The unfortunate part is that I was half naked at the time. As for calling me angel? Ask Big Jake, one of Porter's logging crew.

"Hello, Porter. What are you doing in town?" Unable to move my mouth enough to smile back at him, I did my best to sound natural. My whole head hurt, and for the first time of our acquaintance, I wished he hadn't come. Not at this moment, I mean. For some reason Porter is quite protective of me and at times his temper becomes explosive. This doesn't always turn out well for him. I didn't want him going up against Lars Hansen. Not with Lars a sergeant on the Spokane police force and in a position of authority. By rights, Lars's ethics — or lack thereof — should disqualify him for the job.

Porter opened his mouth to answer, then got a closer look at my face.

"Holy —" He leaned forward, gently took the pistol from me, and uncocked it. "China, what's going on? Somebody been using you for a punching bag?"

I shook my head, but he didn't give up.

"Are you all right? Who did this to you?" His gaze searched the room as if looking for blood. "You didn't shoot anybody, did you?"

Sounded like my face looked even more dreadful than it felt. "Too many questions," I said, my teeth clenched together.

Porter'd had his jaw broken by a brute of a man not so long ago. Right outside our office, as it happens. He recognized the look; the tight jaw, the reluctance to move the mouth.

"Monk and Grat not here?" he asked. Acknowledging him as a friend, Nimble finally left the safety of my lap and bounced forward to greet him and give him a sniff. He patted her absently as he studied me. "Want me to call the bluecoats?"

I'd shaken my head in answer to his first question, but said, "No," quite resoundingly, to the second.

His expression hardened. "No police? Why not?"

I looked away.

"I'll get the doc." He started for the door, but I said no again, and without argument, he turned back, hunkered beside my chair and took a closer look.

"I'm all right, Porter. Honest. Nothing is broken." I didn't think so anyway. "Just hurts. Just a slap." I spoke through clenched teeth.

"Just a slap? Angel, your lip is bleeding and you've got a bruise popping up on your cheekbone."

This time when I moaned, it was because of the all-too-apparent marks of violence, not because of the pain.

"Where's Grat? He better the hell not have anything to do with you getting beat up."

"Of course not! How could you possibly think Grat would do such a thing?" I had to grit the words out.

He sensed my shock and had the grace to look abashed. "For God's sake, China, I didn't mean he's the one did the slapping. He'd rather shoot himself than hurt a hair on your head. I figured maybe one of his cases got out of hand. You know this detective business ain't exactly respectable, don't you?"

The bright spot in his declaration was the part about Grat shooting himself before he'd hurt me. Of course, I'd never want him to consider such an action. Or ever give him cause. Deliberately.

"My own fault. I talk too much." I found a hanky and dabbed at my lips. The hanky came away spotted with blood, but not so much I was in imminent danger of bleeding to death.

"True enough." Porter nodded, an agreement I could've done without. "Where is Grat?" he asked again. "Or Monk. Better get 'em back and tell 'em what's goin' on. Catch the sonsa . . . feller who did this before he gets away."

I shook my head no. It was becoming a habit.

"What do you mean, no? Listen, I hate to say it but those bruises are going to turn purple as a . . . a . . . pansy."

Who knew Porter Anderson knew pansies came in the color purple?

"Trust me," he went on. "I've got experience in these things. There's no way you can hide them under that powder stuff you women fluff on your faces. Be better if you let me get a handle on this for you."

A question was hidden in there. It just didn't have the correct punctuation mark at the end.

I grabbed hold of the desk and pulled myself to my feet. Could I stand? Yes, with a little assistance. Porter's hand under my elbow, I went over to the door, locked it, and put the closed sign in the window.

"Go upstairs. Ice." I waved toward the stairs. "Talk there."

"You bet we will. Here, let me help."

Impatient as I tottered into the hallway, Porter swooped me up as though I weighed no more than a bouquet of those pansies he'd mentioned, and trotted up the stairs with me in his arms. I'm convinced he'd sooner have slung me over his shoulder like

148

a sack of flour, but he was learning finesse. He intended to marry his sweetheart in a month or so, so maybe she was teaching him manners. The thought made me smile.

And wince as my lip cracked open again.

Once in the apartment, he dumped me onto a kitchen chair and went to the icebox to hew a few chips from the block of ice with the pick. He wrapped them in a linen dish towel and handed it to me, oblivious to the fact that the dish towel was one of my best and I'd have preferred not to get blood on it.

"Thanks." I held the ice to the side of my face. Immediately, the numbing cold began to take away the pain.

Porter was clad in his usual logger's duds. Shortened pants, a bit frayed around the edges, heavy caulked boots, and a red-plaid shirt. He barely reached medium height, but was strong as one of his own logging mules. His nose had been knocked askew in a fight and never mended quite right. His skin was darkened by a sun that had bleached light colored streaks in his brown hair. I loved him like a brother, heaven only knows why.

Helping himself to a cup of the morning coffee kept warm in the pot simmering on the back of the stove, Porter plunked down in the chair across from me.

"Mouth working yet?" he asked, taking a swallow and grimacing. Monk had made the coffee this morning. He believes in a brew strong enough to float horseshoes when fresh, the leftovers growing more potent as the day wears on.

Tentatively, I wriggled my jaw. The ice was doing its job. "I don't know what to do, Porter."

"I suppose you mean whoever slapped you not only wasn't some Joe Blow off the street, but is somebody you know and you're scared will come after you again." He studied me. "And he got away with it. It being assault and battery. Think that's the official charge."

He saw too much.

"Which also means," he continued, "this somebody is in a position to do Monk and Grat harm, otherwise you'd have them onto him like stink on a polecat. I figure you plan on hiding what happened from them. Am I right?" He hardly waited for my nod.

"Grat and Monk, they ain't going to like it when they find out. Them two, they're about as tough a pair as I've ever met." He pondered a moment before adding a qualification. "Except for me and my men. But they can handle themselves, and most anyone else, too.

"And that means," he went on, "considering you ain't calling in the bluecoats, it's either one of the police or it's a man with a whole lot of influence in this town. Have I got it about right?"

Unquestionably, he saw too much. My goodness! He might as well have written out the whole plot.

"I can't tell you," I said.

"Won't tell me, is what you mean to say."

"Yes."

He glared at me, then said roughly, "Dammit, China, keep the ice against your face. It ain't gonna do any good when it's an inch away." He sounded just like Grat.

Eyes rolled up while seeming to think, he swilled another gulp of wretched coffee before slamming the cup onto the table. The inky brew splattered as far as my shirtwaist. I don't suppose it mattered. The coffee joined a few drops of blood so I'd have to change anyway.

"I've got it." His shout made me blink. Nimble, who had followed us upstairs and was lying under the table at my feet, punctuated his exclamation with a startled howl. "Lars Hansen, he's the one hit you. Sounds just like him, now I think about it. Sneakin' low-down bearbaiting sonsa . . . skunk."

Sometimes I wish he'd go ahead and say what he wanted instead of cutting his descriptive phrases off just when they got interesting.

Anyway, the mere mention of Lars's name set me shaking again. A dead giveaway to one who knows me as well as Porter does. So then I had to hold him back from taking matters into his own hands. And I had to tell him everything. More than I'd shared with either Monk or Gratton up to this point.

"But Grat and Monk can't know, Porter. Promise me you won't tell them."

"You're not protecting him, are you?" He sounded offended. "Lars Hansen ain't worth one wiggle of your little finger, China, and that's the truth."

"Not Lars. Them. My uncle and Grat. And someone else, too. Especially the someone else. A person who can't protect her . . . um . . . fight back. Please."

I daresay I didn't find it easy to persuade him. But at last I extracted a promise. "I won't tell your men," he said. "Not right now. But I ain't making any promises for myself. I see the bas . . . see Hansen, I'm taking him on myself."

"So I'll just have another person to worry about." I frowned at him.

"You don't need to worry about me. I can take care of myself. Take care of him, too."

Harrumph! One would think his experience with a broken jaw — even though Lars hadn't been responsible for it — would've shown him he wasn't invincible.

After what felt like a very long hour, Porter, satisfied I was in no danger of keeling over with a belated concussion or something, finally left. He was meeting with none other than Sawyer Kennett about cutting timbers for Sawyer's Flag of America mine, he said. I could only pray he wouldn't go in search of Monk or Gratton — or most importantly, Lars Hansen — afterward.

Worry, worry, worry!

Could this day get any worse?

After shucking my shirtwaist and the linen towel into a dishpan of cold water before the bloodstains set, I went into my bedroom to assess the damage Lars had inflicted on my face. One thing I can say; all the numbness had faded after Porter's ice treatment. Yes, indeed.

I didn't look as bad as I expected judging by Porter's reaction. Yes, there was a bruise on my cheekbone and my lip was swollen, but I certainly wasn't disfigured. A dab of rice powder would help tame the bruise.

And the lip?

Let's just say I probably didn't want to kiss anyone today. Unless Grat —

Pushing the vision out of my mind's eye, I donned a clean, though well-worn white blouse and tucked it in. After which, I went downstairs, unlocked the door, and turned the closed sign to open. I had no more than sat down when someone, instead of walking right in, knocked. Nimble, made uneasy by the earlier events, pushed her way into the kneehole of my desk.

This visitor's rapping sounded tentative rather than demanding. A good omen, or so I hoped. But it wasn't.

Neva stood on the doorstep.

One quick look and fury raged through my veins. My eyes widened. Jumping to my feet, I gasped. "Neva! What on earth? What . . . who . . . who did this to you?" I could barely get the words out as I hurried over to her.

"Please, Miss Bohannon, may I come in?" she whispered. She cast a frightened glance over each shoulder.

Looking for whom? I admit I, too, scanned quickly in every direction. No police officers. No older men or hovering mothers. No other suspicious characters, either, not that you'll hear me complaining.

I helped her inside, supporting her until she sank onto the office chair like a marionette without strings.

Standing back, I examined her more closely. Instead of one black eye, she now sported a matched set. She'd walked to the chair as though her tummy hurt, and even as I watched she caught her breath and put a hand to her slim waist. The state of her wrists, both of them, visible now, made me gasp in shock.

But she wasn't crying. In fact, there was not a tear in sight.

"Is this your mother's work? Or your grandfather's? Or . . ." I stopped. Might she, too, have received a visit from Lars Hansen? But surely he wouldn't —

Yes. He would. He'd hit me, whom he often professed to hold in high regard. Why not a girl, even one barely more than a child, whose own mother struck at the least provocation?

"Or did someone else hit you? And these!" I lifted one of her hands. "Who did this, Neva? And why?"

She glanced at the swollen, blood-streaked abrasions around her wrists as though she hadn't realized they were there.

"They did it together," she said, "but I didn't tell."

CHAPTER 12

Bewildered, I studied Neva's poor bruised face. As though she'd just awakened, she stared, with an awed expression, into mine.

"Who —" we said together. Then shook our heads. I was beginning to think she must be the little sister I didn't know I had. Except for her horrid relations. Put Uncle Monk side-by-side of them and I felt certain she'd rather share mine.

"Didn't tell who what?" I asked.

Neva smiled. A little crooked, but a smile nevertheless.

"I didn't tell them where I took Mercury. Someplace safe. Someplace where he can heal."

My mouth dropped open, astonishment most likely landing me right beside the village idiot. "You stole Mercury?"

She didn't take this insult lying down, I can tell you.

"No, I didn't steal him," she said in a tone

156

of great affront. "You can't steal your own horse." Her brows drew together. "Can you?"

"But . . . is Mercury yours? I thought —" I paused a moment, absently giving Nimble a pat as she deserted me to go sit beside Neva. "Legally yours, I mean, with a bill of sale or some other means of proof?"

"Yes, he is." Her head lifted proudly. "Well, mine and Robbie's, so I guess he's all mine now. But my mother and granddad said we were too young to race him under our own colors, so they took over. They started charging Robbie and me for Mercury's keep, too, and then took most all the profits when he won. And he almost always does."

By this time I wasn't even surprised by her relatives' actions. I focused on other aspects. "What means of proof do you have, Neva? And how did you and Robbie acquire the horse?"

She was still wearing her trousers. Pulling up a pant leg, she revealed a scuffed, down-at-the-heel boot, which I guessed were Robbie's hand-me-downs. She reached into the boot and withdrew a calico bag, the top tied together with a brown string. She opened it. Paper crackled. I heard the clink of a few coins, and saw the shape of a small notebook.

She handed me the paper. Short and to-the-point, with a notary seal, it stated exactly what she'd told me. The horse named Mercury belonged to Neva and her brother, Robbie. It was signed by a Mr. Gordon Robert O'Dell.

"This is from my dad's dad, from when he died last year. My mother tried to hide the paper from Robbie and me," she said, "but I know where she stashes things. Her secret cache. Money, too, I mean, like Mercury's winnings."

I couldn't help a quick glance out the window as Neva's story developed. Was someone peering in? No. Just a fleeting shadow from a passerby.

Or was it?

I felt certain if Mrs. O'Dell or Mr. — what was her granddad's name? I couldn't remember — weren't pursuing her now, they would be soon. And after last night's excursion, the Doyle & Howe agency was bound to be one of the first places they looked. For their own sake, they'd best not catch her sitting in my office.

I turned the sign from open to closed and pulled down the shade.

"Come with me, Neva," I said. There

158

seemed only one logical thing, one safe thing, to do.

"Where?" She gazed around as if too tired to move.

"Upstairs, out of sight. My uncle and I live here, on the premises. I'll bathe your face and wrists with witch hazel, for starters, while you tell me all about Mercury. But don't tell me exactly where he is. It's best if I don't know."

She got up. "Why?"

"Plausible deniability, my dear. What I don't know I can't tell."

I'm not sure she understood the excuse I'd given, or sensed any danger in it, but she came with me willingly enough. We paused at the top of the landing.

"Miss Bohannon," she whispered, staring around the comfortably furnished, open room, which still smelled of our breakfast ham and coffee. Her nose twitched delicately as she licked her lips. "Please, do you have any food you can spare?"

As if I weren't already mush, my heart melted. "I most certainly do," I said, propelling her directly into the kitchen and consulting the watch pinned to my blouse. "It's almost lunchtime. You must be famished."

She smiled blindingly. "Oh, yes, Miss Bohannon. I am. I haven't eaten since —" She stopped and frowned. "I don't remember."

She watched me, her huge, dark eyes following my every move as I bustled from icebox, to sink, to bread drawer. Every once in a while her throat moved as she swallowed convulsively.

While Neva made drastic inroads on the sandwiches, I had to settle for an egg scrambled up with bits of bacon. I couldn't open my aching jaw far enough to chew through the sliced ham with horseradish mustard.

Afterward, she became sleepy even as I washed her abrasions and wrapped bandages like cuffs around her wrists. A few dabs of witch hazel laved her bruises.

But it was time for answers. I got her settled on the overstuffed couch in the darkened front room and sat in Monk's leather chair across from her.

I had to laugh and touched my own bruises. "Aren't we a pair?"

As though reading my mind, she straightened. "I didn't ask, Miss Bohannon, but my mother . . . did she pay you a visit? Did she —" She gestured toward my face, battered, perhaps, but no match for hers.

"No," I said, hoping at least this bit of news would reassure her, "but I think both our conditions stem from the same originating source."

She blinked. "What do you mean?"

"I mean our visit to the morgue last night. Apparently there were objections in some quarters."

"He's my brother," she said, sitting up straighter. "I had a right."

"I agree. But if anyone — I mean *anyone* — asks about our visit, our answers must coincide."

She blinked again.

"Our answers must match. Be the same. No variation."

"Oh." She nodded. "Yes. But they will. I wanted to see my brother and you went with me because I was scared to go by myself. That's all." She hesitated. "Right?"

"Right." I smiled. "And no mention of the lacerations we noticed on Robbie's throat. Or of the note I left for the coroner."

"Yes, but . . ." Her dark brows drew together. "Why not? How will the police know to do anything if they don't know Robbie was killed on purpose?"

Good question. A better one might ask what would the police do if they knew we knew? I couldn't bring myself to frighten her so badly. Let her believe it was just her family with whom she had to deal. Or did that leave her open to —

161

My mind stuttered. She was fourteen. My first case had dealt with a murdered fourteen-year-old girl. Youth would not keep her safe.

"Some of the police here have their own interests in mind," I said.

"What do you mean?" She picked at the bandage on her right wrist.

"I mean they've been known to take payoffs to close their eyes to criminal actions."

"Like throwing races?"

Nothing wrong with Neva's grasp of the situation. "Yes. And worse."

She frowned. "All of them?" she asked on a note of wonder and pained disappointment.

"No. Not all of them, thank God. And I'm hoping the coroner is one of the honest ones. I left him a note in hopes he'd investigate further, and take his findings to someone he knows will follow through. But I don't know what kind of man he is, which is why I didn't actually sign the note."

"Oh, Miss Bohannon, he's just gotta be honest," she said fervently. "Do you think he will . . . what you said . . . follow through?"

"I think he may already have. If he went to the district attorney, it may explain why

Lars — Officer Hansen — was so upset with me. With both of us. He may have guessed I started the ball rolling when he felt sure the danger had passed. And call me China."

Neva's face lit up. She smiled. "China."

There was more. I had to tell her about Lars striking me and what he'd said. I had to connect the dots leading from her mother and grandfather to the man she'd seen in the stable and on to Lars. And lastly, I tried to console her with the idea of Robbie's death not being murder, exactly, but perhaps a bit of an accident when a plan went awry.

I don't think she quite came to grips with the latter. As she said, "Dead is dead."

And then she cried.

Before I put her to bed in my room, she mentioned Mercury again. He was close, she said, right here in town with someone she trusted. Sticking to the prudent side of things, I refused to listen when she tried to tell me where.

After checking the state of my powdered face and deciding it didn't look too bad, I left Neva to a well-earned nap and took Nimble downstairs with me. I had typing to do. Clients to serve. Business to conduct.

I turned the closed sign to open.

Just in the nick of time, as it happened. Within seconds my fourth unexpected visitor of the day trooped in. Correction: I should say visitors. The whole Sawyer Kennett family had come to town for Porter's meeting with Sawyer. And, as with Porter, I was happy to see them.

Mostly.

The Kennetts were former clients of the agency. I'd been a decoy in place of Gincy Kennett when her life was threatened by a gang of thieves trying to take over Kennett's silver mine. Instead of her being thrown off the steamboat *Georgie Oakes* to drown in Coeur d'Alene Lake, I'd had the honor. In living through the experience, I'd not only met Porter, but bought enough time for Gincy and her children to get beyond as nefarious a bunch of outlaws as you'd care to meet. In typical frontier fashion, there'd been a shoot-out, in which her husband participated along with Grat and Monk. Somehow, as unlikely as it seems, we all survived and became friends.

Oh, did I mention the silver mine Sawyer Kennett owns is the fabulous Flag of America located in the Coeur d'Alene Mining District? He's rich as Croesus, and as common as an old boot. I think he's the reason people like Mr. L. L. Branston, or Mr.

Warren Poole, for all their airs, don't intimidate me. And after all, my family had once been wealthy, too. La-di-da.

I stretched my sore lip in a welcoming smile and rose to greet them. "Hello, hello. When did you get to town?"

Sawyer answered. "Caught the afternoon train in yesterday. Grat around? Got a job for him if he thinks it's worthwhile." He bent to greet a joyous Nimble before she gamboled over to jump on Sawyer Jr.'s leg. She loves playing with children and doesn't often get the chance.

"He's at the Interstate Fair. Or more precisely, the Corbin Park racetrack," I said. "He and Monk have been hired to stop the bunco men from robbing fairgoers blind."

Sawyer grinned. "I wish them good luck."

Wincing from the pain in my lip, I smiled too. "I think they'll need it. The job won't last long, if you can wait a few days. The fair ends on Sunday."

"Yep. I know. We wouldn't miss the Spokane Derby. One of Gincy's relatives has a horse in the big race."

Gincy Kennett, meanwhile, ignored this exchange to study my face. "China," she finally said when she could get a word in edgewise. Taking my chin in a gentle hand, she turned my face further into the light, examining me with the sharp eye of a physician — or a mother. "What on earth happened to you? Your poor face!"

Her observation drew Sawyer's attention. "Looks like somebody punched you." He sounded awed. "Holy . . . uh . . ." He snorted. "What did the guy look like when Grat got done with him?"

I can't imagine how Sawyer knew it was a man who'd struck me. Or why he, like Porter, would assume Grat—

His wife brushed him aside. "Have you bathed those bruises with witch hazel? Put some ice on your lip?" Without waiting for a reply, she glanced at her husband. "We need another ice plant in Wallace, Sawyer. Let's start one. As a city, we can't keep enough on hand to use for medicinal purposes."

"Where would we put it?"

"How about our warehouse down by the river? It's standing empty."

I sighed. At least my wounds had served some purpose. Beyond diverting their attention from me, they'd given the Kennetts a new way to make money. As if they needed any more.

Sawyer echoed my sigh. "We'll talk about it when we get home."

Gincy nodded. "Yes. Let's get to the bottom of China's injuries first."

Or not so diverted after all.

She'd keep picking at me until I told her something, completely disregarding the fact I'd just as soon not discuss it. However, Gincy is very focused. She refused to let the matter drop.

I eyed the Kennett children. Sawyer Jr. wasn't paying much attention because Nimble had him occupied. Liddy, the little girl, wanted her mother to pick her up. Gincy did, even as she sent her boy outside to play with the dog.

"There's nothing in the yard he can hurt, is there?"

"I don't think so. Except there's an ax," I said. "He might hurt himself."

"Oh, he won't pay any attention. Now then, China. Speak up," she urged me.

In the end, I couldn't tell them the truth. So I flat-out lied.

I'd had an accident with a broom handle, I told them. "The silliest thing. Too embarrassing to talk about. I'm becoming terribly awkward, I'm afraid." I tried to sound amused as I glossed over the incident. Instead, I rattled on about L. L. Branston's early morning visit, and spoke of Porter Anderson. I finished up by urging Gincy to tell me all about Rider, a horse bred and trained by the Coeur d' Alene Indians.

I don't usually ramble on so long. Sawyer bestowed a questioning look on me, but he let my garrulousness pass.

I made no mention of Neva O'Dell, owner of the current favorite in the derby, upstairs at this very moment peacefully sleeping in my bed, nor of Lars Hansen being present when I had my "accident."

Sawyer's interest was piqued by L. L. Branston's name. "Believe your early morning visitor must be the same man I won five hundred dollars from last night in a poker game. L. L. Branston? Arrogant . . . uh . . . feller. A little on the stout side. Flashy dresser. The kind of cardplayer who oughta stick to penny-ante games."

I remembered Branston's gold brocade vest. Yes. It had been a bit flashy. "I doubt there's two men of the same name in town. Especially two with enough money to risk losing five hundred dollars." I was a little surprised to learn Sawyer had been hobnobbing with members of Spokane's upper crust. Didn't they get together at some sort of men's club?

But then I remembered the way he'd become very involved in a poker game aboard the *Georgie Oakes,* part of the reason I'd gotten thrown overboard. Yes. He did like to gamble, and for high stakes, too.

Sawyer laughed, apparently not bothered by the same memories as I. "I gotta say he wasn't best pleased by the loss. Had to borrow money to pay his debt. This Poole feller was ribbin' him about adding it to what he already owed."

Hmm. So Poole was another gambler. Did rich people have nothing better to do with their money than lose it to one another?

Gincy, who'd listened to his tale — and yes, Sawyer was bragging a little — without interrupting, now said, "I'll relieve you of a few of those dollars, and buy the children new clothes this afternoon. Sawyer Junior wears out britches like he's working in a hard rock mine. He simply can't go around looking like a reservation derelict."

Sawyer, without another word, drew a wad of money from his pocket and peeled off several bills. She, oh so casually, stowed them in her pocketbook.

What a difference between them and my poor young client, Neva Sue O'Dell.

CHAPTER 13

The office seemed awfully quiet after the Kennetts left; Sawyer on his way to the racetrack in search of Monk or Gratton — or perhaps to take a punt on the next race; Gincy intent on a shopping expedition.

Left behind by her playmate, Nimble, worn out and more relaxed than I, napped under my desk. It all felt eerie to me, with a queer tense aura of waiting.

Fretting with the desire to talk with my uncle, I decided to go to Corbin Park. With so much else on his mind, chances were Monk wouldn't even notice my bruises. I'd casually happen to mention the warning Lars had issued. Get the worst part over with. I'd simply omit the rest of what happened. Anyway, there was a method to my scheme. Even if my uncle put Lars and bruises together, as long as Porter kept his mouth shut, I could still deny it. There'd be nothing to prove otherwise. No sense in hunting for trouble.

Leaving a note on my bedside table for Neva, who slept with little spurting snores, I powdered my bruises again before Nimble and I — the dog revived from her nap and ready to go — set off to catch a streetcar out to Corbin Park.

Away from the office, my tension eased. The sun shining out of a clear blue sky felt like an extension of summer, so warm and soft on my shoulders. Autumn in Spokane is a beautiful time of year. As long as the weather held for a few more days, I felt sure Mr. Branston's concern about the race meet being a rousing success would be pointless. The track itself would be fast, the footing sure. Grat had said the commissioners had hired a man to harrow the dirt between races.

Gratton and Monk had only to keep the bunco men at bay and all would be well.

We alighted from the streetcar near the fair gates. I paid my admission and Nimble and I made our way toward the track. Our progress was slow, impeded by what seemed half the population of Spokane wandering about. Nimble did her part to keep the area tidy by stopping to sniff — and preferably eat — every dropped peanut shell, chicken bone or crust of bread she found. I could

171

hardly blame her. An aroma of fresh coffee hovered in the air. The scent of roasting peanuts tempted me, a reminder of the bag Grat bought for us the other day. The one sacrificed to Jimsy Woodsmith's capture.

Babies cried in the area where the Best Baby contest was being judged. Losers in the contest, perchance? Above their cries, organ music soared over the fairgrounds. Beyond the fruits and flowers tent, children squealed in high glee. Grat had mentioned a merry-go-round had been brought in, along with games like ringtoss and a shooting gallery. He'd also said the pickpockets searched for easy marks there. I hugged my pocketbook closer to my side.

I was nearing the track where I expected to find Monk when, almost exactly where I'd seen them yesterday, I spied Neva's mother once again talking to Mr. Warren Poole. He frowned down at her, while she shifted from foot to foot and gazed up at him as if trying to appeal to his better nature. If he had one, which I doubted, considering his previous rudeness to me. Mrs. O'Dell looked a great deal like Neva — or rather Neva looked a great deal like her — both of them with masses of dark hair and big brown eyes.

My curiosity drew me toward them. Mrs.

O'Dell's expressions changed with the earnestness of her speech. The corners of her mouth turned down as though she was about to cry. Poole reached in his pocket of his fine gray suit for a handkerchief and gave it to her. She dabbed her eyes, and gave it back, managing to brush against him as she talked. He nodded once. Small smiles followed. She certainly had a lot to say and I wanted to listen.

Especially when one considered what I'd just seen her do.

By fortunate chance, a young couple strolling ahead of me hailed a peanut vendor not three feet from my targeted pair. The vendor stopped his cart and began pouring hot peanuts into a small brown paper bag. I slipped in behind the couple as if I were next in line and perked my ears.

As it happens, I have excellent hearing and Poole and Mrs. O'Dell, no doubt striving to hear each other over the merry-go-round's music, children, and general hubbub around them, spoke quite loudly.

"I've paid right on time up until now," Mrs. O'Dell whined. At this juncture, the corners of her mouth turned down. "And see, I have money. Take this on account. I'll have the rest on Sunday, I promise."

"Best spent fifteen cents of your life. What

girl can resist a man who buys her the tasti-
est peanuts at the fair?" The vendor broke
my concentration. His jocular words made
me miss whatever Poole replied to Mrs.
O'Dell, especially as Nimble took it upon
herself to agree with the vendor by letting
out a loud whine. Apparently she'd acquired
a taste for peanuts. Although considering
she'd choked on one —

I peeked around the young man.

Poole's frowning glance regarded the scattering of wrinkled bills Mrs. O'Dell thrust
toward him with a measure of disdain. "It's
not enough. You're not a beginner at this
game, madam. You know the procedure. All
payments must be paid in cash beforehand."

I sucked in a breath. I hadn't expected to
hear so blatant a confession of wrongdoing,
even though they weren't aware of being
overheard.

"Please, sir —" For an instant she sounded
so much like Neva when the girl was ap-
pealing to me for some favor that I had to
take another look. "— my son has just been
killed. The horse —" She hesitated. "The
horse is a little lame from the . . . the accident. We're certain he'll be ready to run
on Sunday, but not this afternoon. Please,
sir, can't you take today's fee and add this
to it for the derby entry instead?" This time

the corners of her mouth turned up, the slightest amount, in a quavery little smile.

She avoided, I noticed with a wry smile of my own, telling the man Mercury was gone and she didn't know where. Score points for Neva.

"How do I know the horse will be ready on Sunday?" Poole asked.

A pertinent question, to be sure.

The sides of Mrs. O'Dell's nose pinched with the force of her inhaled breath. Her mouth clamped into a severe straight line. "He'll be ready. I promise. Please, will you let me stay in the race?" She put her hand on his sleeve and looked up at him with rounded eyes. Her lashes fluttered. "I'll do anything you want if you will."

What was she saying? I saw a brief flash of what might have been distaste cross Poole's face. And maybe Mrs. O'Dell saw it, too, because her hand dropped to her side.

"Please," she said again. "Mercury will make the race. I'll see to it."

I wondered how she planned on guaranteeing a lame horse's ability. The horse had been the odds-on derby favorite. Until the accident, at least. By this time the punters must've chosen a new horse to favor. So what made her certain Mercury could, or should, race now?

Hah! As if I had to ask. Neva had told me Mercury's well-being didn't matter. Or even, in this instance, whether he won or not. The only concern was how the money got bet. I doubted the event that caused Robbie's death was even unique. Just more deadly this one time.

"Next," the vendor said in a carrying voice. I had to step forward.

"Dime bag, please." I fished in my pocket for a coin, slowly, so as to draw matters out.

At last Poole accepted Mrs. O'Dell's money. "You'd better be right," he said on a note of sour warning. "I'm holding you responsible."

Her persuasion attempt successful, Neva's mother brushed past me with no sign of recognition. I think she was a little upset, for I heard her muttering under her breath as she went by. "Damned girl! I'm going to beat her within an inch her life."

Not a figure of speech, judging by precedents set and the fierce look on her face. She may have hidden her anger from Poole, but she wasn't bothering now.

Poor Neva. No wonder she dare not go home. But what to do with her? Monk was bound to object to yet another houseguest, one who wasn't even family. I just seemed to be digging myself into a deeper hole.

"Here ya go." Squinting at my face, the vendor handed me the bag of peanuts. As I turned away from his cart, I came face-to-face with Poole. I fear I blanched.

"You again," he said, not as if he were pleased to see me. He pointed his long patrician nose at Nimble where she was pawing at my skirt asking for a treat. "See you keep hold of your dog. I won't have her running loose."

"Yes, sir. I intend to." To my horror, I sounded rather breathless, but he strode on without further ado. Apparently, I hadn't really registered on his consciousness, not that I'm complaining. I felt a little like laughing, truth be told. He'd been thoroughly snookered by Mrs. O'Dell, and served him right.

Holding the bag of hot, fragrant peanuts, I continued across the sere and sorely trampled grass toward the racetrack in search of Monk. Puffs of dust spurted from beneath Nimble's feet, rising in little clouds.

As luck would have it, I found Gratton first.

And Lars.

Together.

Why? The question screamed through my head.

If I turned aside, my aversion would be

obvious. Too, I didn't want Lars to believe he'd frightened me badly enough I'd never tell what he'd done. He hadn't. Or so I assured myself. Fiercely.

Even if it were true.

As for Grat, he'd probably just think I was pouting over our words this morning. Sunk no matter what I did.

Straightening my shoulders and pasting on a smile — but not too big a smile in consideration of my lip — I forged ahead.

Nimble, tail between her legs and drooping ears showing her distrust, sidled past Lars to jump up and place a dusty little foot on Grat's knee.

Careful not to let my glance stray toward Lars, I centered all my attention on Grat. "I need to talk to you," I said.

"Here I am." He smiled a little and reached down to pat Nimble.

"Hello, China," Lars said. "You're looking pretty as a picture this fine afternoon. In high complexion, I see."

Inwardly, I railed. Outwardly, I ignored him.

"In private," I said to Grat.

Lars jerked, although I'm certain he hadn't meant to. His cold blue eyes narrowed.

Good, I hoped he was worried.

Grat, covering the movement by scratching Nimble's ears, flicked a glance first at Lars, then at me.

Took a second look.

His expression closed. "Be right with you," he said and turned to Lars. "We done here? Because I got the work I was hired to do waiting for me." He sounded icy cold and decidedly unfriendly. "In fact, there's a woman over there, the one in the yellow calico dress, trying to find herself a mark right now. Maybe you'd like to take care of her yourself. An arrest might look good on your record. Unless," his voice lowered, "you're taking half of what she steals to pretend you're blind."

"Watch your step, Doyle," Lars said. "There's a line you best not cross. Not if you want to continue doing business in this town."

"You telling the power brokers what to do now?" Gratton snorted. "I don't believe it."

For the first time in the months I'd known him, Lars refused to rise to Gratton's bait. He shrugged. "Try me too far. In fact, I wish you would. You'll see. Bad things have been known to happen."

"You threatening me, Hansen? Gettin' pretty low, aren't you?"

"Me threaten you?" Lars laughed as he

179

emphasized the you part. The thing is, Grat wasn't in on the joke. I understood what he meant. He meant to get at Gratton through me. "You ain't understanding me, Doyle. Not at all."

With an obnoxious smirk that included me along with Grat, he swept nonchalantly off in the opposite direction of the woman wearing the yellow dress. He was whistling like he hadn't a care in the world, exactly as he had this morning. The tune was a slightly off-key rendition of "The Sidewalks of New York."

How could I ever have been even slightly attracted to him? The mere idea made me sick.

Nimble, certain she'd done her part to chase him away, growled low in a self-satisfied manner. In the background, the carousel's music soared from high to low, children laughed, a baby cried. Another loser in the Best Baby contest, perhaps? A sudden roar of men's voices over at the track indicated another race had either started or been won.

Grat seemed to gather himself. Then, "Who hit you, China? Him?"

"What? No. Not . . . nobody hit me. Why —"

"Do you think I'm an idiot? Do you think

I can't see the bruises through the powder on your face? Hell, China, you never daub your face up with a lot of female goo."

He sounded furious. He was wrong though. I did upon occasion powder my nose. Just not with such a heavy hand.

"It's not what you think," I said. How I detested Lars in that moment, more even than in the instant when he'd struck me. He'd put me in a position where I had to lie for him.

"No? Tell me the truth, sweetheart. I know something's up because you didn't say a word to Lars. Not one word."

"He . . . I . . . ," I floundered. "I'm still angry for the way he treated Neva and me last night. He was unkind to Neva and rude to us both."

Grat shook his head. "Huh-uh. Try again. How'd your face get bruised?"

"I . . . I . . . it was the stupidest thing. I was sweeping the floor and caught the broom head on a chair leg. The handle whipped out of my hands and slapped me. A silly accident is all."

He didn't say anything, just looked at me. Then, "Not a very likely story, China."

"Well . . . well . . ."

Why did I bother? I had intended to tell him Lars had come around to the office this

181

morning. I'd just meant to omit the part about him actually striking me. Grat was bound to pass anything I said on to Monk and I didn't want either of them to go off half-cocked.

On the other hand, maybe I wouldn't say anything to either man. Someone, aside from me, was too apt to get hurt.

"Do you know you stutter when you lie?"

I swallowed. Our conversation was not going the way I'd planned. It seldom does when Grat is involved and on his high horse.

"What did Lars want?" I asked. When one runs into a brick wall, a change of direction is called for.

In something of a miracle, Grat let me off the hook. "He told me a racehorse was stolen from the course stable last night, and more or less accused me or Monk — or maybe you. I'm not quite certain what he was getting at — of having a hand in the theft. What he wanted is the horse back."

"A stolen horse?" My response turned into a harsh cough. "Why on earth does he think any of us had anything to do with a stolen horse?"

I swear I saw his eyes twinkle.

"Because the horse in question is Mercury, the derby favorite. Seems it belongs to your young friend's folks." He paused for effect. "And apparently she's gone too. The girl, that is."

"Oh," I said, and rewound Nimble's leash around my wrist. The little chore took all of my attention. I felt certain Lars hadn't known Neva and the horse were missing earlier this morning. I shuddered to think of what my face might look like if he had.

"You've got nothing else to say?"

I shrugged carelessly. "What should I say? I don't know where the horse is. And for your information, the horse belongs to Neva, not her mother. Neva told me her other grandfather gave the horse to Robbie and her."

Gratton went silent, although he never stopped scanning the fairgrounds for signs of bunco men and thieves. "You're not concerned about Neva?" he asked after a while. "Not afraid she's been kidnapped or hurt or lost?"

"I'm afraid," I said clearly, so there wouldn't be any mistake, "the biggest danger to Neva is if someone, for instance Lars, finds her and drags her back to her cockeyed family."

CHAPTER 14

Gratton didn't bother arguing about Neva and her situation. How could he? He knew Lars too well to even try, and a passing acquaintance with Mr. Louis Duchene and Mrs. Hazel O'Dell must've confirmed my opinion.

His lack of resistance, if I'm honest, took the wind out of my sails. I'd been expecting him to guess I'd had a hand in Neva's apparent disappearance. I was a little taken aback when he simply nodded and said in an absent manner, "She's had a hard time, eh?" He then pointed out Monk's location and said, a bit abruptly, "I'll see you later."

His quick reaction to a particularly careless dip working alone may have had something to do with his seeming unconcern. I say careless because the mark, a skinny man in a thick woolen suit, caught the pickpocket in the act and yelled for help. The pickpocket was almost as good at his trade as

Jimsy Woodsmith. But this time, he, a common crook overconfident of his abilities, had picked on the wrong man. The last I saw of Grat he was frog-marching the young man away with his arm twisted high on his back, his coat pockets bulging with the telltale shape of stolen wallets. The catch meant Grat would be gone from the fairgrounds while the thief was booked into jail.

I continued on to where Grat had pointed, namely, the racetrack starting line. I found Monk there, keeping a close watch on the bookies' cash drawers. A good deal of money was being wagered. I saw bills passing from hand to hand at a terrific rate. Spokane's reputation as a town where horse racing was king seemed to have drawn every sportsman — and sportswoman, too — for miles around. They all seemed ready to spend money and enjoy themselves, which didn't include getting robbed. My uncle served as the all-important first line against thieves. One would've thought to find a large police presence, but there wasn't a bluecoat in sight.

I had to smirk. The punters didn't realize how lucky they were when Gratton — with my help — put Jimsy out of commission.

"China," Monk said, sounding a little surprised as I approached, Nimble prancing at my side, "what're you doing here? No new clients showing up at the office today?" He answered his own question. "I guess everybody is right here."

"At least nine tenths of them, Uncle." I staggered as a seedy runt of a man ran into me, the odor of whiskey enclosing him in a cloud of fumes. Monk shouted after the fellow, who disappeared into the crowd, while I checked my pocketbook and found it intact. Fearing Nimble would be trampled, I gathered the little dog in my arms and held her, although she put up quite a fuss.

"The Kennett family is in town to take in the fair and races," I added, "and Sawyer wants to speak with you or Gratton about a job. I thought he might've met up with you by now." I was careful to keep my face averted, hidden by Nimble's body. Monk didn't seem to notice as his attention was directed toward the crowd of men clamoring to place wagers.

"Haven't seen him. Anyone else?"

"Yes. Porter Anderson. He's meeting with Sawyer regarding some mine timbers. But he came by the office first." I hesitated. "He said he was going to look you up, too."

"Must've got delayed." Monk inhaled a sharp breath and started forward as two men collided. One stumbled and almost fell

186

as the other pushed against him. But the pusher helped hold the stumbler upright, they shook hands, and all seemed well. My uncle stopped and relaxed.

"I'll be glad to see them both," he said. "Anyone else?"

"Yes." I wasn't mentioning Neva. She was my responsibility, but then there was Lars. I had to tell Monk about him. Partly, anyway.

"Who?" My uncle, perhaps sensing something from my tone of voice, did look at me now, a glance more felt than seen as I had my head discreetly lowered.

"Lars."

Monk's expression grew cold. He grunted. "Hmph! You'd think he's stirred up enough trouble for one day. What did he want this time?"

"Aside from the pleasure of intimidating me?" In retrospect, his visit struck me as unnecessary. "He was warning me to stay away from Neva O'Dell. For some reason, he seems to have suddenly grown angrier about the incident at the morgue last night."

"He has? Hmm." My uncle appeared distracted as he watched the crowd. A race was about to start, I realized, and people tense with anticipation pushed forward to the track rail. My uncle reacted as well, his head turning, watching, his gaze flicking in

187

constant motion.

"Yes. I don't want to overreact, run scared where there's no need, but Monk, he seemed . . . oh . . . vaguely threatening." I touched my sore lip with my tongue. In fact, there was no vague about it.

Monk tensed and his face went hard. "He did, did he? What did he do?"

I waved this off with a flap of my hand. "Yes. What's more, I just ran into Grat and Lars was with him. Lars was saying Neva's horse is gone from the stable, and Neva herself has disappeared. You know him and his method of speaking double-talk on every subject, but I believe he was accusing us, or maybe just me, of stealing Mercury."

"Us? Steal Mercury?" He frowned at me. "You don't say?"

"I do say."

"I wonder why? Seems pretty far-fetched even for him."

I had his attention now, want it or not. I buried the bruised side of my face in Nimble's fur.

"Why he'd come up with that, I mean," he explained. "You haven't stolen the horse, have you, China?"

"Uncle Monk!" Nimble wriggled as my voice rose.

Monk had the grace to look abashed

188

although, knowing him the way I do, I doubt he felt it. "Just thought I'd ask."

"Well, I didn't. I have no idea where the horse is."

Something in my inflection must have warned him. "But you know who took him, right?"

I hesitated. "Let's just say I know the horse isn't stolen at all. Mercury was lamed in the fall that killed Robbie, and the owner has taken him away to protect his leg and give him time to heal. I believe the intention is to have the horse ready to run on Derby day."

"Duchene or Mrs. O'Dell have a change of heart?" He looked surprised. "Last I heard they were bound and determined on running him, lame or not."

"Oh, them," I said as if they didn't count. "Turns out neither Mrs. O'Dell nor her father actually owns the horse. Neva and Robbie did. Now Neva does."

He didn't get the chance to ask how I came by this information, although a lifted brow warned of questions to come. Then a waving arm and a shout summoned him. One of the bookies bellowed at him to come verify the odds on his chalkboard to a customer.

"Damn," he said. "China —"

The bookie shouted again. "Hustle it up. Race won't last forever."

"We'll talk later," Monk hurried to say. "Meanwhile —"

"Meanwhile?"

He went so far as to chew on his mustache, a definite aberration by a man who took great care of his facial embellishment. "Meanwhile, lambie, be careful. These people . . . they ain't —" What he meant to say faded as he started toward the bookie's stand.

"You bet," I said. I don't know if he heard me.

With Monk so busy, I felt my task complete. He hadn't, thank goodness, noticed the damage to my face. Telling him details of my set-to with Lars could wait for a better time. Maybe, if I delayed long enough, I'd never have to tell him.

With both Monk and Grat warned of Lars's latest harassment, I found myself wanting to get home and talk more with Neva. I set Nimble down and we started toward the gate.

What on earth was I going to do with the girl? With the way Lars was watching the office, I didn't dare keep her with me.

The crowd roared as a seven-horse field broke away from the starting line. Unable to resist the excited swell of noise, I turned to watch them race past. A palomino had broken first, but in the quick look I got at the field, I figured a small brown horse would soon take the lead — and keep it. Then Nimble, excited by all the noise and movement, tugged so hard on her leash she almost slipped her collar. I spared a moment's gratitude for Mr. Poole's admonition to keep her close.

Poole . . . Could he possibly be Robbie's murderer? Not that I thought he was guilty of using his own two hands. He was a particularly sharp-spoken, obnoxious fellow, but was he also the man Neva had seen giving money to her grandfather? After spying him hobnobbing with Mrs. O'Dell — twice — well, it roused my suspicions.

The trip back to the office from Corbin Park seemed endless. The streetcar, stopping often to pick up or drop off passengers, was crowded, loud, and smelly. I carried Nimble because the seats were full and I was afraid she'd be mashed like a potato. She didn't appreciate my efforts. My wiggly little dog and I both were relieved when we got off and sped homeward.

Besides, if Neva woke up, I imagined she'd be frightened at finding herself alone in a stranger's house.

I'll admit my hurry made me careless, not paying much attention to my surroundings. Mind you, I had the foresight to watch for suspicious characters lurking in dark alleys and whatnot while traversing the streets. I've been accosted a time or two, and have no desire to be taken by surprise again. I keep an extra hat pin handy, just in case.

But this time, if it hadn't been for Nimble, I would've walked into an ambush right on my own doorstep, figuratively speaking, and who knows what would've happened. Nothing good, I'm sure.

But I did have Nimble, bless her heart.

All appeared well as I unlocked the office, although Nimble scratched at the door in her anxiety to get inside. The sun had dropped behind the taller buildings to the west of us, darkening the room. I fumbled about as I pulled the chain to turn on the electric fixture in the middle of the ceiling. It buzzed softly as the bulb warmed. The odd buzz continued when the light reached maximum illumination. Call me slow off the mark, but that's when I finally realized what I heard was Nimble growling, sort of gargling, really, low in her throat. She sounded a bit like a bumble bee. I studied her, my own apprehension growing. Her nose twitched, her eyes bugged, and the hackles on her back lifted like porcupine quills, curly hair notwithstanding. Her whippy tail stuck straight out behind her.

Appearances can be deceptive. All was not well.

Sometimes this detective business is for the birds.

My first hopeful thought was of Neva, thinking she'd come downstairs and had startled the dog. On second thought, I knew if Nimble had caught the girl's scent, she'd be bouncing around happy as a spring lamb. My third thought, also concerning Neva, had me in a bit of a panic. Head cocked, I listened hard. Sweat sprang out on my body.

And yet . . . nothing. Too much nothing?

Was Nimble, by some odd chance, still reacting to our set-to this morning with Lars?

Unlikely.

My gaze flicked around the room before coming back to Nimble. She was staring fixedly into the hallway opening off the office. A foyer at the back door led into this area, along with the entry to a storage room. *And the stairway up to the second-floor apartment.*

Next, the four or five papers scattered over the top of my desk clamored for attention.

I'd typed them earlier and put them in a basket, lined up in precise order, a couple to await Monk's signature, the others Gratton's.

My heart pounded. For the second time in one day, I opened the desk drawer and retrieved the S & W .32 revolver. Muffling the sound in the folds of my skirt, I cocked it.

Nimble beside me, we moved as quietly as possible toward the darkened hall. Why, I don't know. The dog's toenails clicked on the wood floor. I might as well have stomped as the light glared down from overhead, my every move visible. Each step I took was obvious. And I felt eyes watching me. Whose eyes?

I stopped before I reached the doorway.

"Come out." My voice shook, though only a little. I made a determined effort to hold it steady. "I know you're there."

Nimble growled again, tugging at the leash still looped over my wrist.

I wanted, in the worst way, to run for safety. Seek out Cosimo Pinelli, my cabinet-maker friend next door, and ask him for protection. But I couldn't take the chance. I couldn't abandon Neva — if she was still asleep upstairs. If she was even still alive.

"Come out," I said again after a few

seconds. And then found myself regretting the demand as feet shuffled. Nimble lunged toward the sound and I, in a moment of cowardice, detached the loop from my wrist and let her go.

Quick as a hornet, she dashed into the hall. Fierce growls rang out, accompanied by the sound of ripping cloth. A sharp wail from the dog, then a curse delivered in a man's voice. More barks. More growls. More curses.

I took the opportunity to advance, the pistol held in both hands in front of me. Rounding the corner, I spied a tussle of heroic proportions.

Nimble, with her leash dragging loose behind her, had managed to entangle a slightly built man in the strap. She'd wrapped the leash a couple times around one of his ankles, then changed sides and done the other, effectively hobbling him. He was barely able to move his feet. He'd grabbed hold of an umbrella I left hanging from one of the coat hooks near the door. Bobbing up and down like an egg in a pot of boiling water, he poked the pointed ferrule at the dog every time she gnashed at him with her teeth. She dodged the umbrella easily, until it flopped open and scared her. She yelped like she'd been wounded.

I pointed my pistol at the man. "Stand down, sir," I said, "and drop the umbrella."

"Call off your blankety-blank dog," he replied, ignoring the pistol and jabbing at Nimble with a vicious expression on his face. Only he didn't, of course, say blankety-blank.

He had no weapon I could see, just the umbrella waving about. I released the .32's hammer and stuck the pistol in my pocket. Nimble and the man continued to wrangle until I grabbed up the broom I used to sweep the back stoop. With a swing in the fashion of the Northsider baseball nine's best batter — who just so happens to be Gratton Doyle — I slammed a home run and disarmed the fellow. Then, having gained some experience in such things, I crammed the broom handle between his legs and tripped him.

The broom may have slipped upward a little — maybe it even slipped twice. When he got his breath back, the cursing resumed. This time directed at me.

But not before I heard a rustle at the top of the stairs. I glanced up as Neva came out on the landing, no doubt drawn by all the shouting and barking. She took one look at the man, turned dead white, and disappeared into the apartment.

So she was not coming to my aid. Why not?

I eyed the man now sitting, rather gingerly, on the floor in front of me, his back to the stair. Busy fending off Nimble's teeth, he hadn't seen the girl. And I thought I knew why she was keeping out of sight.

I didn't blame her. In fact, I was glad. She didn't need to be a part of what happened next.

CHAPTER 15

"Get 'im off me," the man yelled, snatching his ear away from Nimble's snapping teeth in time to avoid a bite. "Effing sonsa—"

I whomped him good on his shoulder with the broom handle, narrowly missing the dog. Which was all right. It gave me a couple seconds to catch her as she shied away. I released the leash from her collar, still leaving the man entangled in the strap, and dragged her to my side.

"Shut up," I told the man, and gave Nimble a little shake. "You, too."

The dog did better than the human in obeying me. Surprising in itself since the back door was agape inviting her escape. More so when I told her, "Upstairs," and she actually went.

"Now," I said and, interrupting my captive's fresh tirade, took out the pistol again. "You may loosen your legs and come into the office."

"I bet I can't walk," he complained. "You damn near ruined me."

"But I haven't killed you," I pointed out. "Yet. Even though I would be perfectly justified in shooting an intruder. A thief. A possible murderer. A molester." This last came out in a harsh whisper.

His eyes rounded. "Say, I ain't . . ."

"Shut up," I said. "Do you think I can't see the pry marks on the door?" Monk was sure to be upset when he got home. The door had been replaced only a few months ago after a crazed murderer took an ax to it. "The office. Go."

I don't know what the intruder read in my expression, but at least his infernal yappity-yap complaints broke off. He struggled to his feet, making a theatrical production of rising. I helped him toddle into the office via a couple quick nudges of my pistol. Maintaining a discreet distance between us in case he thought going for my gun seemed the prudent thing to do.

Once released from the gloom of the semi-dark hall, I found time to examine my catch. I already knew he was small in stature. As I'd begun to suspect, I also found him to be at least as old as Uncle Monk. More decrepit in his movement, although I might be blamed for some of his trouble walking. And if so, I didn't care.

He wore run-over-at-the-heel boots, dungarees, and a faded green calico shirt. An old felt hat with a sagging brim had covered his head when I first spotted him. At some point during the melee, it had fallen off. He was dark-skinned and dark-eyed, his hair in the process of turning white.

I scooted a chair into the middle of the room with my foot.

"Sit," I told him.

Glaring at me, he complied, careful as to how he positioned his backside.

"Who are you?" I waggled the pistol at him, making certain I had his attention. "And why have you broken into the Doyle & Howe Detective Agency?"

He told me to do something I thought was probably anatomically impossible — as well as extremely rude.

"Two questions at one time too much for you?" I paced a slow circle until I stood behind him, out of his sight no matter how far he twisted his neck. "Who are you? What's your name?"

He ignored me.

No particular surprise. I poked the .32's barrel into the back of his neck and shoved.

Hard.

He winced and grumbled something

meant, I'm sure, to be menacing. It failed to impress.

A second poke became necessary. "Your name, sir?"

"Duchene. Louis Duchene."

I can't say as I was surprised. Neva's grandfather, just as I'd suspected. And my, how he resented giving in to me. When I walked around in front of him again, hate seemed to shoot from his eyes. I'd known he needlessly used violent means against his granddaughter. Now I wondered if he were touched in the head.

While I pondered this question, footsteps sounded on the boardwalk outside. I looked up as a man shuffled past the windows. Then another. My captive's mouth opened and he sucked in a breath as though to call out.

"Don't you dare." I shook my head and waved the gun. His mouth closed.

A curious passerby had only to look in and he'd see me with my pistol aimed at Mr. Duchene. Not a good idea, in case I had to shoot the old rapscallion. Witnesses were not part of my plan. And yet, I worried about this witness business working two ways. If no one could see what I did to Duchene, they couldn't see what he'd do to me if he got a chance.

Resolve hardened in me. I'd just have to see he never got the opportunity, that's all.

Without ever taking my eyes off him, I went around the windows, pulled the shades and locked the door.

"What're you doin'?" He eyed my precautionary arrangements, sounding the tiniest bit nervous. I was nervous, too.

"I'm making certain we don't have any interruptions. You know, during our little . . . talk."

"I ain't sayin' nothin' to you." His words came out tough, but he eyed the gun in my hand with a certain amount of trepidation. Very wise of him.

"Indeed? We'll see."

I walked around behind him and poked the nape of his neck again. It could've used a good wash, by the way. Dirt was ingrained in the wrinkles. And he smelled. Manure, cheap tobacco with an overlay of cheaper booze, and stale sweat. In fact, sweat beaded his face now. Whatever kind of man he was, at least he didn't discount a woman just because she was a woman. His wariness indicated he knew a female of the species could be as lethal as the male.

Monk's saddle, a leftover of his stock inspector days, lay in a corner of the office. He'd returned from a trip up north to a

Stevens County ranch just before he and Gratton contracted with the racing commission, and he hadn't had time to put it away. I'd been complaining, but now I considered it fortuitous. His lasso was tied onto the saddle skirt with a thong. Just what I needed.

Since Monk used a quick-release knot to hold the rope in place, I had it loose in a couple seconds. Before Duchene could sense what I had in mind, with a flip of my hand I slipped the loop over his head and settled it around his neck.

"What the —" At the rope's first touch he made as though to leap from his seat.

A sharp jerk brought him back down on the chair, writhing like a fish on a line. Holding the rope snug, I jumped forward and tapped him a couple times on the temple with the pistol barrel. He must've had fragile skin, maybe because of all the weathering. Blood trickled a fine line down his face.

"Sit still."

He subsided. Oh, the taps may have hurt, all right, but I felt certain the wound looked worse than it really was. Probably.

"You little bitch. When I get loose I'm gonna . . ."

Another jerk on the rope cut off his

obnoxious line of discussion. Before he could gather himself — and he may, in all honesty, have been a wee bit dizzy from a lack of air — I put the pistol aside, though handy in case of need, and quickly wrapped the rope around his upper body, his arms held immobile. Yanked it tight. Checked to make certain that regardless of the sounds he made he wasn't strangling, put my foot against the chair seat, and yanked even harder. Then, round and around I went; neck, torso, waist, legs and feet. I trussed him up like a Thanksgiving turkey.

Oh, and I didn't forget to thank my stars he was a small man. And verging on old. If he'd been in his prime, I'd probably never managed it. As it was, he fought me tooth and toenail, which is about all he had free.

One problem. I wasn't able to stopper his mouth. So I stuffed Mavis's dusting cloth, retrieved from the under-the-stairs storage, in it.

Spent, I went into the hall and sat on the lowest step leading to the apartment. I put my head on my knees and waited for my heartbeat to slow, my sweat to dry, and my trembling to still. What a day this had turned into!

Before many minutes passed, a shuffle of bare feet alerted me to Neva pacing in the living room above me. Funny. Even the slight noise she made sounded frantic, poor girl. It wasn't fair to leave her wondering what had happened. Thinking, shame on me, I went up.

Her bruises had darkened as she slept, but even so she looked better than she had earlier. Not so haggard. Fourteen-year-old girls should never look haggard. There ought to be a law.

"That's my granddad down there," she whispered to me.

"Yes. I know. What's he doing here, Neva?"

Her voice shook. "Looking for me?"

"Maybe. Possibly. But why? I don't think he knows you're here. Not really. He seemed to be searching for something else."

"Something else? What?"

"If I knew I wouldn't be asking you. But I know it can't be the horse." She winced as my voice sharpened. "Sorry. Not your fault."

Not quite true. I wouldn't be involved if it weren't for Neva and her pathetic plea. Sighing as I steered her into the kitchen and indicated a chair, I relented. "The papers on my desk are scattered about. He seemed to be rifling the hall closet when Nimble and I arrived. And he hadn't headed up-stairs. Yet. If he'd been looking for you, he would've gone there first thing. And," I added dryly, "I don't think he would've left you to get your sleep out if he'd suspected you were here."

I moved the coffeepot to the hotter part of the stove and shoved a stick of wood into the firebox. Neva needed something warm, and so did I after my labors.

She chewed at her lip. "No." She touched one of the bruises on her face. "He wouldn't let me sleep."

"All of which tells me he's after something else. What is it, Neva? What is he looking for?"

"I don't know."

Her voice had risen. From the office below, came the sound of chair legs chittering on the floor. Muffled, pig-like grunts rose in volume. Mr. Duchene trying to release himself, no doubt. Had he heard Neva and recognized her voice?

Putting my forefinger to my lips, I shushed her. "Have you heard him mention anything about Doyle & Howe Detective Agency?"

Her eyes fixed on the floor, she shook her head. "Just last night when he told my mother the man who paid them the money said to stay out of the detectives' way. I heard Granddad say he told him to 'specially warn my mother after he saw her talking to Monk yesterday."

I seized on one minor tidbit. "He? He who?"

Poole? Had to be. After all, hadn't I seen him hobnobbing again with Mrs. O'Dell right after she talked to Monk today? The timing seemed to reinforce the warning.

Still, something didn't quite jibe, but whatever it was drifted out of my mind as Neva shook her head again and said, "I don't know. Just 'he.' Miz Bo . . . China, what are you going to do with my grand-dad?"

The very question puzzling me. To give myself time, I poured us each a cup of rather stale coffee. Neva guzzled it down like a parched desert survivor. I had some oatmeal cookies with raisins in them. Like-wise a little stale, but I fetched a handful from the jar, dumped them on a plate and set them in front of her.

Absently, she took one. I wouldn't have minded a nibble myself, but my mouth was still too sore.

Neva, grown a little braver by now, looked up at me. "Are you going to have the police arrest Granddad? I know he deserves it."

"He deserves worse than a little jail time, the ornery old coot." I thought a moment. Lars. He was mixed up in this somehow. In which case — "But I don't think the police would serve any purpose."

Something, fear most probably, widened Neva's dark eyes. "Are you going to turn him loose?" The question came out as a gasp.

"I expect I'll have to — eventually." I didn't like the thought any more than she did, judging by the way her fingers closed around the cookie, turning it to crumbs in her hand.

Shaking the crumbs off, she jumped to her feet and glanced around.

"What?" I blinked my eyes wide and gawked about, astonished by her sudden action. Nimble scrambled under the table, shuffing up the remains of Neva's cookie with her little pink tongue.

"My boots," the girl said. "Where are my boots?"

"The bedroom." I gestured. "But why . . . what . . . I'm not letting him go this instant, Neva. Calm down."

"No. I have to go." Face white, she headed for my room. "I can't let him see me here. I have to hide. I have to — he'll —"

She verged on hysterical. "I won't tell him. I won't!"

Bewildered, I followed her. "Tell him what?"

"Mercury. I won't tell him where I . . . I won't."

"Of course not." I paused. "But where will you go?"

I don't think she was even aware of the tears leaking from her eyes.

"I don't know," she said on a hiccupy sob. "I'll find some place. Maybe with —" Then more firmly. "No. Not there. I don't know."

A name and face leapt into my mind. On one hand, what I had was a Damsel in Distress. Over there, on the other hand, a mushy heart when it came to the helpless.

"I do," I said.

Chapter 16

I doubt Porter Anderson's name comes up very often in a discussion about the ideal guardian for a young girl, but there you are. On the spur of the moment, I couldn't think of anyone more fitting for the role than he. I have personal experience with him as a rescuer, a protector, and a friend, so I may be prejudiced. If I am, I'm not the only one. His wife-to-be has also benefited from his inborn "Sir Galahad" trait. It's what I was counting on. The only problem I could see would be in convincing him of his aptitude. I'd have to present Neva's sad tale with a lot of heroic flash and dare.

I didn't want to place Porter in jeopardy, mind you, but he's the sort of man who laughs at danger and is willing to take risks. He's well able to take care of himself, of course, which makes his attitude understandable.

Convincing Neva of Porter's suitability, I

soon discovered, saddled my plan with a problem.

I finished detailing Porter's stellar attributes, only to find Neva's wide — truthfully, a little cow-like — eyes staring at me as though I'd gone mad. "But Miss Bo— China, I don't know this man. Even if I did, I can't do it. It's not right. He might get hurt." Then she dealt my argument what she no doubt supposed was the final blow. "It isn't respectable!"

I cocked my head. "You're probably right. But what's more important, Neva, respectability or safety? I know which I'd choose if I were in your place."

She blushed. "But Mrs. Ba . . . this woman I know already thinks I'm a tramp. And my family. Mrs. B . . . she doesn't like my clothes. She says —"

Neva was so upset she couldn't even complete a full sentence.

"Then we'll need to keep this episode a secret. Porter is good at keeping secrets. You'll see."

She kept saying no, while I kept saying yes.

I brought forth several convincing arguments on why she should do as I said, even as I bustled around my bedroom gathering a few things I knew she'd need over the next few days. The girl had nothing. She'd escaped her granddad this morning without brush, comb or change of knickers.

I put a couple dollars in the bundle I made up for her while she stood with her back to me, listening to her grandfather thump and snort in the office below. Her shoulders were so stiff it was a wonder the muscles didn't break in two.

"I know it sounds a bit far-fetched, Neva. And not quite the thing. But that's why it's precisely what you need to do. No one would ever expect to find you with Porter." I handed her the neatly tied bundle, along with one of my old jackets. She'd come away in her shirtsleeves and I wondered if she even owned a coat. Well, she did now.

She took the bundle I handed her and absently donned the jacket. "Maybe this man won't want to help me." She looked almost hopeful.

"He'll do it." I knew my way around Porter Anderson. He was much more mal-leable than say, Gratton Doyle. One look at Neva's blackened eyes and scraped wrists and he'd be won over. The only problem lay in discovering his whereabouts so we could do the handover.

But first, I had to spirit Neva from the

building without her grandfather being aware.

I went down first. A good thing, too, as Mr. Duchene had managed to not only scoot the chair farther into the room, but turn it around until he faced the hall. Neva would've been visible from where he sat.

"You've been busy." I showed him the cloth — a tea cloth, actually — I'd brought downstairs with me and whipped it out in a flourish. "Won't do you any good, though. You're not going anywhere."

He mumbled something behind the gag in his mouth.

"What's this, you ask?" I dropped the cloth over his head and tucked the edges under the rope circling his neck. It all made a rather tight fit. He should've been saying thank you, since the rope was a bit scratchy. I'm quite certain those mutters meant something else, however. "This should help keep the light out of your eyes."

Everything I said seemed to infuriate him which, I have to say, didn't bother me one whit. The chair rocked wildly as he threw his whole body back and forth. Being attached to the chair didn't deter him, so it was no surprise when they toppled over with a resounding crash. I didn't care.

He groaned. Rather theatrical acting, in

my opinion. His muffled complaints grew louder.

I stifled a laugh.

"Don't go anywhere," I told him. "I've got something I need to do, but when I get back, we're going to have a talk." I paused. "I don't know about you, but I'm looking forward to it." Leaving him where he lay, I went to get Neva.

Neva's mouth gaped open as she caught a glimpse of her grandfather lying on the floor trussed up like a hog-tied calf. She took a strangled breath.

Holding a finger to my lips to indicate silence, I entered the room and turned off the light, hiding the old man from view. We left the building via the back door. I grabbed the girl's hand and led her through Mr. Pinelli's side of the yard into the back alley. We crossed behind the buildings backing onto ours, then cut around the sides until we reached the next street. In this round-about fashion, we finally came to Beaver's Family Hotel.

Like nearly every other building in Spokane, the Beaver was only a few years old. After a fire during the summer of 1889 burned the entire downtown to the ground, people rebuilt using brick. The hotel, the simple, box-like two-story structure made of gray bricks, sat in the middle of a patch of green lawn.

Porter always stayed here when he came to town, possibly because of the evening meal the small, friendly hotel offered as part of the room fee, sort of like an upscale boardinghouse. Besides, he'd told me, he liked the food. I was counting on his reluctance to change his habits. Besides, it was nearing supper time. He should be there now.

Leaving Neva out of sight behind a large bush shedding copious amounts of frost-loosened leaves over the porch, I entered the hotel alone. The lobby was deserted, but in the brightly lit dining room off to the side, a man wearing a jacket and tie was setting plates and silverware on a long table. Several lone men, two older women, and a family consisting of mother, father and five children, chatted as they waited on him to complete the chore before they took their chairs. More chairs, standing empty, sat off to one side in case of more guests.

No sign of Porter Anderson. Drat. I'd hoped to avoid having to search for him.

Trying to remain unobtrusive, I sauntered over to the unoccupied front desk. I suspected the clerk was the one setting the table, which suited me fine as it kept him

215

busy in the dining room. The register stood open for all to see, if one were proficient at reading some rather appalling hen-scratches serving as signatures. Upside down, no less.

I'd seen Porter's handwriting before and recognized his scrawl. A number three was written in a box next to his name. Porter lodged in one of the ground-floor rooms, just down the hall from the desk.

Laughter rose in the dining room. I took advantage of the noisy hilarity to wave Neva inside, pulling her along with me in the direction of Porter's room. She didn't make it easy, resisting all the way. Thank goodness a rug ran down the center of the hall, muffling the clomp of her boots.

We came to number three. Checking quickly to either side, I tapped on Porter's door.

Too light a tap, perhaps, as he didn't answer. I knocked again, a fraction harder.

"Porter, are you there?" I kept my call just above a whisper.

From inside the room, I heard a thump.

Knocked again. "Porter? It's China. Let us in."

Footsteps shuffled. The door opened. Porter's face appeared in the opening.

I gasped. "Porter Anderson, what in the world . . . Oh, no! What have you done?"

"What are you doing here?" He scowled instead of answering my surprised query like any gentleman ought. "Go away."

"No. I need to speak with you."

"Can't you see —"

"Right now," I said firmly.

His mouth twisted as resignation set in. "Come in then, before somebody sees you." He grabbed me by the arm and yanked me into the room. If I hadn't had hold of Neva to keep her from running away, she would've been left standing in the hall.

"Who have you been fighting with?" I asked, afraid I knew.

Seeming to see Neva for the first time, Porter eyed her with no particular favor. "Who's this?" he asked instead of answering my question.

"Miss China," Neva said, prim as any old maid, "he doesn't look very nice to me."

I couldn't say she was wrong.

Since we'd met this morning, Porter had acquired a beauty of a bruise over one eye, a cut lip that made mine look like a pretender, a gash on his chin and . . . did I see the remains of blood in the folds alongside his nose? Narrowing my eyes and inspecting him closely, I decided this appendage appeared more bulbous than usual. And those were just the wounds visible upon a cursory examination. Who knows what else he'd suffered? It seemed to me he was listing to one side.

Porter stared hard at Neva. "Ain't we a pair?" he observed, then, his gaze lighting on me, included me in this lucky group. "A crew of beat-up no-hopers for certain."

"A trio of them, at any rate," I said, smiling a little. "You, sir, look like you've been run over by a train."

"He looks to me like he lost a big fight." Neva moved to stand behind me as she spoke. She may have had experience with fighters, both as winners and as losers.

Porter's jaw jutted forward. "Who says I lost?"

"Huh," Neva said, putting so much feeling into the sound it was as though she'd uttered a whole paragraph.

"Say, China, who is this mouthy little —" He paused a moment. "— female?"

"This is Miss Neva Sue O'Dell." I pulled the girl forward. "She owns Mercury."

Porter's brow puckered.

"Mercury is a horse, and is the odds-on derby favorite," I clarified. "Or he was. Neva owns him. The thing is, there's a certain group of people who don't want him to win. In fact, they want him to lose so badly Neva's brother, the horse's jockey, was killed

218

in their last race. The horse was lamed."

"What?" He scratched his head. "Well, I guess I might've heard something about a young jockey dying. An accident, I heard. You're saying it wasn't?"

His exclamation made me think I was on the right track with my heroic flash and dare ploy.

"But then somebody wanted him to race today and win, thereby skewing Sunday's odds. The upshot is, Neva has put her horse in hiding until the derby, and she also needs a safe place to stay until then."

"Yeah? This somebody got a name?"

"Of course." My lips pursed into a thin line. "We just don't know it yet. Or at least we don't know everyone involved in the scam."

He looked Neva over, then switched his attention to me again. "She been staying with you? Workin' for you, is it?"

"No. She can't stay with me, I'm afraid. We found out it's too dangerous." I smiled at him. "She's going to stay with you."

Putting out a hand as though to ward me off, he backed away like I'd just threatened to shoot him.

It hadn't come to that — yet.

Some kind of weird stuttering came out of his mouth, the gist of which seemed to be, "N-n-n-n-no." Then louder and firmer, a definite "No."

"Shh," I said. "Not so loud. Everyone in the hotel will hear."

"Good. I hope they do. Oughta put a spoke in this particular wheel and a good thing, too."

Nevertheless, his voice quieted.

Beaver's Family Hotel wasn't exactly the epitome of luxury. Porter's small room had a bright blue hand-pieced quilt covering the bed, a single chair and tiny washstand. Oh, and a picture of Christ over the bed.

Since it was the only place available, I sat down on the bed and prepared to have a cozy chat. Still examining Porter, Neva sat down next to me. She didn't seem as frightened by him now, perhaps because he was as critical of my plan as she.

"Please, Porter," I said. "Look at her. She's young, she's scared, and she's in danger. Can you pleeeease help her?"

Neva hunched her shoulders and without any further effort whatsoever, managed to look pathetic. As if she weren't, in truth.

I held up one of her arms and pushed the coat sleeve back. "Look at this. They tied her up and whipped her."

Porter swallowed like he had a bird caught in his throat. "Yeah, well, looks to me like both you ladies've been running with the wrong crowd."

"Her family did this, Porter. I'm telling you, she's not safe with them."

Neva's head lowered and she turned a dull red. "She's not lying," she said, her voice so low Porter had to lean closer to hear. "My granddad, he used an old rope to tie me up this morning and took a strap to me after . . . well, after. He said another whipping would bring me around soon enough, even if a fist wouldn't. But I got loose."

I hadn't heard all of this before. It fit with the scene my imagination had worked up. "You see?" I said to Porter.

"Yeah. I see, all right." He looked uncomfortable. "But, China, I ain't the proper person to take care of a girl. The Kennetts are in town until after the race. Why don't you ask Mrs. Kennett?"

"My first thought, but I can't risk putting the Kennett children in the middle of anything dangerous. I mean, look at Neva. She's only fourteen, but certain people have no qualms about hurting her, and killing her brother."

"Granddad and my mother didn't kill Robbie," Neva said, her halfhearted support of them coming as something of a surprise. "But they fixed it so somebody else did."

221

More mention of an elusive somebody.

I nodded, commiserating with her pain. "Your people are in over their heads. Which doesn't excuse them of culpability in his death. Or their treatment of you. Or even of Mercury."

I had another little thrill of pride in knowing I'd hoisted the old man in some of his own petard. So to speak.

Porter drew up the lone, rather spindly chair and sat facing us. "This is a fine pickle you're in, sister," he said to Neva. "None of which makes me the proper person to mind you." He looked at me, unconsciously rubbing what I imagined was a sore spot on his belly. "I can't keep her in here with me, China. You oughta know better than to suggest otherwise. Hell, she's gotta eat sometime. These folks know me here. I ain't having them think I brought a . . . ah . . ."

"Working girl?" I supplied the descriptor he was searching for.

Face red, he said, "Yes. One of them in here."

"It would be proper for your niece to join you in town, wouldn't it? Oh, not in the same room, but what about in two rooms next to each other. That would work, right?" I turned to Neva. "What do you think?"

Her smooth brow wrinkled up like an old

lady's. "I'm not his niece."

"Well, for heaven's sake!" I'm afraid I got a little huffy. "You can pretend, can't you?" I caught Porter in my gimlet stare, as well. "And you."

"We ain't all as devious as you are," he muttered. "Comes harder for some of us."

I managed to ignore his entirely mistaken opinion of my character, sensing agreement just around the corner.

"But you'll do it, won't you?" I smiled at him, unable to keep my relief from showing. I'd won him over.

He glowered, although not even Neva seemed disturbed by the fierceness. "Yeah. I suppose. Dang it, China, you know how situations like this chap my hide."

"Do they?" I kept my face straight with an effort. Of course I knew it. Why else would I be here? Sir Galahad indeed!

"But," he said, and shook a thick forefinger in my face, "I ain't staying here at the Beaver with her in tow. They know me too well. Me and the girl will move on over to the Michigan Hotel. Mostly out-of-towners patronize the place and since I've never stayed there before, nobody'll think anything of it. I can just mention my niece is a little under the weather and they can bring meals to her room."

"Excellent plan," I applauded. I noticed Neva was looking a bit mulish and thought I'd better include her. "Don't you think so?"

"I guess," she admitted. "You aren't going to be hanging over me all the time, are you?" she demanded of Porter. "I'm used to doing for myself."

He opened his mouth to speak, then closed it again. He shrugged. "If you're in so much danger you gotta disappear for the next couple days, I figure you're smart enough to keep quiet and out of sight. I'm there just in case." He looked at me. "Good enough for you?"

"Yes. Wonderful. You're a good friend, Porter Anderson. The best." I laid on praise like thick, overly sweet frosting atop a cake and meant every word.

His face turned a startling shade of crimson, but it was agreed.

Porter never did admit to me how he'd gotten beat up, but my imagination supplied the gory details. He'd gone after Lars Hansen. My fault. Winner or loser, I wished he hadn't. I didn't want a target painted on the back of any of my friends. On the Doyle & Howe Detective Agency?

That's different. Danger is our business.

CHAPTER 17

Porter showed me from the hotel via a side door I hadn't known existed. Like an accomplished spy, he first checked around corners and side-to-side for any possible witnesses. He found none, no big surprise, which didn't actually relieve me as much as one might think.

"Don't you worry," he said with a conspiratorial grin as he sent me on my way. "Me and Neva will leave from here, too. Nobody ever uses this door except for the help. Doubt anybody'll be watching."

He seemed to be getting into the spirit of the enterprise.

Time had gotten away from us while I'd been seeing to Neva's situation. I suspected Porter had missed his dinner by this time. Anyway, full dark had fallen before I finally started home. Doorways and side alleys were blacker than a witch's armpit. I don't have a great deal of experience with such things, but I'd heard Gratton use the analogy to describe dark nights. Anyway, only a few areas were spotlighted by lamps shining from windows of shops staying open late. Shadows lurked, created by the fluctuating beams.

And now, I berated myself in disgust as I walked rapidly homeward, I'd succeeded in scaring myself. I touched the outside of my pocket, reassured by the feel of the .32 revolver resting within easy reach. I'd long since vowed I'd never be taken by surprise again. If accosted, it'd be the accoster who got the surprise.

So what about the overwhelming impression I had of being watched? My nerves shivered as though bitten by an invasion of insects. I know it's not unique to sense such things. Even Gratton, as prosaic as he is, had once told me he could tell when someone was stalking him. Not by physically seeing or hearing such a person, but by the feel of the stalker's malign touch.

I hurried my steps, stopping at a corner where I'd normally cut across a yard. It seemed as though trouble waited for me there. Big trouble, because when I glanced ahead, I saw the gigantic shadow of a man cast on a building's wall, like a negative of a photograph. Something dangled from his massive hand.

Faster and faster, I lengthened my stride, taking the long way while keeping to the light and the sidewalks where people milled about in a before-supper rush. Finally, the sense of being watched faded. I even relaxed, certain I was safe with home only a couple blocks away.

Had he not been so large, I probably wouldn't have noticed the man who joined the stream of walkers in front of me. At first glance there was nothing alarming about the way he shambled along, sometimes going a little faster, sometimes a little slower. I figured he was just another tired workman trying to get home after his shift. But then, during a break when no one else was near us, without notice he stopped in his tracks and spun toward me.

Embarrassing to say, I ran into him.

"Excuse me," I said, horrified by my clumsiness. Preoccupation in watching for bogeymen leaping from dark alleyways had diverted attention from my immediate surroundings. Not a wise choice, as it turned out.

More embarrassing, as I stepped back, our feet somehow became tangled. I lost my balance, falling over and landing at his feet like a two-year-old toddler. To anyone watching,

I'm sure he appeared the perfect gentleman as he reached down to help the awkward young woman to her feet.

"Thank . . . ," I started to say as I looked into his muddy brown eyes. Evil eyes. What I saw glittering in their depths stopped my words. But his eyes weren't the worst. Or maybe they were. Who knows, since I could only see the upper part of his face? A bandanna covered the rest from his nose down. The "accident" had been deliberate, I realized, flinching from the knowledge.

"Oh, no." I ducked, trying to scoot backward and slapping at his hands as he succeeded in picking me up.

"A message for you, lady." His voice rumbled a deep bass note. "And one for the O'Dell girl."

He kept his hold on my elbows. I twisted, doing my best to break free. Didn't work. The man had a grip like a giant vise.

I had no chance to reach my gun. No chance at all.

"Let me go," I demanded, "or I'll scream." I might as well have saved my breath. He didn't let go and I didn't scream.

"The message is, no more nosing around for you. This is the only warning you get. You don't, you'll be sorry. Tell the girl to give back what she took and do as she's told. She don't, she'll be sorry."

My heart gave a jump. "What did she take?"

He shook his head. "She's gotta give it back. Quick. She don't, she'll be sorry."

"You're repeating yourself," I said.

"By tonight," he added. "You tell her."

He let go of my arms and, taking long, fast strides just short of a run, sped back the way he'd come.

As for me?

I must've stood stock-still for a full two minutes, air gusting from my lungs as though I'd run a footrace and trying desperately to recover my equilibrium until I could go on. People detoured around me as if I were some kind of bulky, dangerous-looking package dropped in the middle of the road.

One woman said, "Some people!" as she went around me.

One man said, "Get moving, sis. You're blocking the sidewalk."

And finally, I did. Move, I mean. At least I no longer troubled to watch for the bogeyman. I'd already met him.

When I arrived at the office, the shades were still drawn, although the overhead light was on. Probably not a good sign as I'd made a point of turning it off before Neva and I left. A golden glow shone on the walk outside. I drew both a shuddering breath and the pistol before unlocking the door.

I slipped into an empty room. No one leaped out at me. Monk's rope lay uncoiled on top of his saddle, as if tossed there to get it out of the way. The fallen chair sat upright in its regular position in front of my desk. And Louis Duchene, naturally, given these circumstances, was no longer tied in it. All was quiet. Too quiet?

Just then the stairs leading to the apartment creaked as someone started down. I snatched up the .32 and pointed it toward the hallway. Fear struck at me like a jolt of electricity as I prepared myself to shoot.

What about Nimble? Why hadn't she barked a greeting? Why hadn't she come to greet me?

A man came through the door. I barely got my finger off the trigger in time.

"Monk!"

"China!" His exclamation was equally as heartfelt. "Where the devil have you been?" He stared at me. "Put that gun away before it goes off."

"Are you all right?" I let the pistol hang at my side but I didn't put it away. Not yet. "Where's Nimble?"

He shook his head. "The dog's in your room. Asleep on your bed." He eyed my set face, perhaps, finally, seeing the bruises hidden beneath the layer of powder. "I'm fine. She's fine. What did you expect?"

My voice shook. "Maybe to find you — or she — not so fine."

He huffed out a slug of air. "Well, she is, and I am too. Relax, lambie. Your eyes look like chunks of polished turquoise. The door locked?"

I took a moment to remember before nodding.

"I'll turn off the light," Monk said, and despite his seeming calmness, I sensed great tension in his words. "You go on upstairs. Looks like we've got some talking to do. I figure you have at least one more question you're chomping to ask."

Sarcasm. A faint lift of his lips indicated a wry smile.

"And I've got one or two of my own," he added. No surprise there.

"Yes. All right." Exhaustion gripped me as, without argument, I obeyed Monk's injunction to go up. I kept the pistol with me. It would stay with me, too, until we finished this affair with Neva and she was in the clear.

Not, in retrospect, that the pistol had done me a particle of good so far.

■ ■ ■ ■

Nimble awakened at the sound of my voice and came to greet me, her whippy tail wagging in an ecstasy of joyful reunion. I kissed the top of her bony little head and lifted one droopy ear to whisper, "I was afraid he'd hurt you."

Or killed her.

With the dog gamboling at my feet, I went to remove my coat and hat, brush my skirt and wash the grime from the street from my hands. By the time I left the bathroom, Monk was in the kitchen, puttering around with the stove and gathering sundry items out of the icebox.

"You can cook?" My mouth gaped open. He hadn't lifted a finger, as far as I knew, in the months since I'd lived here. Well, made coffee, really strong coffee, a few mornings, and burned some eggs in a skillet. But not anything I'd call real cooking.

Monk snorted. "How do you think I managed before you came?"

"Well . . . er . . . Mavis?" I knew he cooked camp food, bacon and beans and cornbread and such, I just hadn't thought about his everyday life.

Color rose over his cheekbones. I guess I

wasn't supposed to mention his longtime affair with Mrs. Atwood.

Acting as if he hadn't heard my comment, he sat me down at the table and proceeded to concoct hash from leftover beef, cooked potatoes and an onion. I vow, you could've wiped my eyes off with a broom handle. He was just dishing up when we heard noise from below and Nimble, plenty alert now, set up a ruckus.

I leapt to my feet, hand diving into my pocket to retrieve the .32.

"Calm down," Monk said. "It's only Grat. I called Moseley's Tavern and told him to come on over tonight. Whatever's going on concerns him, too, right?"

My eyes bugged yet again. My uncle had overcome his aversion to using the telephone? Astonished by the idea that wonders can and do happen, I returned to the table. "You're not going to talk me out of helping Neva O'Dell, you know."

My uncle sighed as if he were tired to his very soul. "I figured as much, China. You're worse than an old hound dog. Put you on the trail and you don't stop till the game is treed."

A promising concept. He sounded resigned and not likely to argue. My tension eased the least little bit. "Just like you."

I thought I saw a smile turn up the corners of his mouth, but his mustache made it hard to tell. Anyway, Gratton came in just then, smelling strongly of beer and looking every bit as tired as Monk. They were earning every dime of their pay. Branston had been working them long hours.

"China," Grat said. Gray eyes scanned my face, my form, as though checking for damage. "What have you been up to? Do you know Monk called Moseley's looking for me? I figured you must be in a pile of trouble and here you are . . ." His gaze sharpened. "Are you in trouble?"

Apparently he didn't see Monk shaking his head. "Don't know why you're both so surprised I used the telephone. I ain't an idiot, you know."

I kept my mouth shut, but Grat said, a little heatedly, "No, just a stick-in-the-mud. As for China —"

My uncle ignored the stick-in-the-mud comment. "Easy, Grat. It's no emergency. Not yet. Let's hear what China has to say. Turns out there's been some queer stuff going on around here."

Grat sat down and folded his arms over his chest. "Such as? Aside from this cock-and-bull story our office manager came up with to explain those bruises on her face."

234

My uncle whirled from where he'd been turning his hash in order to brown, not burn, the other side. "Bruises you didn't think to mention earlier, China. Which is why you got your face gobbed with powder." He waved the pancake turner. "You better start from the beginning, lambie. What's this all about? It isn't every day," he said as an aside to Grat, "I come home and find a man tied up tighter than a drum and lying on our office floor." His mouth twisted as he elaborated. "His head wrapped in a tablecloth and him cussin' fit to still a mother's heart."

"Harrumph," I said. "He must've spat out the gag."

"What?" Pure shock swept over Grat's face. "Who? Why?" he demanded.

They stared at me. Even Nimble felt the weight of their gaze. She wriggled on her belly until she was hidden by the hem of my skirt.

How to begin? With a question, naturally.

"I take it Mr. Duchene didn't free himself under his own power. You let him go, didn't you?" I bent an accusing stare on my uncle. "I wish you hadn't. Not yet."

"Who?" Grat asked again, although I was sure he'd heard me perfectly well. "Duchene" — he looked toward Monk — "he's

235

the old geezer who owns the derby favorite, right? Or says he does." Obviously, he remembered what I'd told him this afternoon.

"We talked to him and a Mrs. O'Dell the other night," he went on.

"That's the feller," Monk said, and I nodded.

"I walked into the office when I got back from Corbin Park this afternoon and found Mr. Duchene rummaging through the hall closet," I said. Did I sound self-righteous? Maybe. So what?

"The papers on my desk were scattered about. Nimble —" I felt her tremble against my ankles as I said her name — "like the brave girl she is, tried to defend me and her territory. I don't know . . . things were in a bit of an uproar. Nimble barking, the old man cursing and poking at her with an umbrella. Mercy, Mr. Duchene was so angry. I was afraid he'd hurt her. So I grabbed the stoop broom and swatted him with it."

I physically felt Gratton's attentive stare sharpen the second the words came out of my mouth. Drat! It was too darn akin to the broom story I'd told to account for my own bruises. Probably, in fact, what had given me the idea.

"In other words," Grat said, oh, so dryly, "you overcame the man and tied him up."

"Yes." I smiled at him.

We were silent, me reliving the battle — with some pride, I must say — and Monk and Grat with twin flummoxed expressions on their faces.

After a moment, my uncle stirred, giving his hash another flip. "Why put the tablecloth over his head?"

"He hadn't gone upstairs yet. If I hadn't walked in on him, he would've found Neva there, sleeping in my bed. It's important for you to know he wasn't looking for her, or maybe just peripherally. He seemed to think we have something of his. Something else, I mean. Or perhaps something of Mrs. O'Dell's."

I paused. Whatever he'd been looking for wasn't his — or hers — at all, I thought. The man who'd stopped me seemed to prove as much.

"Yeah?" Grat asked. "What was he looking for, then? And why did the girl come here?" Without thinking, he took a swallow of the coffee Monk had poured for him. His face twisted.

I preferred water, with a chip of ice in it. My mouth was crackly dry, so I got up to run the tap. "Neva trusts me and wanted

237

my help. I don't know why Mr. Duchene broke in or what he was looking for." The story was becoming more complicated by the moment.

I spent a moment with the ice block and pick. "As to why I put the cloth over his head," I said, "it's no big secret. I didn't want him to see Neva when she came downstairs. That's all."

"Well, it sure enough discombobulated the man." Monk gazed around as though he'd find the girl hiding under the sofa like a clump of dust and dog hair. "Where is Neva now?"

"I took her where she'd be safe."

He eyed me sternly. "And where is that?"

I felt a curious reluctance to tell. I'd never accuse Monk or Grat of blabbing a client's business to anyone, but they didn't seem to take Neva's dilemma seriously. Or her fear for the horse.

Or not yet. I expect they would when I got around to telling them about the "message" I'd received on the way home.

I threw up my hands. "What difference does it make? Suffice it to say, she's where she won't be tied up and beaten."

"Tied up?" Grat glared at nothing. "Who —"

"Yes. Tied up. By the very same grand-

238

father who I left in like condition on the office floor. Served him right, too. Oh, Grat, Monk. You should've seen her poor raw wrists and her bruises. The one's you could see, at any rate. She had — has — others. Neva really is a brave, strong girl. She deserves our help. All of our help, not just my poor efforts."

Muttering to himself, Monk brought the hash, still in the skillet, and some leftover gravy to the table, inviting us to dig in. We had a tomato, too, a big one, brought in to ripen before autumn's first killing frost, and a loaf of fresh bread. My adventures of the day, I discovered, had made me hungry, and my mouth had already healed enough to making eating a pleasure. Well, except for a slight sting as juice from the tomato settled into my split lip.

We ate in silence until the only thing left on the table were dirty dishes and a few crumbs.

Grat pushed back his chair. "So, China, you're sure Duchene was looking for something? Not just curious or trying a bit of petty thievery?"

"Given the circumstances, you tell me. You're the detective." Perhaps I said this a bit too emphatically because I earned myself a sharp stare.

"And he didn't mention the missing horse?"

"Not a word."

His left eyebrow arched in question. "I'd give a dollar to ask him why he didn't."

"Me, too." My agreement was heartfelt.

Monk cleared his throat. "Sorry. If I'd had more time to think about it, I probably would've kept the old man here till I could get some sense out of him. And you, lambie. But you weren't here, and he was choking and wheezing something fierce. Didn't want him dying on the premises, if you want to know the truth. It'd cause all kinds of a stink."

Grat and I nodded, and without even thinking, I said, "I'll wager he was putting on an act. The other man implied —"

That was as far as I got.

Grat, as though wishing to snatch himself bald-headed, scrubbed fingers through his thick dark hair. "What other man?" he demanded.

CHAPTER 18

I'd planned all along to tell Monk and Gratton about the man on the street, but this was too abrupt. I'd meant to work my way into the story.

Me and my big mouth.

"Yes, what other man?" Monk echoed Grat's question. "Are you telling us someone else was here? Did Duchene have a partner? How —"

"No. Not here." To give myself a little time, I got up and started clearing the table. I'd taken one load to the sink when Grat stopped me by the simple expedient of grabbing my wrist and holding it when I reached for his empty cup.

Truthfully? I didn't mind. Gratton has nice hands, warm and firm and dry. Sort of comforting, ordinarily, although for some reason this time I felt a kind of tingle.

"So you met up with someone other than this Duchene character. Who?" he demanded. "Where?"

"When?" Monk asked.

"You two should try writing a column in the *Spokesman-Review.*" I tried, maybe not too successfully, to make light of the incident. "All those simple little interrogator questions."

"Tell us everything, sw . . . China," Grat demanded, "not just a few handpicked parts."

"Sit down, niece," Monk said in evident agreement with Gratton, "and answer."

I did sit. I did answer. And I was actually glad Grat kept holding my hand. When I'd told about the man — not much to it really, the interlude had happened so fast — I faced yet another barrage of questions.

Monk's were perhaps the most practical, although Grat, being the man of action he is, were more to the point.

"Did you have your pistol on you?" He'd given me a derringer not long ago, which was a pretty little pistol, but not especially accurate. Between the three of us, we'd decided the .32 was a better choice.

"Yes." Heat rose in my cheeks. "I couldn't get to it. I told you. I was on the ground."

"He didn't hit you?" Monk asked to make sure. I'd already told them he hadn't.

"No. He didn't hit me. Just tripped me

242

somehow so I fell. But —"

"But?" Grat urged.

"He was very intimidating. You have no idea." I couldn't meet their eyes.

"Oh, I think I have," Monk said. "Don't forget, I saw you when you came in. You were determined not to show it, but lambie, you looked damn scared."

"Of course I was scared," I burst out. "And I hate being scared. I hate men looming over me and wearing masks. Most of all, I hate being manhandled and talked down to. I hate . . ."

"Whoa," Grat cut in. "What do you mean, manhandled. I thought he didn't hurt you."

"Well —" I stopped. There'd be bruises on my upper arms when I undressed tonight, but I'd never in this world allow either Gratton or Monk a glimpse of them. "I mean he was just —"

"Yeah. Intimidating."

From the way the two men looked at each other, they clearly weren't buying all my story.

"He was saying 'give it back,' eh, but not like he was looking for the horse," my uncle said thoughtfully, going back over one of the things in my report.

"Not unless they expected to find him in our office." I'm afraid I sounded a bit tart.

"And even he didn't seem that stupid."

The corner of Grat's mouth turned up in a grin.

"And don't forget he brought Neva into it, too," I reminded them. " 'The message for you,' he said, 'is no more nosing around. This is the only warning you get. You don't, you'll be sorry.' Then he said, 'Tell the girl to give back what she took and do as she's told. She don't, she'll be sorry.'

"That's as word perfect as I can remember, so he definitely wasn't talking about Mercury. It sounds to me like whatever is missing has to be small and easily transportable, don't you think?"

"Yes. And he believes Neva has it," Monk said.

"Or maybe he suspects China does." Grat wasn't smiling now. "Otherwise, Duchene wouldn't have been grubbing through the office and reading the mail."

Monk agreed. "Lambie," he said to me, "you do manage to get yourself in predicaments, don't you?"

"This isn't my fault," I said.

"Never is." Monk gave me a level stare.

"I mean it. I haven't been nosing around, asking questions. I've just been trying to help Neva." The memory of my note to the coroner crossed my mind and I felt just the tiniest bit guilty.

"You're sure you've never seen this feller before?" Grat again.

"No, I'm not sure. How would I even know, but I don't believe so. The only thing I can tell you is he has a deep voice and big, rough hands. They caught on my coat. He's big all over. He . . ." I thought a moment. "He has a funny kind of gait. He walked fast, then slow, and when he ran away, he kind of clippety-clopped."

Grat really did smile this time. "Clippety-clopped?"

I slapped my hands on my thighs to demonstrate.

"Sounds like a horse trotting on a paved road," he said.

"Well then, that's what he sounds like — a horse." I went on to describe the working man's clothing he'd worn, as well as mention he had no particular odor. They laughed at the description. I can't imagine why.

The upshot was they'd be on the lookout for a man who sounded like a horse, but didn't smell like one.

I went to bed exhausted and disgruntled.

"Say, China, little Miss Neva O'Dell, who you palmed off on me, is a firecracker. And

245

she isn't easy to keep track of, either."

Porter Anderson sat across from me in the visitor's seat, sipping the coffee I'd brought down from the apartment and chomping enthusiastically on a snicker-doodle cookie. He tilted back, using the chair's hind legs as runners and rocking to and fro. I breathed only lightly for fear a deeper breath would send both chair and occupant crashing to the floor. After the treatment it had received yesterday from Louis Duchene, I could only wonder to find it standing upright at all. Good thing the maker had used sturdy oak and plenty of glue.

It was ten in the morning. Grat and Monk were off to their job at the fairgrounds, and I was tending to the business. Porter was my first visitor of the day. A surly visitor wearing a scowl.

"Keep track of? What do you mean? What did she do now?" Gritting my teeth, I resisted the impulse to tell him to sit up straight and have a care for my furniture. And for his own spine, while he was at it.

"For starters, she was gone when I knocked on her door this morning to see what she wanted for breakfast. She didn't get back until an hour later. I was beginning to think she'd run off. Or that maybe somebody took her." He chewed and swallowed before reaching for another cookie. "And wouldn't he have been sorry?"

The question sounded rhetorical.

It beats me why people can't, or won't, behave in a way that furthers their own best interests. I found myself a bit exasperated with the girl.

"Did she say where she'd gone?" I asked. "Or what she was doing?"

"Not hardly. First she denied she'd been gone, then changed her mind and told me to mind my own business."

"She did?" This didn't sound like the Neva I knew. She always struck me as too reticent to be so blunt.

"In so many words." Porter's face flushed a little. "Said the less I knew the better off I'd be. Said she didn't want me to get hurt." He got even redder. "Hurt! Me!" He wound up with a softer, "I'll show anybody hurt."

He seemed to have forgotten he'd already been hurt, if not directly because of Neva, because of me and my connection to her.

"She's a nice girl, Porter. I expect she was off somewhere taking care of her horse. And she'd feel bad if something did happen to you."

The chair slammed down. "Well, how the h . . . Hades am I supposed to look out for her when she goes off who knows where and without a word? This is quite a job you've handed me, China."

"I know. I'm sorry. I just couldn't think of anybody else I trusted. You took such good care of me after Leila Drake's gang tried to kill me, I figured you're the best. Even if you did get me inebriated." A little buttering up never hurts, right? And the reminder of my introduction to moonshine brought an evil-looking grin to Porter's face, which had been my intention.

"Tell me what can I do to repay you," I said.

The chair tilted again. "Put a spoke in the wheel of whoever is threatening the girl. Quicker she's out of my hair, the better. And take care of yourself while you're at it." He gazed around the room as though searching for something. "I don't know why Monk and Grat are leaving you alone without protection. One of them oughta be here with you."

I hate to say so, and I'd never admit such a thing to Porter, but the same thought had occurred to me. I kept hearing things that weren't there, and flinching at as little as the flicker of a falling leaf.

"Oh, I'm fine," I said, smiling as though I had the utmost confidence in myself. "I have my pistol, and Cosimo Pinelli — you remember him, don't you? Our next-door neighbor? — is keeping his eyes open and his ears cocked in case anything out of the ordinary happens. Why, I'll bet he could repeat this entire conversation."

"Huh. Maybe if he spoke English." Porter snorted, showing he did indeed remember Mr. Pinelli.

The telephone rang, at which he jumped like a frog. I welcomed the interruption — a request from one of Doyle & Howe's regular clients asking us to verify whether a certain gentleman paid his bills. Or not.

A simple bread-and-butter problem, easy to fix. If we were lucky, it would net enough to pay the Washington Water Power Company for our electric lighting this month. As soon as Porter left, I'd probably do the job myself. Anyway, I noted details and told the client we'd be back with him within the week. Porter sat still and looked impressed.

I put my pencil down, set my notes aside, and folded my hands. "Do you want me to speak to Neva? You see, right now, I don't have any idea where she's put the horse. I didn't want her to tell me. What I don't know, I can't repeat. But if you think it'll be helpful, I'll try to get her cooperation."

Porter huffed out through his nose, sounding a small bull-like snort. "Nah. Better if you stay away. Somebody might follow you right to her and we don't want that. I can tell her about you getting stopped, and let her know what's going on.

"She needs to hear the message," he added when I started to protest. "Whatever they think she has, well, better if it comes out in the open."

I couldn't disagree, and not just because my curiosity was killing me.

"Anyhow," Porter continued, "I don't look for Neva to listen to a word I say, so when she sneaks out tonight or tomorrow to check on the horse again, I'll follow her. Don't worry. I won't let her spot me. But at least we'll have a handle on where she goes and who she sees."

I found myself nodding agreement. I didn't like doing this sort of thing, tricking the girl into giving up her dearly held secrets, but like Porter, I couldn't see any other way to keep her safe.

Our conversation grew cheerier after settling a course of action on Neva's behalf. Porter brightened, telling me he was making a stop at Dodson's Jewelers with an eye to buying Alice a pair of diamond earbobs. And then, having eaten a whole plateful of cookies, he departed at last, promising to report back the next morning. I'd have to bake again, perhaps something chocolate.

The small job I'd contracted took only half an hour — hardly longer than it took to create the invoice.

I found myself too restless to sit still and work on the ledger. Restless and itchy, as if sensing some kind of calamity in the offing. Hoping to evade my own thoughts — or maybe they were fears — I decided to take Nimble with me to the post office to mail the aforementioned billing statement.

I'd barely stepped outside and locked the office door behind me than the woman who ran a lovely little café up on Howard Street joined me on the sidewalk. Mrs. Flynn, tall and heavily boned although thin, worked hard to make her little hole-in-the-wall restaurant a success. Incongruous as it may be, given her height and a certain mannish appearance, she catered mainly to ladies. She furnished her place with tables covered with embroidered or lacy cloths, supplied delicate wire chairs, and served a light, delectable menu with the most wonderful pastries. I loved it, and always felt comfortable there when I dined alone.

"Good day, Miss Bohannon, I've been meaning to ask you something — for a favor, actually," Mrs. Flynn greeted me, tilting the brim of her plain felt hat to shade her eyes from the sun. The cloudless sky was the brilliant blue only found on crisp, sunny autumn days. Even the dust from the street, roiled by passing horses, buggies, and heavy freight wagons, failed to sully the clarity of the afternoon.

"Yes, Mrs. Flynn? How can I help you?" Headed in the same direction, we started off together.

Happy as a bird on a wire, Nimble pranced at my side carrying her red leather leash in her mouth. Her unusual looks, by which I mean her wedge-shaped head, curly, pale-gray coat, and whippy tail, always drew attention when we went out, and today was no exception. I smiled at a little boy who, holding tightly to his mother's hand, walked backward, his wondering gaze fixed on her. It wouldn't be the first time Nimble had been taken for a tame lamb.

If it hadn't been for the boy and for Nimble, I probably wouldn't have noticed the man barreling down on us. A ham-handed bullying type of man so rude as to give the boy a shove as they came abreast, knocking the child to the ground.

The mother cried a protest. The boy hollered — loudly.

The man didn't even react to them, which is when, with a chill freezing me where I stood, I realized he was focused on me.

Why? What did he want?

My innate cowardice coming to the fore, I stepped to the other side of Mrs. Flynn, dragging Nimble with me, and using the woman's considerable size and flinty-eyed stare as a bulwark between the man and me.

My hand went to my pocket, ready to draw the .32.

The man paused in mid-stride, then came on.

Fortunately for me, by then the mother's protests had drawn attention. The bullying man's focus changed. He glanced around, saw several people looking at him and pointing their fingers. Perhaps a bit of cowardice wisely afflicted him, too, because after the slightest of hesitations, he walked on without stopping, brushing past us and almost running.

I choked out an audible gasp of relief, and gradually became aware of Mrs. Flynn speaking to me.

"I'm sorry?" I blinked at her. Up at her, I should say, she being several inches taller than I. "What did you say?"

"I said, why was he coming at you, Miss Bohannon? Any fool could see he had evil intentions. What changed his mind was the little boy crying and too many people watching." She sounded quite huffy.

"And you. But I'm afraid you're right," I said. Ever so slowly, I took my hand from my pocket.

"Why?" Mrs. Flynn was nothing if not blunt. "What's he got against you?"

What did he? The exact question I was asking myself. It's a bit disconcerting to be a target and not even know why.

"I don't know," I replied after a moment. "I've never seen him before."

"I think," she said in a no-nonsense tone of voice, "I'd better walk with you, wherever you're going. We don't want him coming back."

"No. We don't," I said, perfectly willing to use the royal "we" in this case. "Although I'm only going to the post office." I stopped in the middle of the sidewalk. "Maybe I should go back to the office and lock myself in."

"Indeed you won't." She sounded affronted. " 'Tis a sorry day indeed when a respectable woman can't walk by herself on the streets of Spokane."

"Yes." I couldn't disagree. "But —"

"No buts. I shall act as your bodyguard, and in return, perhaps you can tell me what you've done to increase business at the Doyle & Howe Detective Agency since you've arrived here. I could use your advice."

"Me? Increase business? I don't think —"

She cut me off in jig time. "Oh, yes. You. Word gets around in the business community, you know, and everyone is aware the detectives' business has improved a great deal lately. Most everyone is crediting you."

My cheeks warmed. "I don't deny updating their billing practices has helped with cash flow, but if business has improved, it must be because the men are getting better at catching out bad people."

"Nonsense. From what I hear, they've always been good detectives. But people are talking now of better, more credible and documented results. Come, my dear." With a sharp glance around, she took my elbow and scooted me along at a faster pace. "You help me, and I'll give you a" — she winced, then went on bravely — "a thirty-percent discount on your meals. And if you bring someone else to lunch, I'll give you both fifty percent."

Puffing with the effort of talking and almost running to match her stride at the same time, I glanced up at her in surprise. "You're very generous."

She grinned. "You know people, Miss Bohannon. Important people. I'm hoping some of the women you bring will be society ladies with plenty of money to spend."

We reached the post office in record time, Nimble flopping down at my feet to rest with her tongue hanging out. I handed over my mail.

The three of us continued on, Mrs. Flynn completing a mundane purchase or two, and then we headed home. Not quite, thank goodness, so rapidly. When we reached the office again, I'd made up my mind.

"I'm acquainted with one or two fairly influential ladies who might take lunch with me," I conceded before we said our good-byes. "Mrs. Biddlestrom, the banker's wife, for one. Perhaps Miss Fern Atwood, an actress I know, for another. She's quite the toast of the town just now. But really, I'm sure it's more a matter of keeping tight control of your bookkeeping. Paying bills on time and receiving all the money you earn. It would pay if you placed an advertisement in the newspapers. Hand out flyers to your customers, perhaps telling of a special day for special items, like ice cream or chocolate cake. I believe you're well on your way already."

Perhaps, if I ever saw Mrs. Branston again,

I could also approach her on Mrs. Flynn's behalf.

Mrs. Flynn's eyes lit up. "There. I knew you'd help. Why, what you've already suggested has been worth the chance of getting stuck with a knife!"

"Stuck with a knife?" Blinking wide, I pulled Nimble closer as I hurriedly shoved the key in the lock.

"Why yes, Miss Bohannon. Didn't you see the knife in the man's hand? He had the blade up his sleeve and the hilt hidden in his palm. If you hadn't stepped behind me when you did —"

Head abuzz, I stumbled into the office.

CHAPTER 19

After collapsing onto my office chair, it took a few minutes before I unfroze enough to remove Nimble's leash and let her into the backyard to do her business. Had Mrs. Flynn been joshing me about that evil-looking man and a knife? I didn't think so. She didn't strike me as the joshing type.

After a while, I went upstairs, put my hat and jacket away, washed my face and re-powdered my bruise. Better. Or so I told myself.

At least Mrs. Flynn had given me something to think about besides Neva O'Dell and her problems. Which, above expectation, had also, apparently, become my problems.

This time, before I turned the closed sign over to the open side, I left the top drawer of my desk ajar and placed the .32 in a position where it was easy to palm. In fact, I practiced once or twice, just to be sure. And this time, when the door rattled a warning before opening, I had my hand on the grip.

Believe me, I breathed no more freely when my next visitor entered.

"Miss Bohannon," said Mr. Warren Poole in a stern tone, as if he were speaking to a recalcitrant schoolboy, "I want a word with you."

Me timbers, as they say, shivered, while Nimble, taking action on her own, scrambled into the kneehole to hide. I expect she didn't like his tone of voice any more than I did.

He looked down his long, thin nose at us in obvious disapproval. His grape-green eyes were cold. Well, he didn't intimidate me! Or not much.

"Mr. Poole. How may I help you?" Ice dripped from my voice. I got to my feet. "Or have you come to complain about my dog?"

"Dog?" he said vaguely, as though he'd never heard of such an animal. "What about your dog?"

"Nothing. That's my point."

We stared at each other for long seconds.

He blinked first. Then cleared his throat. Preened his short beard. Said portentously, "I'm here at the request of a certain Mrs. Hazel O'Dell and her father, Mr. Louis

Duchene, with whom I believe you're acquainted."

I choked back a gasp. Really? Mr. Louis Duchene? Had he mentioned to Poole how he'd come to meet me? Or said how he'd broken into our office and I'd caught him rifling through our things? Had he told how I'd hog-tied him and stuck a gag in his mouth?

"Also, I might add," Poole said, nodding as though agreeing with himself, "I'm here under the aegis of the Spokane Horse Racing Commission, for whom the proprietors of this detective agency work."

I took a moment to decipher what he'd said, then snorted audibly. As if I didn't know whose desk I was sitting at.

"And?" I snapped my mouth shut on anything further. Like Gratton says, when it comes to interrogation, let the other party speak first. And answer questions with a question — if we ever actually got to the crux of the matter.

"Shall we sit?" Poole asked, already pulling up a chair. The same one Porter had occupied earlier. I wondered, given the abuse he'd subjected it to, if the legs would hold under its new occupant. Frankly, I didn't much care.

Seating myself, I waved my hand in invitation. Amazing. One of my suspects had come to me and, although he frightened me a little, I considered this too good of an opportunity to pass up. I'd stand my ground. No running out the door screaming for help.

Anyway, he'd made no threatening gestures. Yet.

"How can I help you?" I asked again once he'd gotten settled, legs crossed, his hat resting on a cocked knee. He cleared his throat.

"Mrs. O'Dell came to me this morning," he said, "saying her daughter has run away. She thinks you had a hand in the child's disappearance."

"Really," I said and shut my mouth on anything further. I forgot to form it as a question.

After a long moment, in which I'm certain he expected a denial, an excuse, a confession, or something besides silence, he said, "Yes. But worse, at least in the racing commission's point of view, the daughter seems to have stolen a horse, Mercury, along with some other things, from her mother. Mercury is the odds-on favorite entered in the derby, to take place on Sunday at the fairgrounds. Perhaps you've heard your uncle speak of the race."

As though I couldn't possibly know such

a thing without hearing of it from my uncle. Bah!

"It is," he added when I remained silent, "an important event in this area. A large segment of the population, sporting men or not, are interested in the outcome. Plus, it brings a great deal of money into the community as a whole."

Especially him, if my speculation was correct.

"Do you mean gambling, Mr. Poole?" Maybe he'd admit his interest.

He hesitated. "Among other things, yes. But not only gambling. More importantly for the city, people also stay in the hotels, they eat in the restaurants, they shop in the stores, all profitable for Spokane citizens."

Including him, no doubt.

"Yes. I suppose so." He'd get no argument from me on this.

"Which is why we, not only Mrs. O'Dell and Mr. Duchene, but the entire city needs the horse back in time for the race."

I sat waiting, not saying anything, as Nimble, hidden from Poole's sight, leaned against my knees. I gave her ear a scratch.

Poole frowned at the small sound. He shifted in his seat, lifted his hat and uncrossed his legs, recrossing them the other way. His whole body tensed. "Well?" he said after perhaps ten or fifteen seconds had ticked past.

I widened my eyes at him. "Excuse me. Did you ask a question?"

Under the force of a frown, his heavy eyebrows puckered, nearly to meet in the middle. "Do not trifle with me, Miss Bohannon. Where is the horse? I demand you tell me."

"I beg your pardon. Demand?"

Without thinking, I'd folded my hands in my lap. Now I reached into the open drawer again and, hidden by the bulk of the desk, transferred the pistol to my lap. If necessary, all I had to do was lift it up. Comforting, to say the least.

"I haven't the faintest idea where Mercury is, Mr. Poole. What on earth makes you think I do?"

He shifted impatiently, the chair squeaking a protest. "Don't lie to me. Mrs. O'Dell tells me her daughter has, for some reason neither she nor her father can ascertain, come to you for some very ill-advised 'help' before. They told me you even took it upon yourself to force the child into viewing her brother's body, giving her nightmares until she can't think straight. Although, according to Mrs. O'Dell, her daughter is not quite 'all there.' Now, apparently, she's a common thief, to boot. And you, miss, right along with her, if you don't speak up immediately."

I could actually feel the blood draining from my brain. My vision went fuzzy. I wished Porter were here to supply the swearwords I wanted to use on this horrible man, on Neva's twice-horrible mother, on her equally horrid grandfather. Everything I'd ever learned about questioning suspects flew from my head. Thank the Lord, I was too stunned, at first, to as much as open my mouth.

In the kneehole under the desk, Nimble growled.

"Get out," I finally managed to say. My lips felt icy, making speech difficult. "You haven't the least idea what you're talking about. To come in here and accuse me of lying, of horse stealing, of I don't even know what else, is beyond enough. I want you to leave. Now. While you still can."

I rose to my feet, the pistol in plain sight. I watched with pleasure as his confidence abruptly waned.

"See here," he said, rising so quickly his hat fell from his knee and went spinning across the floor. "Put that gun away."

"And what? Put it away so you can slap me around like another of your minions has already tried to do? Or do you have a knife ready to stab me with, like the failed attempt by your man only a few minutes ago?"

He gaped in a most unattractive fashion. "What are you talking about, you fool woman?"

"You know exactly what. Don't try acting like you don't. I know you for what you are." My gun hand shook a little. He watched it happen, his eyes flickering.

"Hold on." His feet moved, inching him toward the door. "Are you implying I hired someone to slap you? To stab you? Have you been stabbed or struck, Miss Bohannon?"

Mr. Poole was a decent actor. It almost sounded as though his astonishment was real.

"What's wrong, Mr. Poole? Haven't you gotten the full report as yet?"

We stood glaring at each other, a tableau of distrust. Nimble came out of her hidey-hole to stand beside me, her little white teeth showing in a snarl.

Our standoff was interrupted as the door swung wide. Gratton slammed in, smelling of whiskey and with blood spilled down the front of his shirt and jacket. His fingers were already twisting the buttons on his collar.

His mouth gaped at the sight of the pistol

I held aimed at Mr. Poole. His storm-gray eyes blinked. His jaw set and he sucked in a deep breath through his nose.

Nimble backed a tail's length farther behind me.

"Somebody want to tell me what's going on?" he asked in the mildest tone imaginable. His gaze shifted from me to Warren Poole.

"A misunderstanding, I believe," Poole hastened to say.

"Not a misunderstanding." I shook my head. "He just accused me of, among other things, being a liar and a horse thief." I couldn't bring myself to mention the two men he'd hired to intimidate me.

"He what?" Grat didn't sound so mild now. He rocked a little on his feet.

"Listen," Poole said, a trace of desperation in his voice. He could see the expression on Grat's face as well as I could. "I just . . ."

"Going on and on," I continued, "about how important it is to find Mercury, in order to insure the success of the Spokane Derby, the racing commission, and the entire city of Spokane."

"It is important," Poole said, and Gratton, darn him, nodded.

"Forgive me if I'm not impressed. All of

this is in total disregard of Neva O'Dell's rights and well-being," I added scornfully. "You see, Mrs. O'Dell and her riffraff piece of . . ."

"China," Grat said in warning.

". . . scum father, along with their emissary, Mr. Poole, have yet to even inquire as to where Neva might be or if she's all right. I can't tell them and wouldn't if I could, but do they care whether she's dead in some alley, or perhaps her body thrown in the river? Doesn't sound like it to me. And these are the kind of people whose word Mr. Poole is only too eager to believe. Why, I don't believe he even knows Mrs. O'Dell picked his pocket yesterday." I forced a laugh, high-pitched and a little out of control. "Or that the money she used to finance Mercury's entry fee was acquired only ten seconds earlier from his own purse."

"What?" Poole and Gratton said together.

"How did you know I —" Poole stopped. Perhaps he was remembering the last time he'd seen me and what had gone on just before. Comprehension dawned.

"Disillusioned?" I asked him. "Or what does it take?"

"You . . . she . . ." He stopped, his eyebrows drawing down into yet another scowl. "It appears I may have been duped. I'd better go," he said stiffly, applying a demeanor of polite rectitude. A bit difficult for a man attempting to retrieve his hat from where it had rolled into a corner.

"It does," I said. "You should."

"I do beg your pardon, Miss Bohannon." He gave the slightest of bows aimed in my general direction. "I sincerely hope you can expunge this incident from your memory. Forget it ever happened."

The nerve of the man. I had no words.

"China," Grat said, "can't you —"

Pooh. I knew what he wanted me to say. After all, this man was one of his employers. And, drat it, influential in the city.

"Think of all this as an unfortunate misconception?" He could call it an apology if he wanted, but I wasn't sorry for a single word I'd said. And I'd certainly never forget any of his.

Poole, with what dignity he could muster, sidled from the building.

"What other things?" Gratton asked.

"Excuse me?" I looked at him blankly, shivered, and finally deposited the pistol back in the drawer.

"What other charges did he lay against you?" Oblivious to the disgusting state of his jacket and shirt, he gathered me into his

268

arms. "Shh," he said with a soft Irish brogue, "don't you fret."

Mercy, he stank. Even so, I liked being held.

"I don't really remember." Not true. I remembered all too well. "I was too angry to pay attention beyond the lying and the horse-stealing accusations. I still can't believe he didn't even ask the most important question. Or what should've been most important."

"About Neva?" He sort of rocked me in his arms.

"Yes. Nor did her mother or her grandfather, the evil old coot. All they care about is the horse and the money he earns for them."

"If I can catch up with them, I'll ask a few questions of my own," Grat said. He kissed the top of my head. "I assume Neva is all right, or you'd be raising the roof. Do you know where she is? Or the horse?"

I pulled back and scowled at him. "Not precisely, no. Twice no. And I don't want to. All I want is for Neva and her horse to both be safe."

"Yeah. Me too." He stared down at me, expression serious. "My advice? Don't go borrowing trouble. And stay far away from Neva O'Dell."

No need to worry, I told myself. She's with Porter.

CHAPTER 20

I stopped shivering after a while and Grat let me go. I hadn't given a thought about being seen through the window until now, but we were in plain sight of any pedestrians passing on the sidewalk. A man peeked in, grinning to see Grat holding me.

Grat's arms stiffened. I looked up to see him glaring out at the peeping Tom; a glare fierce enough to send the man scurrying on his way.

Stepping back, I smoothed my skirt and ran my hand over my unruly hair.

"I'm surprised to see you here at this time of day." I smiled shakily at Grat, forgetting about my lip until it zinged. "I'm glad you arrived when you did, though. I was on the verge of shooting Mr. Warren Poole." I gave a dramatic sigh. "And then where would we be?"

He grinned. "My guess is you'd be in jail. Don't worry. I'd help break you out. And hide the body, too."

"Why, thank you, kind sir." I poked at his jacket. One of the pockets was missing, completely torn away, the woolen fabric ripped and hanging loose. "What happened to you? Have you been in a fight?" I studied him a moment. His face was all right, but his knuckles were split and bloody. Turning purple with bruises, too. "Sure you have. And I'm not sure you won."

He shrugged out of the jacket and started on his shirt buttons, fingers stiff as though they might hurt. "Not sure I did either. This isn't my blood though. Mostly. Funny thing is, I usually know how a fight starts. And why."

"But not this time?"

"Nope. It kinda crept up on me."

Galluses hanging loose, his shirt, stuck to him with dried blood and whiskey, tore loose from his chest as he shed the offending garment. He grimaced.

Me? I admired his manly chest and forgot to blush.

"Damn." He held up the ruined coat. "Look at this. I'm gonna need a new jacket before winter."

Sartorial splendor is not one of Grat's indulgences.

"Worst part is, this feller made off with

my handcuffs." Grat scowled in disgust. "Only reason I came over to the office is to arm myself with another pair." He brushed at his chest. "And make myself presentable. Otherwise I would've missed this dustup you had going with Poole."

Gratton keeps a change of clothing at the office just for occasions like this. He went to the storage closet — the very one I'd caught Louis Duchene ransacking — and donned a shirt. Old, although not raggedy, it went well with the barn jacket he found there, the two pieces making a matched set. At least the garments were clean and didn't stink.

Galluses up, jacket on, he sat on the corner of my desk idly swinging his free leg.

"Now," he said, "I think you'd better tell me why you had a gun on Poole."

I wanted to. I really did. But something was tickling at the back of my mind and it just didn't seem right to tell a half-developed tale. I needed to think what bothered me most about the encounter with Warren Poole.

Lying. Horse stealing. Weren't those accusations enough?

Somehow, for some reason, no.

"You're right," I agreed. "And I will. I just need to collect my thoughts."

"Not thinking up some kind of story to put me off, are you?" He arched a brow.

"No." It didn't seem worthwhile to take umbrage because, after all, he was right. I'd done it before. Told him stories, I mean. And truthfully? Probably would again. "Will you come around after the fair closes this evening? I'll have everything sorted out by then and I can talk with you and Monk together."

He gave me the eye, but nodded. "Guess it'll have to do."

He stood, ready to leave, but I called him back.

"Wait. Aren't you going to tell me what happened to you?" I wasn't about to let him leave without me hearing the whole story. He'd lost his best set of handcuffs, which were not cheap, and considering the damage to his clothing, I would've thought he'd be ranting. It really wasn't like him not to be. Which meant he was putting on an act.

He shrugged carelessly. "Guess we can wait till later."

And maybe we could've, but I said, "A tall bruiser with big fists and a knife didn't happen to waylay you, too, did he?"

I wished the words back as soon as they escaped.

His smile faded. "How —" he said. Then, "Too?"

What a time I had wiggling out of that mistake! The regular kind of excuses poured from my mouth: slip of the tongue, good guess, stood to reason, meant something else, he misunderstood. Grat didn't believe a single one. He knows me too well.

It didn't take nearly as much effort to extract his tale of woe, one way in which his anger worked for me. Nor to learn whoever we found running this race-fixing affair — my money was still on Warren Poole — had meant it when he said . . . or no. Wait. It was Lars Hansen who'd cautioned me to have a care for the people I talked to.

Lars or Poole, either one, it seemed to mean Monk was most likely in danger of being the next victim. As for Neva, thank the good Lord I'd gotten her to safety with Porter before the gang caught up with her.

Grat's account did nothing to relieve my worry.

He had been escorting a drunk from the fairgrounds because the inebriated man had been bothering a respectable woman with a couple terrified little boys in tow, he told me.

"Should've been the bluecoats' job," he grumbled, "but it landed on me. This yahoo had an open bottle of whiskey. The fool about drowned me with it, waving the jug around like a club. Spilled hootch all over my clothes. Threw it in my eyes. I figured him a danger to anybody even halfway close, so I decided to hurry him out through the stable yard entry. Get him away from the woman and her boys."

I hadn't known about a stable yard entry. In retrospect, I suppose it was how Neva spirited Mercury away.

"The big galoot was waiting around the side of the barn. I had the drunk — only he turned sober as a judge when we got out of sight of the crowds — by his collar and his belt, about to give him a toss, when the other feller clobbered me. He almost took me down with a kidney punch." He rubbed the offending area reminiscently.

"But I fended him off with an elbow. I'd gotten the cuffs on one of his wrists when the little one came at me." He took a moment to observe his bruised knuckles. "I subdued him, but then the big guy grabbed on and he had a knife."

My eyes widened.

He grinned at me again, as cocksure as ever. "Don't look so stricken, China. Here I am, fine as frog's hair. He got his knife tied up in my jacket pocket before he could do any real harm. Got a scratch is all. I pulled my gun and both of them took off running like stripe-ended apes. Only I'm out a pair of good shackles." He shrugged. "And a jacket. So there you have it."

I swallowed. Judging by the amount of blood run down his front, the fight hadn't been as simple or fast as he described. A knife in his pocket? It had been so close. A quarter of an inch from his skin. From his heart?

"I don't think that is it. Monk will be next on their list. Please, warn him to be on the lookout when you get back to Corbin Park, will you? And maybe travel together tonight after the fair closes?"

"Monk can take care of himself." Grat knew I'd be worrying. "But I'll tell him. I figured this to be personal, not random. I'm not a fool. And neither is my partner."

I wasn't reassured. Nor was he, according to the look on his face.

The afternoon shadows lengthened to evening. Streetlights came on, casting small pools of light at street corners. Traffic dwindled as folks went home to supper. The fairgrounds at Corbin Park would probably still be crowded, although the last horse race of the day would've been run in full daylight.

But the carnival and food vendors were no doubt doing good business. I almost imagined I could hear the merry-go-round's calliope from here and catch the scent of burning fat and hot roasted peanuts. An illusion.

I felt exposed, alone in the office. Uneasy. Vulnerable. What if the big galoot, as Grat had called him, came back? I'd rather have been busy, some of my tension, false alarm or not, relieved in work. Alas.

At six o'clock, having had neither visitor nor telephone call in the last hour, I turned the sign to closed, pulled the shades, and locked the doors. Both doors, back as well as front. The men had keys.

Nimble and I went upstairs to make a start on supper. Monk and Grat would be home soon. As long, I reminded myself, as all was well.

I'd had plenty of time to think during the last few hours. A thing or two stood out and I couldn't wait to discuss them with Monk and Grat. Too bad it meant confessing what I'd been doing the past couple days. My menfolk weren't going to be happy.

I peeled potatoes and put them on the stove to boil, grated cabbage and apples together with a creamy sweet-tart dressing, and whipped up some biscuits. We'd have pork chops. Monk always liked my pork chops. Anything to put him in a better mood to receive my news. All mindless work.

When Nimble, distracted from her close supervision of my cooking by the sound of a key in the lock, ran down to greet the men I put the floured and seasoned chops in sizzling bacon fat to cook. Two sets of footsteps thumped on the stairs. Both sounded firm and healthy.

The knot in my stomach unfurled itself.

Monk was quite boisterous when he entered. Boisterous for him, I mean. An act. He looked worn to the bone.

"Something smells good," he said. "I'm hungry."

"Ready in ten minutes," I promised.

I rushed around, laying the table while Monk and Grat took turns in the bathroom. It was all so normal. Mundane. How could anything be wrong when the world continued on its ordained course? I had to remind myself that a boy was dead and a young girl on the run, sheltered from harm and in the care of strangers.

Oh, yes. And a horse was missing from his stall.

A half hour later we finished our meal, and while Nimble chewed a meaty bone under the table, small talk ceased and the confab, to use Monk's term, began.

"You first, China," my uncle said, settling back and, patting his belly, loosening the bottom button on his vest. "Seems this deal started when you met up with the O'Dell girl."

"Unless it began with the Doyle and Howe Detective Agency hiring out to the Spokane Horse Racing Commission for the duration of the fair," I shot back. I'd detected a little something in his tone that concerned me.

"You heard Branston on the scope of our job. Nothing out of the ordinary. Sounded pretty straightforward to me." Grat sat back in his chair and took a swig of coffee, hot off the stove. Cowboy fashion, and just like Monk, he drank it much hotter than I can abide. "Still does," he added, twirling his cup. "And we needed the work."

"Doesn't it strike either of you as strange that the racing commission would hire detectives and then not use them to investigate the death of a jockey? Dead during a race discovered to be rigged, no less?" I frowned at him.

Grat's face reddened.

"Accidents happen," Monk said. "Nobody thought the death anything but an accident until you and the girl started poking around

280

and stirred the coroner into action. The police had gone out and looked around. Said everything was A-one."

I couldn't help it. I glared at him. "Even though I reported what Neva told me. That her mother and granddad had demanded Robbie throw the race, and he wouldn't. And they'd taken someone's money to do it, which probably didn't settle well when the scheme played out like it did."

"Not much doubt about that," Grat said, catching the tension between my uncle and me. "But the order of who found out what when didn't exactly come together in a straight line."

I had to admit he was right.

Monk slapped his hand on the table, making the dishes jump. Me too. Nimble scrambled from under the table and took her bone into the other room.

"You haven't been very forthcoming yourself, China," he said. "Otherwise, finding a man tied up in my office when I walked in might not have been such a surprise."

"Yes, well, that's why I wanted to catch the two of you together." I got up and went into the parlor where I'd stashed some notes on the case. Typing them is how I'd spent a good part of the afternoon. Each copy said the same thing. I handed one to Monk and one to Grat. "This is everything I know."

"Know?" Grat asked. "Or speculate?"

"Maybe some of each. Read it and see."

Monk, having settled his spectacles on his nose, had already made good progress. After all, I really didn't know much. After a bit, he looked up, sputtering with anger. "Lars slapped you?"

"Ignore that. Pay attention to the fact he threatened me. And you. And Grat."

"And you're just now telling us?" Grat seemed about to blow up.

"Read on," I said airily. "That's just the beginning. Time wise, after Neva's and my trip to the morgue, that is."

Next came my personal observations of Mrs. O'Dell and Poole. Check.

Neva's battered little self, mentioned more than once. Check.

Manhandler man looking for some un-specified item. Check.

The big man with the knife. Check. This one drew a great deal of comment, some of it a little crass.

Poole's visit this morning. Check.

Grat's set-to with a couple of toughs. Check.

Monk looked up from his reading. "So where's the girl?" he asked.

"Where's the horse?" Grat asked.

"I can't say."

"Can't?" Grat asked.

Monk completed Grat's question with, "Or won't? See, being lost in the fog just don't sound like you."

I smiled at them. "Can't. I made sure of that."

Grat shook his head. "You may be sorry."

"Will I? But listen, I've been thinking. Does it strike either of you as odd that Poole didn't ask for the return of whatever the first man said is missing? But equally as odd is the first man, the one who tripped me, never asked about the horse?"

They stared at me in silence. Thinking, I hoped.

CHAPTER 21

My uncle Monk, being a person of equable disposition, soon recovered from his fit of pique just as I'd counted on him to do. He was back to calling me "lambie" long before Gratton left for his own place.

I walked Grat out, loosing Nimble in the backyard for her evening perambulation while he watched over us. Have I mentioned the night and the wind rustling through the bushes always makes me uneasy? Well, they do. I see shadows lurking and bogeymen waiting in the dark places between buildings. Grat knows my fears. And, after being ambushed earlier by those two men at the racetrack, he may have been acting a bit more cautiously than usual.

His head cocked to one side, he scanned the area for anyone or anything that shouldn't be there.

It was all rather silly, I scoffed to my inner self. Me with my fears; Grat with his. I knew for a fact he had his own. In truth, Nimble would've let us know of strangers soon enough, had there been any. Instead she darted from bush to bush marking territory and choosing just the right spot to do her business. The same spot she always chose to do it, I might add. Her light-colored fur made a pale blur against the night.

"See," Grat said, as if he'd known we were safe all the time and was just catering to a Nervous Nellie out of the goodness of his heart, "there's no one out here. Nothing to worry yourself over."

"Yes, no worries." I shivered anyway. I'd come down without a wrap and, with the turn of season, the weather changed fast. There'd be frost tonight, with the temperature already dipping.

Grat, seeing my shiver, wrapped his arms around me. The rough fabric of his old barn coat scratched my arms through the thin cambric of my blouse. Even so, it felt good. He hugged me against him and rested his chin on the top of my head. I nestled, making myself comfortable.

"Only two more days." He blew one of my curls out of his mouth.

"Two more days?"

"Until the fair closes. Come Sunday evening our job will be done, your little friend will be safe, and the horse will have either won or not."

"A case of 'let the chips fall where they may.' "

"As far as we're concerned, yes."

But I sensed a lack of conviction in his words, very like what I, myself, felt. What might a man who'd had a surefire money-making scheme thwarted by a young girl and her horse do in reprisal? He'd manufactured one death already — or had his cohorts do it for him. If his temper got the best of him and his wrath fell on Hazel O'Dell and Louis Duchene, Neva would be left alone to fend for herself. And her horse. If his wrath fell on her, well —

We, meaning Doyle & Howe, *and Bohannon,* couldn't let that happen.

"You're sure you don't know where to find the girl?" Grat asked, rocking me slowly as we stood on the back stoop. A rhythmic motion almost like we were dancing. "Or the horse? Although I suppose they're together. Maybe we ought to keep a watch on them. Make sure they're protected."

I thought I should come clean. "I only know where she is in a general way. I do know she's under the protection of a trustworthy person."

"You're sure?" Grat, finally, had decided

to take the situation seriously. And about time, too.

"Very."

"What about the horse?"

"No idea about him, I'm afraid. Neva says he's safe."

His chest, pressed against my back, rose and fell as he chuckled. "You're not going to tell me who this 'trustworthy' person is, right?"

"Right."

His breath stirred my hair. "Stubborn female. I hope you're doing the right thing."

"Me, too." Nobody hoped it more than I.

Gratton whistled to Nimble, who came running. She had to stop once or twice to sniff her favorite spots, and Grat took the opportunity to turn me around and search out my lips. Not difficult. I wasn't exactly hiding from him.

The kiss lingered on even when Nimble pawed at my skirt. I was breathless when Grat broke contact. There. Hadn't I known his kisses wouldn't hurt my lip?

"Umm," he said against my mouth. His voice was a sort of low growl. "Nice. We should do this more often."

"Yes," I breathed. Oh, yes, please.

"But not right now." He set me aside, and with a soft good night, held open the door for Nimble and me to go inside. "Lock the door."

He waited until the tumblers had clicked over before I heard him striding off at a swift pace.

I don't like waking up to a messy house, so before I went to bed, I spent a few minutes emptying ashtrays, washing up our supper things, and generally tidying the apartment. Monk's snores already threatened to raise the roof. He'd freely admitted being on his feet all the long day wore him out, and I had no fear of waking him as I went about my chores. That would've taken an explosion.

Which is, according to Porter Anderson, just about what it took to rouse me at five o'clock the next morning. If shooting off a gun beneath my bedroom window qualifies as an explosion, anyway.

When the gunfire cracked — the report bouncing from building to building in the street below — I startled awake, half leaping, half falling from the bed, drawing the blanket with me. Nimble, caught in the blanket's folds, dropped to the floor yipping as though being slaughtered.

"China." I heard my name called in a hoarse voice from outside. "China Bohan-

288

non. Dang it, wake up!"

I'd grabbed my pistol from the nightstand beside my bed, ready to do battle, before I recognized the voice. Or thought I did. Very cautiously, I crept to the side of the window and peeked around the edge. A man wearing familiar logger duds jerked about impatiently in the road below. The sparkling white bandages swathing his head in an Arabian turban gleamed beneath the waning moon.

Not a promising start to the day.

I raised the window. "Porter?" Nimble jumped up, front paws on the sill, to look outside with me.

Porter saw us and waved.

"What are you doing here?" I called softly. I still hadn't heard Monk stir and I hoped to keep it that way. He needed his sleep. "What's happened?"

"Neva O'Dell, the girl you saddled me with, that's what happened. I need to talk to you. Come down and let me in."

I held up a finger indicating he should wait, although he probably couldn't see it in the dark. Feet freezing, I shivered as frosty air seeped into my otherwise cozy room. "One moment," I said.

"Hurry it up."

I closed the window and threw on a ratty

289

old robe, one my evil stepmother, Oleatha, had bought for me in better years. Or maybe not better. It was frilly and baby girl pink, a color she knew I detested. However, the robe refused to wear out, so there you are.

Shoving my feet into a pair of rabbit-fur-lined moccasins with beaded toes (made specially for me by a Coeur d'Alene Indian lady), Nimble and I dashed downstairs to let Porter in. Preferably before his noise brought the police down on us.

I threw the lock, opened the door far enough for Porter to slip inside, then locked it again.

"Got any lights in this joint?" he asked crossly as he stumbled against a chair. Feeling around, he plopped gracelessly onto its seat.

"I do, but I'm not turning it on. I don't want to draw any more attention than you already have. What's the matter with you, anyway? Shooting in the street and causing a ruckus. And what happened to your head?"

Even so, I found the kerosene lamp we keep handy due to the regular occurrence of power outages, and held a match to the wick.

"Aren't you going to ask if I'm badly hurt?" he demanded as soon as the room brightened.

"You're too loud to be badly hurt." I'm afraid a lack of sleep caused an equal lack of diplomacy. "Although I'm sorry for the bandages. What happened? And what in the world were you shooting at just now?"

"Nothing. I was shooting at the ground, trying to wake you up. Throwing rocks at your window didn't work. I was beginning to think you'd been kidnapped, too."

I sucked in a breath. "Are you saying someone else has been kidnapped?"

"Yeah. Me and Neva O'Dell."

"You were kidnapped?" I repeated. Had I heard what I thought I'd heard? "And Neva, too? Oh, no."

"Well, maybe not me. Not exactly. I just got thumped on the head, but she was and still is kidnapped," he said. "I think." He grabbed at his head and groaned a little, muttering a string of words I couldn't quite hear. Just as well, no doubt.

Fumbling for support, I gripped the edge of the desk. "I'm sorry, so sorry I got you into this, Porter. I never thought —" I patted his bowed shoulder. Porter is a rough-and-tumble sort of man, unaccustomed to being on the losing end of things. And to have failed to protect a girl like Neva, well, he must be devastated right now.

"Tell me," I said, so he did.

Neva sneaked out the first night, too, Porter started his tale. "I heard her tiptoe past my room just before daylight. By the time I got dressed and downstairs, she'd disappeared. An hour later, she came back. Didn't hear a peep out of her the rest of the day except when I asked what she wanted to eat. I had room service bring her meals to my room and she ate there. I went out. None of the hotel staff ever got a look at her."

I brushed that aside. "Did she say where she'd been?"

Porter shook his head. "I didn't ask."

"Really? Why not?"

"Didn't figure she'd tell me. She'd already said you" — he put a particular emphasis on the word *you* — "told her not to tell anybody where Mercury was."

"I did. But what made you think she went to see about Mercury?"

"On account of the raw carrots she said she likes to munch on when she feels peckish." He huffed. "Thought she was fooling me, but I'm telling you nobody gets that peckish for that many carrots — unless it's a horse."

"Ah."

His shoulders lifted in a shrug.

"So, acting like a blind fool, I had room service bring some up," he said. "The way she grinned when she got them showed she had a scheme of some sort planned. Anyways, I made sure to be awake when she snuck off this morning, and I followed her. Right on her heels."

"And?" I leaned forward to hurry his story along.

"And, after a while we got close to the river, downstream from the mills and such. Bunch of people are camping there along the bank. Pretty rocky ground to sleep on, though, if you ask me."

I didn't care about rocks.

He put a hand to his forehead and felt around. Poor man. I bet he had a raging headache.

"So I followed her into some trees. There was a tent pitched in a clear spot between them and she headed right for it, only she didn't go in. She stood outside and whistled like a dove. Good at it, too. Couldn't have told her from a bird if I hadn't been watching." He stopped.

After a few moments, I said again, "And?"

His answer came slowly. "And that's the last I saw of her. Next thing I knew I was laying on the ground with a lady winding this bandage around my head. She said I must've lost my footing and thumped my 'beaner' when I fell."

It was still quite dark in the office, but even so, I was aware of the glare he directed toward me.

"Hit my 'beaner' my left toe," he said on a wealth of disgust. "Somebody sneaked up and coldcocked me from behind. And I never heard a thing."

Nimble took the opportunity to leap onto his lap and lick his face. He muttered something about a "dang dog, get off," but he didn't mean it. I could see his hand moving over her fur, holding her steady as he petted her wiggly little body.

I made my way around the desk to my own chair and sagged onto it. As was becoming habitual, I rested my fingers on the keys of the typewriter sitting there in front of me. "You don't think Neva did it, hit you, I mean, do you?"

"A little bit of a girl like her? Not likely. Besides, she was in front of me when I went down."

I had news for him. For a little bit of a girl, Neva, in the short time I'd known her, had survived a remarkable amount of abuse. But the fact remained, Neva couldn't be in two places at once. "How did the lady come to find you?"

"Said she heard me cry out." He snorted. "Me. Cry out."

"Did you? Although —" I stopped, thinking.

"Although what?"

"Oh, nothing I guess. Cry out just seems an odd way to put it. But," I added hastily, "she wouldn't know you're not crying-out kind of man. Too delicate of a word, for one thing."

He made a "bleh" of disgust. "Accused me of being drunk is what she did."

"I don't suppose you saw anybody come out of the tent. It would be helpful to know who Neva was meeting."

"Didn't see a soul," he reiterated. "Like I said, until the lady. But you ain't heard the best part yet."

"Best? You mean there's something good?"

"Huh. I mean funny. Funny in that I woke up in a different place than when I got bushwhacked."

"What? They — or someone — moved you?" Would Neva do such a thing? Could she?

I answered the question myself. She was the most determined girl I'd ever met. She'd do most anything.

"Yep. I'm guessing it was Neva and her friends. Anyway, I woke to no tent, no trees, no Neva. I was outside a tidy little house with a doctor's sign in the front. The doctor was the nice lady who bandaged my head." He frowned. "Nice even if she did figure me for a drinkin' man."

"A lady doctor?" I was delighted — and sidetracked.

Porter got me back in line. "Cracky, woman, are you even listening to me? That's what I said."

"Sorry. Sorry. Let me get dressed, Porter. We'll go back to the river and find the tent. See who's there. We can take Nimble to warn us and I can watch your back."

"Already went back," he groused. "First thing. They'd cleared out. All that's left is ashes from their fire and a tent-sized area with most of the rocks cleared."

"Oh. Then we should go back to your room. Maybe she's returned."

Morning was coming. Dawn light showed his pained scowl. "Do I look stupid, China? I checked there before I came here. No Neva."

Reaching around Nimble, he fished in his pocket and drew out a paper. "This is what I found, shoved under my door."

I took the note and held it close to the lamp.

"Return the horse and the book to the

296

O'Dells immediately," it said, "or at noon
the girl will lose her eyes."

CHAPTER 22

Neva. Whoever had written the note warned us he had Neva. And said he . . . they'd . . . take the sight from her beautiful eyes.

The note fluttered to the floor from my nerveless fingers. Nimble, abandoning Porter's lap, jumped down and sniffed it.

She sneezed. Then again, so hard she bumped her nose on the floor and squealed. I winced. For a small dog she has a mighty voice.

"China?" My uncle called from above. "Is that you?"

"Yes, Uncle Monk. It's me," I called back, my voice quavering. "And Nimble."

Overhead, his feet thumped on the floor as he pulled on his boots, a sound I'd heard nearly every morning since I'd been here. The light went on at the top of the stairs. They creaked as he started down.

Neva. My mind raced like a mouse in a maze. How can we . . . I . . . save Neva?

"What's going on?" Monk had reached the bottom landing. "What are you doing up this early? Is that dog of yours sick?"

"No, Nimble's not sick." I sounded faint to my own ears.

There we were. Me in my pink robe, Porter with his bandaged head, and Nimble with a small trickle of blood coming from her nose. Monk, entering the office, blinked his surprise at the tableau.

"Porter? What're . . . What's the matter?"

The note still lay on the floor.

"You'd better read this." I retrieved the bit of paper as if it were poisonous and handed it to him.

His face changed as he read. "Where'd you get this?" he asked.

"I didn't. Porter did."

"Found it stuck under my hotel room door," Porter said.

Monk turned his attention to Porter. "Why you?" He glared. "What happened to your head? Been scalped?"

"Just what I'd like to know," Porter said with an expression like he'd been eating hot, raw onions.

Monk's mustache did a twitchy little lift. "You don't know if you've been scalped?"

I daresay the nice lady doctor had applied

enough bandages for one to see Monk's point.

Porter's mood didn't lift at Monk's small joke. "I was answering the only question that matters," he said stiffly. "The one about the little girl."

"Yeah? I didn't hear an answer, just another puzzle." Monk looked us over. "Well, come on up to the kitchen. All of you. Porter, you're gonna tell me how you got involved with Neva while China puts the coffeepot on. And you — meaning you, China, and you, Porter — can explain to me what this note means." He turned to retrace his steps. "Besides a threat to a young girl. And no cock-and-bull stories saying you don't know. I won't stand for it."

Whew. In my experience, that's about as fierce as Monk ever becomes. On the surface, at least. I'd seen a different side to him a time or two.

We all traipsed up to the apartment, Nimble still snuffling as I lifted and carried her tucked under my arm. Book, I was thinking. What book? What had Neva kept from me?

Outside, the sun peeked over the top of the new brick building to our left, welcome daylight shining through the windows. Porter had already had an adventure, if one wants to call having his head bashed adventurous, and my uncle and I were done with sleep. I bustled about, tripping over the hem of my hideous robe, gathering pans and eggs and bread for breakfast. Nimble apparently decided her nose wasn't so bad after all and trailed under my feet in anticipation of fallen tidbits.

I didn't disappoint her.

Monk declared he needed his strength fortified by eating before talking. We were about halfway through a meal I merely poked at, when Gratton announced his early arrival by knocking into the coat tree in the rear hallway — same as he did every time he entered by the back door.

Dismayed, I jumped up and dashed to my room. What would he think if he saw me wearing this awful robe, my hair unbrushed, my face unwashed? I wanted, no, needed, the confidence of presentability while enduring our next confrontation.

I had no doubt there'd be a confrontation.

My uncle and Porter chuckled as I departed. I didn't care. After last night, I hated to spoil Grat's impression of me. I wanted him to think me . . . desirable. The mere thought made my innards feel itchy. But it was a cinch a tatty pink robe would do nothing to enhance the impression.

So I brushed, I washed, I dressed in my second-best skirt of dark-blue gaberdine with a pleated ruffle at the hem. I'd made it myself and it had taken me days, but it fit well and was the right length, sometimes difficult to find in a ready-made. I wore a blue-sprigged muslin blouse and a wide belt of blue leather with it and felt much more able to face what came next.

More able to rescue Neva? If I had to, I would. I'd promised she'd be safe and I meant, no matter what, to keep my promise.

After all my effort, even though he winked at me, I don't think Grat noticed my appearance. Too busy gobbling down my abandoned breakfast, I guess. I didn't care. In my worry about Neva, I had no appetite anyway.

But I still craved coffee. When only empty cups remained on the table, the note came out again for Grat to read. Porter had already filled him in on the circumstances of his head, since the bandages were the first thing Grat asked about.

Grat tapped the note on his nose as he thought. Then, in a funny sort of sequence, his eyes narrowed, his nose wrinkled, and he sneezed. Explosively. And again. And yet again.

I snorted. Nimble stared at him before curling up for a nap on my feet.

Eyes watering, he scowled. "Are you laughing? What's funny?"

"Nothing." But I couldn't help adding, "At least you didn't hit your nose on the floor."

"What?"

"Never mind." Composing myself, I saw Porter grinning, too. His grin faded when I said, "About Neva. What are we going to do?"

"We? You're gonna stay out of it, China. It's getting too dangerous." Monk shifted in his chair and brought out one of his wretched-smelling cigars, which, in consideration of my sensibilities, he rarely smoked inside our living quarters. "As for the horse, it's an easy answer if you ask me." His nod included Gratton and Porter. "Give the horse back to the O'Dells. Horse for the girl. No problem."

"What about the book? Horse and book the note says. Are you forgetting that? And I'd agree," I said, "if only any of you knew where Neva hid Mercury. Do you, Porter? Do you Gratton? Uncle Monk?"

Their silence was telling.

"All I've got for sure is a theory." Porter shook his head, wincing as he did so. "But then I wouldn't know the horse if it walked up and bit me. Neva never said a word about him, other than he was safe. That's why I followed her this morning. And because I didn't like her sneaking out by herself."

How badly was he hurt? I wondered. In truth, he looked rather pale. Also, very unlike him, he'd left part of his breakfast on his plate. Who had bashed his head? We knew it hadn't been Neva. Whoever she'd found to help her with Mercury had to be the culprit.

"So the horse is there?" Grat seemed to be sniffing the note — rather cautiously, I might add. "With some of those gypsies camped by the river?"

Porter shrugged. "Probably. But don't ask me. If he was, I expect she moved him first thing when she caught on I'd followed her there."

"If she had time," I said.

A sulfur match scritched as Monk lit it on his boot heel. He held the flame to the end of his cigar, noxious smoke rising over the table in a blue haze. "What I want to know is how you got involved, Anderson." He shot me a wry look. "China twisted your arm, I suppose."

"Why, I did not, Uncle. I persuaded. And

asked nicely," I said, even as Porter nodded. I hesitate to say which of us he agreed with.

"Seemed like a good enough plan at the time," he said, fiddling with his coffee cup until I got up and fetched him a refill. "After I saw the girl's scrapes and bruises, it didn't seem right to do nothing. China and me, we figured even if anyone suspected her of hiding the girl, nobody'd guess I was in on it. And they wouldn't have, either," he added bitterly, "if Neva hadn't gone running off after the horse. I figure somebody spotted her, then me, and put two and two together. Bad luck."

Grat disagreed — sort of. "Some bad luck," he corrected Porter. "But not, I think, all. I can't help thinking other forces might be involved here. For one, somebody who knows both you and China and that you're in town. Somebody who might have his own ax to grind."

My jaw clamped. Without thinking, I touched the sore spot on my cheekbone. "You're not talking about Sawyer Kennett, I assume."

"I met Kennett to talk about cutting some new timbers for his mine shaft," Porter said. "He ain't —"

Grat smiled. "Not Kennett. You assume right, China."

"Lars Hansen," Monk said, tapping his cigar until ashes floated down and landed on his pant leg. He brushed them away.

Porter banged one fist into the other as though he wished it was Lars's face. "How'd you folks . . ." He stopped just short of admitting how he'd gotten thrashed before I took Neva to him. "Hell, yes," he went on. "Right up his alley. Clobber somebody over the head, or bump them off."

I ran my tongue over my cut lip. There was a ridge, but it didn't actively hurt anymore. Lars was an ass, all right, but — "Let me see that note again, please."

Grat handed it over.

The vague observation that had eluded me before finally surfaced. What can I say? It was early. I hadn't had enough sleep. Fear for Neva overrode the clues. "Whatever else Lars has done, however else he's involved, he didn't write this note," I said.

Grat cocked his head. His lips twitched.

"He didn't?" Porter said.

Monk blew out a puff of smoke. "What makes you so sure?"

I ran my thumb over the paper, evaluating the texture. "For one thing, the paper is fine, handmade parchment. In other words, stationery, the good kind. The second thing is, I can't imagine he's started wearing women's perfume. Expensive women's perfume." I flapped the note again, puzzled. Did Mrs. O'Dell own a bottle of Jicky by Guerlain? I could hardly believe so, and yet —

Grat chuckled. "Got it in one."

"Got what?" Porter said.

"This paper reeks of perfume," I explained. "So much that Nimble got a bloody nose trying to clear the fumes away, and even Grat had a sneezing fit. So, not Lars. And not Mrs. O'Dell. This perfume comes straight from Paris. What's more," I paused, trying to think, "I've smelled it on someone recently."

"Where?" Monk snapped. "Who?"

I pondered. Where had I been? Who had I seen? The list seemed endless.

Finally defeated, I slumped. "I don't remember."

CHAPTER 23

No matter how I tried, the memory of who had smelled of Jicky and where I'd met her continued to elude me. I daresay three men peppering me with questions didn't help. They strained my poor gray matter to the breaking point.

After a while, to my relief, they decided it wasn't worth their time and gave up. Monk and Grat had no choice but attend the job they'd contracted. First on their docket, before the fair opened, they had an early meeting with both Warren Poole and Mr. Branston.

Porter, complaining of a headache, thought to drink a little whiskey for medicinal purposes, and ask his wide acquaintance if they'd heard any scuttlebutt making the rounds regarding Mercury.

Grat, before he left, grasped my shoulders and fixed me with a dark stare. "You be careful, China. I'd say close the office, lock yourself in, and lay low, but I don't expect you'd pay me any mind."

He knew me too well.

His smile crooked upward on one side. "You'd just give me some story about having to follow your conscience."

I'd been known to say something like that, once or twice. Why not? It was the truth.

"But I still wish you'd stay put."

"I wish I could." I eyed him levelly. "But nobody is doing anything about Neva. You know I can't just ignore what's happened, Grat. Somebody has to do something."

"I'm hiring Bill Jackson to see if he can trace Neva," he said. "He'll be on the job within an hour."

Bill Jackson, an old friend of my uncle's, used to be a brand inspector, too. He'd put himself out to pasture ten years ago as too old and too beat-up to be effective anymore, although he helped Doyle & Howe with surveillance and whatnot upon occasion.

"I'm sure he'll be a big help," I said. Inwardly, I had doubts.

"Meanwhile, keep in mind the note is meant to scare you — scare all of us," he said. "Whoever wrote it has no intention on following through. Nobody'd harm a young girl like Neva. Why would he?"

He meant to reassure me with logic. The

trouble is, Grat needed reassurance himself. I heard the worry in his voice, saw it in the way the muscles in his jaw tensed.

A stray thought came to me. "I wonder —"

"What?"

"If any of the police would help. They aren't all like Lars. Are they?"

"No. They're not. The problem is telling which is which."

He tapped my cheek ever so gently — a bare touch on the bruise Lars had inflicted — with a couple fingers. "Whatever you do, sweetheart, do not leave this building without your pistol in your pocket. Got that?"

"Got it. I won't."

"Promise?"

"I promise."

The men were no more than out of sight than I replaced my second-best skirt, donning an older one with a reinforced pocket specially added to support the .32's weight. Grat's advice — or order — made sense. I fetched my jacket and pocketbook, donned a blue felt hat with a plain band and a pheasant feather, and made ready to start the search for Neva.

Keeping my promise to Gratton, to which Monk had added yet another admonition to keep my pistol handy at all times, the .32

310

was in my right skirt pocket. I'd never have left the building without it anyway. I had money, paper and pencil, and an extra handkerchief in my purse. One never knows when a written missive or something to bind a wound will be called for.

As for money . . . well, who can go anywhere without a bit of cash? One of Gratton's lessons had been about bribes. He maintained that even small ones are sometimes effective.

I left Nimble, whom I warned to hide if any burglars came around, lounging on my bed. Sometimes she's a help. Today, I feared she might be more of a hindrance. Lastly, I locked up, turning our sign on the office door to the "closed" side.

Then I was off, sadly without a clear destination in mind.

Where should I go and what should I do first? It seemed I had only two choices. Or maybe three. I dreaded the third, thinking I'd leave it as a last resort. So of the two most likely, I decided to work backward, from the last known place of action. I'd visit Porter's hotel, where he'd found the note shoved under his door.

The Michigan was several blocks away. At the corner, I hopped aboard a streetcar and took the last remaining seat. The car was crowded at this time of the morning with people on their way to work. As Grat and Monk always instructed, advice I sometimes ignore, I kept my wits about me and didn't let my attention wander. I took careful notice of anyone who seemed the least bit suspicious. Only one got real consideration, a youngish man dressed in a fancy vest over a white shirt, its sleeves rolled to the elbows. He seemed rather familiar to me. But then he winked and his lips formed a whistle, leaving me to believe he was only flirting. I lifted my chin and ignored him the rest of the way.

Then there was the big fellow who kept dabbing at the side of his face with a blue bandanna, and another one who worried me because I fancied I saw a resemblance to Neva's grandfather. He sat several rows ahead of me and kept his back turned.

After a while, when he showed no interest in me, I forgot about him, too.

It was after I reached my stop and started into the Michigan that I grew certain I had someone following me. I don't know what tipped me off. An uncomfortable feeling, I guess, a bit like an itch in the middle of your back you can't reach to scratch.

Once inside the hotel, I darted to the side and, through the wide, plate-glass window, watched as people, mostly men, streamed past. One of them was the man with the blue bandanna. He stepped into a nearby doorway, loitering as he built and lit a smoke.

He took up a position near the street where he leaned against the hitching rack. His gaze remained fixed on the hotel's swinging door as if glued there. A woman I also recognized from the streetcar halted in front of the hotel entrance as if undecided whether to come inside. She was sharp-featured and a little too stylishly gowned for the time of day.

Some people, my own uncle among them, would've said, "Never mind her." Not me. Women, I've found, are no more honest than men, and sometimes just as violent. I stood behind one of the stout pillars holding up the Michigan's soaring ceiling and kept an eye on her.

Finally, she did enter. She stood looking around, an expression of utmost displeasure on her face, as though the decor was not to her liking. After a minute, she went over to the desk clerk and spoke to him. His shrug raised the shoulders of his cheap-looking suit almost to his ears. He shook his head. She bent toward him and whispered. He pointed his nose toward the ceiling and made broad shooing motions with his hands. "Certainly not," he mouthed so precisely I had no trouble reading his lips.

"You'll be sorry," I heard her say, voice rising like a fishwife's on a beach as she departed. She went out, shaking her head for someone's — I couldn't see whose — benefit before crossing the street to the other side. If she was indeed a conspirator, she wasn't a very good one.

Interesting.

Before I approached the clerk — and believe me, I had to work up my nerve to do so as I didn't look forward to a bum's rush — I took a piece of the paper from my purse, folded it into a square, and wrote Porter's name on the outside. Then, since I expected that if I were being described to someone my blue felt hat would get a mention, I removed it. Carrying the hat behind my back, I took a deep breath and approached the front desk.

"Good morning," I told the clerk, stretching my nearly healed lip in an entirely false smile.

"Yes, madam," he said. "How may I help you?"

He didn't smile back. Not, perhaps, a good beginning.

"I have a note for one of your clients." I

waved the document I'd had the foresight to prepare, and using my best approximation of a British accent, I said, "If you'll give me his room number, I shall deliver it to his door myself." Workers are often impressed by hoity-toity speech.

Other times they are not.

"You too?" he said. "I suppose you're looking for this Anderson character. He seems to be popular today."

My accent didn't falter. "I beg your pardon?"

"Beg it all you want. You're the second female in a row with an almost identical spiel, and the third person today. Well, I won't allow it. Not again. I chased the other woman off just like I'm gonna chase you." He made those obnoxious shooing motions again.

I ignored them.

"May I infer the first person did indeed leave Mr. Anderson a message?"

"Yeah, he did, and Anderson pitched a fit. Came storming out of his room asking who it was, when it was, and where did the fellow go. I ain't leaving myself open for that again."

Seeing the bum's rush didn't work on me as well as it had on the sharp-featured woman, he started around the tall desk he'd been using to buttress his authority. He must've been standing on a box, because when he stepped down and faced me, he was only a few inches taller than I. Not so very intimidating, if it hadn't been for his rather protrudent blue eyes.

I stood my ground. After all, I had justice on my side.

"What did you tell him?" I asked.

"Tell who?"

"Mr. Anderson. What did you tell him about the person who delivered the message?"

He looked me over. Paused. Squinted. "What's it to you?"

"Don't you mean, what's it worth to me?"

He stared at me, silent. Then, "Maybe."

I could've used some of Grat's advice right now. For instance, how much did he consider an acceptable amount to bribe a hotel clerk?

Opening my pocketbook, I made a show of looking through it, finally withdrawing two silver dollars. It probably amounted to a day's wages for a clerk. I gave him one of the dollars, dropping it into his rather grubby palm. "You can earn the other by telling me about that messenger. Deal?"

"Chicken feed," he said, even as the dollar disappeared into his own pocket. "But you look like a nice lady. What do you want to know?"

Oh, so now I'd become the nice lady. Progress. Relieved, I took a deep breath. "You referred to the person who did leave a note under Mr. Anderson's door as he. So, a man. Did he give a name? Had you noticed him hanging around the hotel?"

The clerk shrugged. "Never seen him before. He didn't introduce himself and I didn't ask."

"What did he look like?"

Another of those care-nothing shrugs. "Can't remember. Just some feller off the street."

It was an effort to contain the scathing remarks that formed on my tongue. "Young or old? Short or tall? Ethnicity? Color of hair or eyes? Crippled or well?" A thought occurred to me. "A smoker or chewer? What was he wearing?"

"Don't want much, do you?"

"I want my money's worth."

"Huh. Well, he was young. But not too young. Medium tall. Couldn't see his hair or eyes. Had a hat pulled down low."

"What kind of hat?"

He started to shrug again before his memory kicked in. "Derby. Gray. Not crippled. Talked like he came from back east somewhere. Might've smoked." He paused to correct himself. "Yeah, he smoked. Had a Bull Durham tag hanging out his vest pocket."

"Vest? Was he wearing a suit?"

"Nah. Just a vest over shirtsleeves. Kept smiling as friendly as a snake-oil salesman."

I froze. Then, "Come over to the window with me, if you please." I grabbed his sleeve to make certain he did. He moved as slowly as an iceberg, but eventually I pointed out the man I wanted him to see. "Is that him?"

"How . . . That's him, all right." He glared. "I got a notion to go over there and give him what for, getting me in trouble the way he did."

I considered. "I wouldn't, if I were you. He may be dangerous."

The clerk's close-set eyes bugged. "Dangerous?"

"Yes." I loved throwing a bit of a scare into him. "So, did you tell Mr. Anderson any of this?"

The clerk's face grew hard. "No. I told him nothing. Why should I? He was yellin' at me . . ." Oh, Porter, I thought, bad mistake. ". . . and had obviously been drunk last night. So drunk he'd been in a fight and was all bandaged up. I didn't tell him anything." He seemed rather proud of himself for this as he repeated it. "I don't know anything else. Give me my dollar. We're done."

I tossed the coin on the desk where it spun and rang. "We are done. In the interest of fair play, be warned that you may be called to testify about the man outside. Mr. Anderson was attacked, probably by him, while attempting to save a young girl from kidnappers. Hence his bandaged head and short temper. It would be best if you didn't try to obstruct those of us who are trying to help find the missing child."

Neva, I thought, would certainly protest that "child" part.

His eyes bugged even larger. "Testify? Child?"

"Yes." I looked around. "Is there a back way out of here?"

He pointed. "Kitchen at the rear."

I nodded and was already halfway down a narrow back hall when he called out, "Hey, I thought you was a Brit!"

Five minutes later, I'd not only escaped the hotel without being seen, but was well on my way to the river. More specifically, to the meadow on the riverbank where Porter had followed Neva. He said he'd gone back, only to find the tent and the people had moved on. Even so, someone at the campground must know who those people were and where they'd gone. Perhaps they'd be more open to speaking to a lone, fairly innocuous female like me than a tough, angry logger like Porter Anderson.

CHAPTER 24

Morning fires crackled in front of a scattering of tents at the campground down by the river. Wisps of fog rose off the water flowing nearby. Smoke smelling of tamarack wood drifted into the air, surrounding the eight or ten tents grouped among the sheltering trees in a blue haze. Canvas tarps protected backsides from dew-damp ground as people lounged about lingering over late breakfasts. Bacon sizzled in cast-iron pans, coffee boiled, women and children did their chores bundled in sweaters against the early morning chill. A surprisingly large herd of horses spread a significant odor all around. Some of the horses were attached to a picket line, some wore hobbles.

I scanned the animals, looking for a sleek bay without finding one. None had the correct coloration. Drat! I'd been so sure —

A movement from a horse tied in the middle of the picket line caught my eye. A toss of the head shook a precisely braided forelock from its eye. A bay, all right. Mostly. I almost laughed out loud because of the series of odd-looking white spots peppering its hindquarters. Clever. Unfortunately, an all-too-conspicuous wrapping tied around the horse's left front leg sort of ruined the disguise.

I didn't let on that I'd noticed a thing. As for anyone noticing me, well, I might have wandered into a camp of the blind.

Nobody can say I'm easily driven from the path I've chosen. I prowled quickly among the tents. The threat to Neva drove me to hurry, while allowing what I saw to connect with what I knew. Monk and Gratton, whether they were aware of it or not, had been good teachers.

Monk advised a detective to look for what isn't there, but should be.

Gratton said to watch for the one thing different from all the others.

So I looked and watched as I strode about. I nodded and smiled at the few people who deigned to meet my eyes until at last, using Grat's criterion, I found that one thing. Such an ordinary thing, at that, and not so very different from its fellows. Even so, it brought me to a halt outside a shabby gray canvas tent whose guy ropes were tight as a tick. A second oddity, I decided as I digested its implications, telling me this particular tent had recently been pitched. The others had been here since the fair began and their ropes were beginning to sag.

Close to a fire burning cheerfully in front of the tent — but not too close — a rickety wooden chair held an old lady. She was drinking coffee from a pint-sized mason jar, and drawing deeply on a shiny brown pipe. At her side, seated on an old rag rug, a young fellow drew his hat over his eyes and pretended I wasn't there. He also had a jar of coffee, hands clamped so tightly around it his knuckles showed white.

I wasn't fooled. He'd been watching me from the moment I arrived.

"Good morning," I said to them both. Neither answered. The old lady blew a puff of rank tobacco smoke upwards into my face, making me cough. The boy — almost a man — uttered what I thought might have been a protest, but at the old lady or at me, I couldn't tell.

I spoke to the boy when it became plain neither of them was going to start a conversation. "I'm China Bohannon. May I assume Neva O'Dell has mentioned me?"

He jerked. The old lady's toes tapped on the ground as though wishing for a chair to rock. "Never heard of you," she said. "What do you want?"

A tiny frazzle of tension eased. I'd come to the right place. The first oddity I'd noticed, the fact this one campfire was built on raw ground, not ashes like the others, had led me well.

"I need your help." My reply may have seemed to answer the old lady, although I looked at the boy as I spoke. "Neva is missing, apparently kidnapped. Someone, a man, delivered a note threatening her safety to Mr. Anderson's room." I paused, unable to keep the condemnation I felt from showing on my face. "You do know he was only trying to protect her, don't you? I wish you hadn't struck him."

The boy sprang to his feet like a particularly lithe feline. "Neva is missing?"

I was able to see his face, now. A good-looking kid, deeply tanned skin, eyes as dark as Neva's own, black of hair, skinny and not very tall, but his adult muscle buildup well along. Probably some Indian blood not too far back. Obviously the friend she'd mentioned, and most probably the person who'd gotten Porter to the lady doctor after he'd been ambushed.

We hadn't the time for me to pull my punches. "Yes. When Mr. Anderson got back to his hotel after the doctor treated him, he found a note shoved under his door."

The kid was no expert at dissembling. In truth, I was glad to see his face crumble and turn crimson at hearing about Porter. "We didn't . . . ," he started.

I cut him off. "Don't bother to deny it. I know, and so does Mr. Anderson, you were only trying to protect Neva. Now, do you want to know what the note says?"

He nodded. His granny — I felt certain she was his granny, if not his great-granny — remained silent, watchful, concerned.

"The note isn't signed, of course, but it says they've taken Neva. It says if the horse isn't returned by noon, he's putting out her eyes." I'd almost forgotten the book, since the main search had been for Mercury. And yet, should he be the center of attention? Or should the book? Mercury or the book? Book or Mercury. My mind whirled. Anyway, I'd found the horse. One out of two isn't bad. Besides, find Neva, find the book. That much seemed simple.

"Her eyes?" The kid's concern stopped at Neva. His skin went from red to sallow. He swallowed with a choking sound. "Who — They can have the horse. Where —"

"Hush, Lorenzo," the granny said. "How

do you know this is the right woman? She could be anybody. Someone that O'Dell woman has hired." She muttered something about "mothers" and "trash."

Good to know I wasn't the only one who recognized Hazel O'Dell for a true villain.

Lorenzo shook his head. "No. This is her. Neva pointed her out to me a couple days ago. She said she trusted her. But she didn't want Miss Bohannon to —"

Impatient, I interrupted. "If you mean Neva didn't want me to know where she hid Mercury, it was my suggestion that she not tell me. I didn't want to know. I didn't want to lie to anyone about his whereabouts. But after Mr. Anderson and I talked this morning, I had a good idea where to find him. And, of course, there he is." I let my gaze flick to the picket line. "What I need to know is who snatched Neva, where they snatched her from, and where they've taken her now. And then I intend to free her. You can help me, if you will. Did you see her all the way home, Lorenzo? Or rather, back to Mr. Anderson's hotel?"

The kid reminded me of a puppy who'd wet on his master's best rug, one with his belly exposed and whimpering, just waiting for punishment.

"No," he almost whispered. "Neva didn't

want me along, in case the clerk caught sight of me. She said she'd be all right. And besides, she was mad at me for what happened to Mr. Anderson. She said I had to take care of him right away, get him some help."

My heart lifted at hearing this. So Neva hadn't been in on hurting Porter, who'd only wanted to see her safe. I'd been right about the kids. They'd been scared. But not, I figured, as scared as they both must be right now.

"So she must have been taken right off the street. Unless the desk clerk at the Michigan withheld most of what he knew." Which he might have done. I tried to think. "Did you spot anyone who didn't seem to fit in? Who struck you — or Neva, for that matter — as suspicious?"

"No. Well, maybe. Neva said she heard someone behind her on the way here yesterday morning, although she didn't see anyone. But she's been awful nervous ever since Robbie died."

"With good reason, I'd say."

Even Granny had to agree, murmuring to herself as she relit her pipe, which she'd allowed to go out. Her bright black gaze darted between me and Lorenzo.

"But no strangers have come around asking for her? Anyone?" I pressed on. "Anyone at all?"

"Aside from Mr. Anderson?" Lorenzo stopped his head in the middle of a shake. "One. Maybe. A big man. I seen him a couple times looking at the horses but he didn't come too close. Didn't ask about Neva, either. I figured he must just be visiting somebody here in camp. Myra Wallace ain't no better than she —"

"Hush, Lorenzo," Granny cut in. "It's not for us to judge."

"Big?" I said. Suddenly cold, I held my hands to the fire, hoping to warm them. "How big. Did he . . . tell me about him, Lorenzo. Because a big man stopped me yesterday morning. A scary big man." I hesitated. "He had a knife."

Granny's chair squeaked as she leaned forward, glaring into Lorenzo's face. "Child, we don't want to be mixed up in this any more than what we already are. I'm sorry for your little friend, but I'm too old to take these people on, and you're too young. Besides . . ." She paused as though to give the final blow. ". . . you're the only boy in this family, in this generation. Who else is going to carry on our name if something happens to you? Something like what happened to Robbie." Her rheumy eyes switched to me. "Lorenzo is a rider, too. He and Robbie were always in competition."

Unsurprised, I huffed out a tiny laugh. "I don't suppose either of you would like to tell me what that name is."

"Bassi," Granny said, reaching over Lorenzo's "Bass," his version having been Americanized. Or maybe he'd heard of the outlaw, Sam Bass, and decided it sounded romantic. For all I knew, the outlaw's name might also once have been Italian.

"Where did you last see Neva?" I asked the boy.

"At the doctor's gate. She said she'd be fine, but wanted to get back to her room before Mr. Anderson woke up. Before daylight, too, 'cause she didn't want the clerk to see her. She didn't want anyone to know she was staying at the Michigan. For all the people who work there knew, Mr. A was using the spare room for business."

No flies on Porter. Even though, in the end, the plan hadn't been foolproof.

"How far was that from the hotel?"

He thought. "About a mile, I guess."

"I'll have to start there." I was thinking aloud, although Lorenzo and his granny watched me with worried eyes. "See if anyone along the way may have seen her." At this stage of the game, about a mile sounded like a lot of ground to cover in the allotted time.

I studied the boy's drawn face. "The note said by noon. I don't suppose you'd like to help?"

He nodded eagerly.

"Lorenzo," Granny said in warning. "Think what you're doing. If they've taken the girl, they may think two hostages are better than one."

For all her wizened appearance, it didn't seem as though the old lady's intelligence was on the wane. And I couldn't blame her for not wanting her grandson involved. Or not much.

Lorenzo, on the other hand, had his mind made up.

"She'd do it for me," he said.

He emptied the remainder of his coffee onto the ground, kissed his granny on the top of her head, and we departed.

Did I feel a frisson along my spine warning of trouble? If so, I was getting used to it.

CHAPTER 25

Ten minutes later, we stood outside the doctor's gate. We didn't go in, but Lorenzo pointed out the direction he'd seen Neva take when they split up. We tramped along as he said she had done, soon coming to a cross street. From there, she could've gone either east or west. One way took a longer route than the other, requiring an extra block or two, but better lit and safer as it dodged a particularly well-known . . . um . . . boardinghouse area.

I stood on the corner and looked around, my neck twisting like an owl's. "Which way?" I asked Lorenzo.

He shoved his hands in his jeans pockets and scuffed his shabby boots on the ground. "Dunno." Silent for a moment, he said, "Wish I had my hound dog, Growler, along. Bet he'd be able to scent her out."

"Me, too," I said, and added, when he gave me a funny look, "Wish you'd brought your hound dog, I mean. I'm afraid this is beyond my dog's abilities."

"Yeah. Neva told me about your dog. Said she'd never seen anything like her before."

I'd come to expect such double-edged comments. "Nimble is a companion dog," I informed him, feeling a bit defensive for some reason, "although she certainly got the best of Neva's granddad yesterday."

He smiled a little. "She told me that, too."

All of which made no headway when it came to finding Neva. There seemed only one thing to do.

"I'll go right, you take the left," I said.

But he said, "No. Right is a bad area for a lady all by her lonesome. I'll take that side."

"If it's so bad, Neva would surely have avoided going there. Wouldn't she?"

He shrugged. "Nothin' she hasn't seen before."

I do believe I was a little slighted. I am no delicate fairy, after all. I am a detective and I had once, although inadvertently, mixed it up with prostitutes. Came out unscathed by the experience, too.

"If Neva felt capable, then I am capable too. Besides, it's shorter, and my feet hurt." They didn't, but something told me this was the correct action to take.

"I should stay with you," Lorenzo said

stubbornly. "We can do both ways together. Take the likeliest one first."

His intentions, I daresay, were right on track.

"There's no time." I glanced at the round silver watch pinned to the front of my blouse. "We can't take the chance of missing word of her. You know what to do?"

He gave in. "Yes. Knock on doors. Go in businesses. Tell 'em what she looks like and that she's been kidnapped. If they saw anything, hurry up and say so."

"Correct. I want people to know she's been kidnapped, not a case of a runaway girl. And if you get any news, come and find me. I'll be asking the same things."

He nodded. "I'll meet you at the hotel."

"Right. This shouldn't take more than an hour. Better not take more than an hour. Time is growing short."

He'd already begun walking away, but he stopped and looked back at me. "What if nobody's seen her? What will we do then?"

I took a deep breath. What would we do then? "Somebody out there has to have seen something. We'll find whoever it is," I said, "and then we'll find her."

Lorenzo had spoken truly. The area I'd chosen to canvass wasn't exactly filled with

333

South Hill mansions. At this time of day few residents were about. Ladies of the night are just that; women known to make themselves scarce during the daytime. When Neva had come through here though, there may have been more activity. Only a hootch factory and a corner grocer appeared to be ready to conduct business, their doors standing open.

I turned into the grocery store to be met by a dour-faced man who looked like he needed to eat more of his own product. His shelves, from what I could tell in the rather dim light, appeared well stocked, and a meat counter contained the usual cuts. A closer look, however, showed cans with faded labels, pork chops with dry edges, and withered-looking hams. Not a shop I would patronize, given a choice. Perhaps that accounted for his drawn appearance.

He may, however, have been a better person than the surroundings indicated. "Lady," he said, "you're in the wrong neighborhood. You don't belong here. Hurry along south for two blocks and then go left. Don't look at nobody and don't talk to nobody."

Talk about a bum's rush! More forceful than the Michigan's desk clerk, he shooed me away so fast I barely had time to question him about Neva.

"Ain't seen her," he said quickly. Too quickly, perhaps? "Don't want to, either. I mind my own business and you should, too."

And that, as they say, was that.

Outside the now-closed door, I brushed imaginary soil from the hem of my skirt in a huff. "Dratted man," I muttered. Perhaps I'd find the person I saw peering above the bat-wing doors in the saloon across the street more cooperative.

I cut across Front Avenue, coming to a halt in front of Bart's Bar, a disreputable joint if I've ever heard of one. My nostrils flared. What a stink! The great unwashed evidently gathered here, to spill booze and smoke rank tobacco. And what else did they do? I didn't want to know. I just wanted to find Neva.

The flappy half door squeaked on its hinges as I pushed it open and took a single step inside. The interior was even worse than the exterior. It featured a splintery board floor, a few rickety tables with overhead coal-oil lanterns — no electricity here — and a prominently displayed lithograph of a rather chubby naked lady.

Averting my gaze, I turned to the big mirror behind the scarred oak bar. Squat bottles of liquor sat on shelves in front of the mirror, which reflected the image of a lone man sitting on a stool.

Our eyes met in the mirror. I don't know about him, but I didn't care for what I saw.

I cleared my dry throat. "I beg your pardon. I'm looking for someone. I wonder if you can help me."

"Looking for me, I expect." The bartender swept my person with a lascivious eye. "You're new. Kind of different. Hansen recruit you? Dammit, he could've said something."

Hansen. I put the name away to think about later and stood my ground. "I have no idea what you're talking about." Maybe I did, but I'd never admit it. Not to him, at least. "I'm trying to find a young girl who vanished from around here sometime this morning. I'm afraid she's been kidnapped."

A change, one hard to put my finger on, came over him. He eased himself from the stool and walked toward me, his gait as smooth and cautious as a cat's. "Guess we're even." He spoke in a quiet voice I strained to hear. "I don't know what you're talking about, either. Are you accusing me of kidnapping this girl?"

I put my hand in my pocket, finding the grip of the .32 exceptionally comforting right at this moment. "Should I?"

"Better not." He stopped in front of me. The sleeves of his rather grimy white shirt were rolled to his elbows, held there by elastic bands over massive muscles. Brown hair greased his collar. His teeth were stained by tobacco.

He frightened me.

I cleared the collywobbles blocking my throat. "I wanted to ask if you might have seen her, is all. She's only fourteen, about yea tall —" I measured with my hand. "— and has . . ."

"Nope." Easy to see he wasn't interested.

"But I haven't finished —"

"If you're not looking for a job, you're finished," he said, even more quietly. "Get out of here, and be quick about it. You're a pretty girl and you're in the wrong neighborhood. Never know but what you might be kidnapped yourself."

"But —"

His warning became clearer. "Lady, it ain't safe. People around here are always on the lookout for someone like you. Scat. Don't stop to talk. Not to anybody."

The conversation ended. Taking his advice, I scat — scatted — tripping over a loose floor board on my way out. He'd given me an unmistakable order. Unnerved by the confrontation, I hurried now, certain the hour time limit I'd set with Lorenzo must be up. The street was curiously empty, but I sensed an air of tension, something like when a crowd of people is standing on the sidelines waiting for a parade of circus elephants to pass. Remember, the way everybody senses unleashed power and always hold their breath?

The only person in sight was a man on the other side of the street. He leaned over a horse trough squirting water into it from a hose. I paused a moment to adjust the pins in my hat before, ignoring the bartender's advice, I crossed over and approached him.

In profile he appeared a little older than I'd thought at first sight and from a distance. He wore a new pair of dungarees and a pale-gray shirt, oddly clean given these surroundings.

"Excuse me, sir," I said. "A word, if you please?"

At the sound of my voice, he straightened and faced me.

I'm sure my heart stopped for a single moment. I know I came within a hair's breadth of fainting.

The man cocked his head as if in question and smiled. When he spoke, his voice seemed loud in the otherwise silent street. "Sure, and I please."

Instead of stopping, my heart now raced. The man acted as if he'd never seen me before. Was it possible he didn't recognize me? Should I carry on as though nothing were wrong. Maybe . . . maybe I could just walk away.

Turn around, China, a voice in my head said. Turn around and run.

This was the saloonkeeper's fault, I thought. He'd frightened me into rushing out and committing a mistake.

I berated myself too, in that brief instant. Detectives ought to be able to see through something as small as a change of clothing or venue. I was a complete idiot and I'd failed in my mission.

My voice came out in a croak. "You know what? It . . . It's all right. I'll go." I spun on my heel. Took one step. Just one single step.

His fingers gripped my arm squeezing my flesh to the bone. My right arm. My gun arm.

I froze. Oh, he'd recognized me, all right, this man whom I'd last seen following me outside the hotel earlier this morning.

"Take your hands off me." My throat was so dry my voice cracked.

"Am I the luckiest sonsabitch you ever

heard of or what?" Mirth put a gurgle in his speech as he started dragging me away.

Where to? I had no idea, and had no desire to find out. I jerked against his grip, which only grew more fierce. I twisted, I turned, I cursed.

"Two of you in one day," he explained, my struggles without effect. "Walked right up to me, both of you, like lambs to the slaughter. Les ain't goin' to believe his eyes when I bring you in." Laughter roared, fitting, I suppose, in such a big man. "And neither will the boss. I oughta get a bonus for this."

"Let me go!" Mind you, I wasn't simply marching along with him, a beaten captive. My shoes made gouges in the dirt as I dug in my heels.

I screamed, too, with all the breath I had. He didn't seem to care. Closed doors remained closed.

He may have had my gun arm immobilized, numbed by his strength, but my left was free. So I fumbled at my hat, plucked out the pin — all nine inches of it — and whirling, jabbed the pin toward his eye with a haymaker swing. My hat went sailing.

But he was too tall, or I was too short. Whichever, I had the satisfaction of opening a long, deep scratch down his face and into his ear. The pin hung, jammed through the cartilage.

Very brief satisfaction because, as though someone had turned out my inner lights, pain hit with blinding force and everything went black.

CHAPTER 26

Consciousness returned in fits and starts. One moment nothing, the next a bit of bewildered awareness of the kind that asks, "Who am I? Where am I?" at which point one knows they're alive. Then finally came the memory of being knocked out by a blow to my head. My poor head.

Men's voices, muffled as though they were talking with hands in front of their mouths, did a better job of bringing me around. I strained to make out what they were saying. Fear grew that something awful had happened to my aural capabilities. If sound can blur, then this did.

"Murphy, you're a damned idiot."

Relief! I heard those words clearly enough.

"What were you thinking?" Anger almost palpable, a man's clipped voice was giving someone a dressing-down. "You shouldn't have brought her here. It's too dangerous. That uncle of hers, Howe, and his partner too, they're like weevils on cotton. They won't let this go. They'll keep on looking for her no matter how deeply they have to bore. Did you even bother to cover your tracks? Did anybody see you?"

Icy hot. That's how the speaker's words manifested in my brain. And familiar. I'd heard him speak before.

Then the content registered. They were talking about me. And thanks to my slowly returning faculties, I realized that I was inside a structure and they were outside it.

"Nobody along Front will talk, boss. They know better," a voice like a foghorn said, easier to hear because he spoke loudly.

"Nobody? Are you certain? Don't forget she's a lady of means, not some piece of fluff who'll never be missed. Pay any one of those rogues enough and he'll squawk like a chicken," the first voice said. "Just like Billy Banks threatened to do."

Oh, he was thoroughly upset, all right, but I had news for him. He wasn't nearly as upset as I.

The next voice belonged to the man who had captured me. "So? We just bury her deeper, somewhere nobody'll find her. Right alongside Billy Banks. She's got it coming, too. Look what she did to my face. Damn near put my eye out."

343

My whole body shook. They killed the other jockey? Oh, God, I prayed. Please help me. I don't want to die.

I didn't get all this dialogue in one straight flow, but in disjointed fits and starts. Their words seemed to go in and out as I listened. Loud to quiet. Hard to soft. Black to white. The pain alongside my head and around my ear made me want to cry.

I scorned the urge and listened harder.

". . . not all," complained the man who struck me as more refined. He paused. "Did you search her? Tell me you at least found the notebook. Dare I hope we can salvage something out of this fiasco?"

I thought I heard satisfaction when the plug-ugly I'd stabbed with my hat pin, the winker from the streetcar this morning who now wanted to kill me, said, "This it?" Paper rustled.

"Idiot!" The epithet — perhaps his favorite when dealing with subordinates — seemed to explode with anger. "Can you even read? Did you even look at this? Of course it's not it. What is this? An appointment book. Here's an entry . . . it says . . ." His voice fell away, before he said, on a note of wonder, ". . . Mrs. Branston?"

Branston? Shock roiled through me. Could the man speaking actually be —

One man, the thug who'd knocked me out and who was still trying to defend himself, came back cockier than ever. "I looked, boss," he said, "but she didn't even have any money to speak of. Couple of bucks is all I found."

"What're we gonna do with them?" The foghorn fellow wanted to know. "The detective's girl. What about her?"

The boss must've been thinking over his options because he didn't say anything for several seconds. A full minute must've ticked past before he came up with fresh orders for his gang.

"Les," he said, "see if you can find the logger fellow, Porter Anderson. Keep an eye on him, but don't approach. Just follow him, see where he goes. Murphy, you do the same with the boy you saw with the O'Dell girl. When you get a chance, I need you to search through their things. I've got to have that notebook."

"What if we don't find it?" Foghorn asked. "Want us to kill them?"

"You'll take care of them if it becomes necessary. If neither Anderson nor the boy has the notebook, I doubt it can be found. Which means —"

The sound level dropped and I lost out on what he deemed necessary.

"But those girls, boss." Foghorn wasn't happy. "They know who me and Murphy are. They open their mouths and even your tame bluecoat can't save us."

"I'm aware of the danger. This entry in the Bohannon woman's book. I'm very much afraid it means she knows or guesses who I am, too."

Well, I certainly did now. I hadn't at the time I penciled in the lady's name.

"So what do you want us to do about them?" my captor, Murphy, asked.

I heard no trace of regret when the boss said, "We'll have to dispose of them, I suppose. Eventually. But only after we either find the notebook or determine it can't be found. Not by anybody."

"How we gonna do it?" Foghorn asked.

Just what I wanted to know. Or maybe I didn't. Logically, the only thing he could do — which he'd already stated in no uncertain terms — did not bode well for Neva or me. Did I really want to know the details? Their voices faded before the boss got around to answering. Footsteps shuffled as they moved away.

It took me a moment to realize I'd actually heard the movement.

I nearly jumped out of my skin as fingers cold as death touched my hand. My eyes,

346

kept closed on the premise it would hurt too much to open them, flew wide. It didn't do much good.

Blind! Not only halfway deafened, but blind, too.

"Miss Bohannon?" a little voice whispered. "China, are you awake?"

Much as I rued it, I feared so.

"Neva?" I whispered back. "Is that you? Are you all right?"

"Yes. Yes. Oh, I'm so glad you're here."

Relief swept over me. They hadn't blinded her. The threat had been a ruse.

I soon discovered I wasn't actually blind either, even if my vision blurred and my eyes felt sandpapered. The main reason I couldn't see was because the room where we were held was dark as aces. It had no windows and only a closed, ill-fitting door. Gaps around the door allowed some light to enter, as well as sound, which accounted for what I'd overheard.

I shivered. A cold wind blew through the structure, too, carrying a definite aroma of horses.

"Did you hear?" Neva choked. "They killed Billy. Are they going to kill us?"

"Not if I can help it," I said, much more stoutly than I felt. "We have to get out of here before they come back. Er . . . where

347

are we?"

I tried to sit up, only to discover my hands bound up tight. At least they were in front of me, which is, according to Grat, the best way to be tied. He said one could always escape if his — or in this case, her — hands were in the front.

Neva leaned against my back, propping me until I finally managed an upright position. A mistake, perhaps. My head swooned.

"I don't know where we are," Neva said. "Some fancy place on the hill south of town, I think. But not in the house. We're in a shed at the back of the fancy house's stable."

"They didn't knock you unconscious?"

"No. Blindfolded me, but I soon scraped a peephole."

"Good for you." I was proud of her, brave child. She sounded strong, though frightened.

"Miss China," she said, "can you tell me . . . do you know . . . if Mr. Anderson is all right? Honest, I didn't mean for anything to happen to him. Lo . . . my friend thought Porter was one of those bad men when he saw him following me. It was dark out, you know. But when I saw who we knocked out, we took him to a doctor. Lo . . . my friend did."

I could see better as my eyes grew accustomed to the light — or lack thereof. I rested my head on my knees. One side, the one with my damaged ear where Murphy had struck me, was sticky with blood. Thank goodness I'd changed out of my second-best skirt.

"Porter has a headache," I told her, "but he's all right. Even though he is quite angry with you, he's looking for you, too."

Porter and I should compare our aching heads, I thought. Only who could we find to judge which of us hurt the most?

"Oh." Neva's voice fell to a small squeak. "I've caused so much trouble. I hope Lo . . . my friend doesn't get taken. Or hurt."

I managed to straighten. "For heaven's sake, Neva. I know your friend's name is Lorenzo Bassi. We're all acquainted with him by now. Probably" — I admit to pinning my hopes on this — "including my uncle and Mr. Doyle. Lorenzo has been helping me look for you. He seems a smart boy. He also knows to get in touch with Porter or Gratton when I don't show up where we agreed to meet at the appointed time."

"You talked with Lorenzo?" She seemed quite astonished.

"Indeed I did. And with his grandmother."

I recounted my activities of the morning, finishing up with, "So tell me, Neva, how did these people find you? Where did they find you?"

She gulped down a sob. "I don't know how they found me, Miss Bohannon . . . China, I mean. I think . . . I think maybe my mother . . . or my granddad told the man, the boss, about Lorenzo. They knew he was here, riding for whoever needs a jockey. He's doing good, too. They know we're friends, Lorenzo and me . . . and Robbie."

The disconcerting gulping sob came again at mention of her dead brother, but then her spine stiffened. "The boss. They don't know I saw him, but I did. He's the one who paid my granddad to throw the race. He's the reason Robbie got killed and Mercury lamed." She took a breath. "My mother, she must've guessed I'd go to Lorenzo and told the boss where he was camped. He had one of those awful men keeping a watch."

Her explanation came with bitter emphasis on the words *my mother.*

"Anyway, I was hurrying to get back to the hotel before daybreak, but what with getting Porter to the doctor and all, I was late. So I took a shortcut."

I nudged her. "The same shortcut I took, I expect, looking for you."

"Along Front Street? Anyway, this man sneaked up behind and grabbed me, threw something over my head so I couldn't see, and tied my wrists together." Her head hung. "My fault. All my fault. I'm sorry, Miss . . . China."

"And so am I. I should have been better prepared. We all should have. I just didn't think far enough ahead." As my uncle might jump in and say, not thinking ahead was one of my troubles. I hadn't thought things out, simply barreling in with a damn-the-consequences attitude. For shame.

I shifted my bottom, an effort both to assuage the self-incrimination and because I was sitting on something hard. My pistol, I realized with delighted shock. How had the thugs missed finding the pistol?

Hah! He hadn't expected a lady to carry a firearm, more fool him. He'd only checked my purse.

"Neva," I said, my voice lowering. "Do you still have Mercury's papers and the other things you took from your mother's cache?"

"Yes. Those men, they slapped me a little and jerked me around while they shouted out questions, but they didn't look in my boots. They just kept yelling, 'Where is it, where is it?' I didn't know what they were talking about." Her face loomed up beside me, dark eyes big with earnestness. "But I do now. They want the little notebook my mother stole. And I know they're not very smart."

I choked out a laugh, even though it made my face and head hurt more than ever. "You can say that again. They didn't search me, either. Just took my purse. We're going to get out of this predicament, Neva. Right now."

"We are?"

Didn't she believe me?

"You bet we are."

I found it encouraging the men failed to find the book Neva had hidden so securely. While on the face of things discovering Mercury's whereabouts appeared their goal, and I'm sure he did play a large part in their scheme, we now knew it was the notebook the boss was really after. I had no idea what it contained, but it must have incriminated him in some way.

Neva might give the book up if she thought it would save our lives. Probably not an act in our best interests. On the other hand, she'd fight for Mercury's papers to her last breath. And if we were to get ourselves out of this mess, she definitely needed to fight.

"Can you stand up?" I asked her, not at all certain I could.

"I think so."

She put words to action, promptly pulling my propped knees out straight and tripping over them.

Neva swore. I thought she may have been eavesdropping on Porter.

The thugs, we discovered, had tied our ankles together. They hadn't crossed our feet when they bound them, more fools they. But they had made hobble-like shackles and tied us to each other.

Even so, on Neva's second try, with an agility I envied, she eased herself to her feet with barely a bobble.

My turn.

Knees first, then I placed my right foot flat on the ground. Whoever tied us had left barely enough slack in the ropes; an inadvertent error, I had no doubt. Slowly, I forced one leg to bear all my unbalanced weight as I struggled upright. Then I stood swaying, heartbeat drumming in my damaged ear, the edges of my vision black until my equilibrium regained itself. It all would've been easier if I'd been wearing trousers, like Neva.

When I had my breath back, I said, "We've got to get these ropes off. Quickly, before they return."

"I've been trying," she said. "But they're tied awfully tight."

"We have to do it, Neva. Try harder."

So we did.

The cord they'd used to bind us was more of the kind used for clotheslines than the rope one used on animals. Unfortunately, this made working our hands free all the harder. The finer diameter meant the knots were drawn tighter, no slippage like one might find in a thick hemp lasso.

Neva, her fingernails bitten down to the quick to start with, got no purchase at all. I fared little better. My nails snapped leaving bloodied stumps. Our wrists remained tied.

"Hellfire and damnation," I said at last. Blood dripped from a couple fingertips down the front of my skirt, adding to the smudges left from when I'd rested my head on my knees. A fine predicament, to be sure.

With our hands tied and our feet bound together, moving about was rather awkward. As for running, no chance. If we were even able to escape from the shed.

"What are we going to do?" Neva, as usual, left our strategy to me. She sounded drained, hopeless. I needed her spunky and full of fire.

"Trust me, we will get out of here. Both of us." I reflected a moment. "In one piece."

Neva may not have been convinced. "How? He put a bar across the door on the outside. We're locked in."

I didn't know how. Yet. I just knew we would. If worst came to worst, I intended to meet whoever unbarred the door with a bullet to the chest. If, that is, I succeeded in working my hands free, able to reach into my pocket and draw the pistol.

And as long as I managed to do it without shooting my own leg off.

CHAPTER 27

Neva's and my first course of action consisted of learning to move together, synchronized so one of us didn't trip the other. Not, I may add, the easiest dance step I've ever learned. I daresay waltzing is a great deal simpler, and accompanied by music, besides.

Nevertheless, in searching for a way to gain our freedom, we managed a complete circuit around the room without doing ourselves harm. We found exactly nothing. Nothing particularly useful, at any rate. Or not at first glance.

Our dreary cell had, at one time, been a tack room built onto the stable proper. Or perhaps it was where the homeowner's stable boy slept when the space wasn't used to hold prisoners — like Neva and me. The room had been cleared of nearly everything, although an overlying scent of horses and manure remained. A mouse-eaten blanket covered a thin straw mattress on the sagging cot. We found a three-legged table which, due to one leg being shorter than the others, rocked almost unseen in a corner, a saddle stand without a saddle, an old grain bin where mice rustled, and one dented tin plate, rusty where the enamel had chipped off. Maybe they'd used it to feed the mice.

Neva, to my dismay, began to cry. Quietly, thank goodness, but with little hiccuping sobs, like bubbles rising to the top in a bottle of soda water.

I had to restrain myself from joining her. She'd borne her despicable mother's and grandfather's abuse, and she'd put a brave face on her brother's death. This was not a good time to break down. Not for either of us. Too bad comforting children was not one of my strong points. In fact, I wasn't any too sure I had any strong points. It occurred to me a little comforting wouldn't have gone amiss for me, too.

"We'll be all right, Neva. Please don't cry." I patted her shoulder with the back of my hand since my palms were tied facing my body. Awkward in the extreme.

"Oh, Miss Bohannon, I've gotten you in all this trouble. I wanted you to find who killed Robbie and now we're going to be killed, too. Just like he was. A . . . and it's all my fault."

I refused to let her sincerity convince me, as for a weak moment I wanted to do.

"It's not your fault at all. I took the job with my eyes wide open. Now buck up. I need your help."

My abrupt demand seemed to help, probably because people ordered her around all the time. She inhaled, then exhaled, letting the air out on a shuddering breath. "What do you want me to do?"

What did I? Think!

I'd kicked the metal plate across the dirt floor, but now I had Neva shuffle along with me to take a second look. "See that?" I pointed down. "We're going take that dirty old thing and start bending it back and forth until it snaps in two."

She reached down and picked the plate up, almost upending me in the process. "Sorry. We are?" She stared down at it, her stance filled with doubt. "Why?"

"Because we're going to break it in half and use the raw edges as a saw. Something to sever these cords on our wrists. It'll take both of us. You push, I'll pull."

So we did. We settled onto the floor again, although Neva, after two or three minutes while we got nowhere, had the bright idea of just bending the plate enough she could finish the job by jumping on it. Which meant we had to stand up again. Her boots did a good job protecting her feet while she jumped, once again, I might add, nearly toppling me. But even when we had our saw, hours seemed to pass before we managed to cut through the cords. Our wrists oozed blood. Our numbed fingers left red streaks everywhere we touched. And even though the stable was cold, we both were sweating like Irish gandy dancers driving spikes. By then, I knew it must be nearly noon.

The hour that wicked man had named in his threat against Neva. Would he be back to carry it out?

What had he written in the notebook he searched for so frantically, that he deemed so precious? Or maybe precious wasn't the right word. I'd bet incriminating hit closer to the truth. Sadly, my curiosity might never be satisfied.

"You need a weapon, my dear," I said when we finally cut through the cord around our ankles. One of mine had been awfully tight. My toes tingled as circulation returned.

Neva's boots had protected her. It amused me that Branston's men had been so close to their goal and totally unaware.

"I wish I had a knife." Neva's teeth gritted. "A great big Bowie knife. I'd . . . I'd . . ."

"I wish you did, too." The three-legged table caught my eye. Limping, I went over and dragged it into the center of the room. "I suggest you kick this apart. Try not to actually break the legs, just separate them from the top. Not as good as a knife, but maybe a pretty good club. I think the wood is oak. Nice and heavy."

Even in the dim light I saw her smile.

She went to kicking and stomping with a will. Badly constructed to begin with, the table soon fell into four pieces thanks to her strenuous efforts; the top and three legs.

I spied the gleam of metal. Whoever built the table used good wood in his project, even though he'd lacked basic furniture-making skills. The table had been cobbled together with nails instead of glue and mortise joints. Some of the nails had worked loose over the years. Two or three protruded from one of the legs.

Neva reached down, picking her weapon.

"Wait," I said. "Choose the other long one. The one with the nails in the end. When the time comes, swing hard and fast and don't, at any cost, lose your grip. Anyone would be scared if they saw that

360

nail coming at them. They'll keep their distance."

I expect I sounded more confident than I felt. I certainly tried hard enough.

"You'll need one, too." Neva tried to hand me one of the legs. "Please. You have to have something."

"Oh, I will. And I do." I smiled as I pulled the .32 from my skirt's hidden pocket. "I've got this."

Neva eyes opened wide. "Ooh, a gun!"

By her reaction she liked it better than birthday cake.

Our relief lasted only a few seconds. That's as long as it took before we heard the heavy plodding of men's boots and the sound of their voices. One of them laughed.

Noon.

My stomach growled — but not from hunger.

Neva clutched her table leg in both hands. She held it poised high above her as though planning to smash it down on her captor's head, a strategy more apt to work if she'd been a foot or two taller. And if she could've traded the table leg for an ax.

"Wait," I said. "Don't hold a weapon like that. These are big men. All they have to do is reach out and take the club from you.

361

Hold it like this." I demonstrated with a hypothetical baseball bat. "See. You can hit harder and faster."

"Got it," she said, adjusting her grip as I suggested. The club trembled in her hands. "I'm going to aim for the first man's knees. He can't catch me if he can't walk."

"Good girl. That's an excellent plan. Keep the nails pointed toward your target. And remember. Hard as you can, fast as you can. We don't want to just make them mad. We want to discourage them from getting close. We want to hurt them."

Her eyes widened, the whites showing all around, as if she couldn't believe my ferocity, then she nodded. "Pound them down. Like they want to hurt us."

I eyed her. Did she realize what those words meant? "Yes," I agreed, "if it comes to that. But our purpose is to escape. Quick as you get the chance, run. Don't wait around for me."

Events moved like a train on a track after that, its speed multiplied by the weight behind it. One of the men, the one I'd jabbed with my hat pin, announced his intentions as they neared the stable door. Loud enough to begin with, his voice was perfectly audible, probably because he wanted us to hear.

"Boss ain't gonna be happy we didn't find his little book." Murphy was the one talking loudest. "But he's gonna be real mad we lost sight of Anderson and the kid."

"Time to finish the hunt right here and now," Foghorn rumbled. "Then it won't matter about them two."

"I'll take the detective's office girl," Murphy said. "I owe her."

My stomach clenched, tied up in knots as he chuckled, an evil sound if ever I heard one.

"Or she owes me," he added.

"You get all the fun. The young one won't be no bother." Foghorn seemed disappointed. "Now the boss ain't here to see, I'll just beat on her till she tells us what we want to know. Boss is a little squeamish, but he won't ask no questions after it's done."

"Never does," Murphy agreed.

This must not have been their first foray into murder. My blood ran cold.

I glanced at Neva, her features uncertain in the gloomy shed.

The door rattled. Metal scraped as one of them pulled the bar from the brackets. A widening glimmer of light shone through the crack between the sagging door and the jamb.

"Ready?" I whispered.

Neva nodded. Her lips pressed tight, as though to hold in a scream. So, I discovered, were mine.

"Hard and fast," she said through gritted teeth.

The door yanked open. The shape of a man filled the opening as the first of them stepped through.

"Fe, fie, foe . . . ," Foghorn was saying, playful-like, as if this were all a game.

Neva's club slammed into his kneecap with a resounding thud. His quote from the old fairytale turned into a scream.

Murphy, my bitter enemy, had followed Foghorn closely. Too closely, as it happened. He stumbled over Foghorn, who crashed to the ground with a thump like a tree falling in the forest. Unfortunately, this was not part of the plan because it meant the bullet I'd aimed at Murphy's midsection flew over his head. Which also meant we lost our critical moment of surprise.

And it meant their thrashing bodies blocked the doorway.

Meanwhile, Neva, silently intense, continued pounding on Foghorn with her nailed club. He bellowed as nails tore through skin and muscle. Blood squirted from his wounds.

"Hands up," I screamed at Murphy.

What a nonsensical thing to say! Of course, he didn't obey. He yelled, leapt over Foghorn, and grabbed for me with complete disregard of my pistol.

His mistake this time. Despite my trembling, I didn't miss again. Well, it would've been hard since some part of him was almost pressed against the .32's barrel.

I pulled the trigger.

He dropped to the ground, at which point Neva, who, in her enthusiasm, had Foghorn subdued, hit Murphy in the behind with her nailed club.

My, my.

What a sight. I wished I had my trusty Kodak camera handy. The table leg, ripped from Neva's hands and dangling from Murphy's buttocks, was a vision to behold.

We reigned supreme, Neva and I. For the moment. I feared our dominance wouldn't last.

I grabbed the girl's hand. "Come on. Run."

Suiting action to words, I dodged around the writhing pile the two men made, pulling Neva with me. Foghorn may have been hurt and bewildered by Neva's whirlwind attack, but he'd soon recover his wits if not his mobility. As for Murphy, I didn't know if his wound was disabling. A glance over my shoulder as we fled showed him getting to his feet, the table leg still attached. A bit slow, granted, but inexorable.

We burst into sunshine blinding in its intensity after the hours spent in our dim prison. A breeze blew, carrying the sweet smell of freedom. I wanted to scream my euphoria.

My exhilaration ended all too soon. I didn't, I realized, know where to run.

"Which way?" My head swiveled. We were on a tree-lined lane — a driveway, I guessed, with a gate at the bottom protecting the owner's privacy. The long drive ran between a stand of golden-leaved sugar maple trees into a wider road, whether a secluded city street, a county road, or the main thorough-fare, I couldn't say. A red tile roof rose over a cluster of evergreens to the south of us, perhaps a hundred yards away. If we went in the wrong direction, we'd probably end up right at the boss's front door.

Neva took the lead. "Here. Follow me."

She ran straight ahead, toward the cross-road, with me on her heels, regardless of the hampering effect of my skirt. I have no idea what made me turn and look over my shoulder. A sixth sense, perhaps? But what I saw made me stumble in a gravel-filled rut in the lane.

Good thing, too. The momentum sent me lurching sideways just as a shot rang out from behind us.

Murphy, one arm hanging from his shoulder like a red rag, was up, the wooden appendage no longer attached to his rear. His pistol leveled as he took careful aim for another shot at us — or not us. At me.

"Duck," I screamed at Neva. "Run."

She had the good sense to dash in a zigzag pattern. I followed suit, leaving the road to her and taking the grassy verge for myself. No sense putting us in alignment, especially since Murphy had made me his target.

I felt a tug on my skirt as a bullet passed through the fabric. Terror seized me. He'd have me next time. But I had to prevent a next time.

I stopped. Turned. Lifted the .32 in both hands. Took a deep breath, let half out, held it. Lined the front sight on Murphy's torso, then raised it just a half a hair's width. I squeezed the trigger.

Emitting a satisfying yell, he spun away.

Without waiting around to see if I'd made my shot or only scared him, I turned and ran again. Harder. Faster. Panting. Sobbing.

And then we, Neva and I, were at the gate which, as if by magic, swung open as we approached. Another bullet whizzed past my head, telling me Murphy remained in the chase. And then we were through.

"Right," Neva called out, breathless with effort. "Turn right."

So I did.

Straight into Gratton Doyle's arms.

"Oof," I said as they closed around me.

CHAPTER 28

My, but didn't Murphy get a surprise when he rounded the corner? Much as we had done, he turned right, expecting, I'm sure, to have a clear shot at Neva and me running for our lives. Instead, he met the combined force of Gratton, in the lead and rushing toward the sound of gunfire, with Monk, Porter, and Lorenzo right behind.

I'm happy to say the meeting wasn't nearly as pleasant for Murphy as it had been for us.

Backing Gratton up was Lorenzo, hollering fit to awaken the ghosts in the cemetery: "That's him. He's the one."

Next came Porter, handing Neva off to her young friend to keep them both out of the way. "I've got the sonsa— gun." Then followed up by getting him.

And Monk, as grim as I've ever seen him, who held his old .45 Peacemaker Colt on Murphy in a way that showed he meant business.

Best of all was Gratton, who simply gathered me into the crook of one arm and held me.

Murphy froze, his eyes bugged out like a squashed toad's.

Turns out the most surprising, maybe even shocking thing — and I'd be hard put to call the surprise pleasant — was the man who stepped from a closed carriage that wheeled up and parked a few yards away. With Murphy captured, his pistol taken away and everyone else's holstered, Warren Poole approached and eyed the prisoner with prissy-faced disgust.

"Another piece of the puzzle slips into place," he said. "This man is Branston's coachman. He is, I suppose, intent on working a scam of his own." He puffed a little sigh. "Such a to-do over a horse and a race."

I made a move, but Grat stilled me. His head made a short motion, one that meant *say nothing.* Why? Put to the trial once again, I managed to cut off a pithy rebuttal of Poole's conclusion.

"Your name is Murphy, isn't it?" Poole questioned the prisoner.

I noticed he kept his distance, leaving the work to the other men, Monk and Porter leading the way since Grat was otherwise occupied. I snuggled closer.

Murphy looked back at Poole. "I need a doctor."

He looked at me, too. Not much liking it, I slid behind Grat.

"Bitch shot me," Murphy said as if Poole hadn't spoken.

"Did she? A lucky hit?" Poole seemed amused.

"Not luck." I couldn't stay silent at this slur on my marksmanship, even if he was more than half right. I peeked over Grat's shoulder. "Accuracy."

You could've knocked me over with the flap of a fan when Poole murmured, "Well done."

Yes. Well, I thought so.

So did Neva. "Miss Bohannon, she's the one got the idea to use the plate for a saw, and the table leg for a club. Left the nails in it too. So now that other one, he's bleeding like a throat-cut hog."

We grinned at each other, even as the men scratched their heads, metaphorically speaking. I guess what she said didn't make much sense, taken out of context. Well, they'd soon understand.

"Other one?" Monk asked her after a moment.

"Yes." I answered for her. "A very large

man who seems to like brandishing his knife at people. The very one who ambushed you, Gratton, if I'm not mistaken. And the same man who accosted me the other day, whom Mrs. Flynn foiled. You remember Mrs. Flynn from the café, don't you?"

"Les is his name." Neva gave a skip, ducking her head when everyone looked at her again.

"Yes. Les, thank you, Neva. Unless he's managed to get away, he's lying in the shed where they were holding us. Last I saw he was crying his eyes out because a girl beat him up with a stick." I took great pleasure in saying those words.

"You?" Monk asked.

"Not me. Neva. You should have seen her. She was wonderful, so brave and strong."

Lorenzo whispered something to her. Something which drew a blush into Neva's pale face. A blush and a real smile to her lips. The first from her I'd ever seen.

Meanwhile, Murphy kept protesting his innocence as if he thought somebody there might believe him. In between, he whined over and over for a doctor. An idiot, just like his boss had said.

"Shut up," Grat told him, even as Porter jerked his wounded arm, eliciting a yelp. Personally, I hoped it hurt a lot.

"I wonder," Poole started, a frown creasing his brow, "how these two ended up on this piece of property. I don't suppose you know who lives here, but —"

I interrupted. "Of course we do. Lloyd Branston lives here. We've met."

Monk's face wore an unhappy expression as he chewed on the ends of his mustache — mustache chewing being totally out of character. "Yes," he said, but tentatively, as though unsure of his ground, "I remember you meeting. He came by the office and talked with us yesterday morning."

"Oh, I've talked to him since then." I looked down to where my watch should've been pinned to my blouse, only to find it missing. My skin gave a shudder, like a horse shaking off flies. One of our kidnappers had touched me. Touched my breast. The thought almost made me swoon. Almost. I had no time for such things.

Breathing deeply, I announced, "We spoke only an hour or so ago." And then, just to make it clear. "In the shed, where he gave his men permission to kill us, Neva and me, if we didn't tell him what he wanted to know. He's looking for a certain item, you see, and wants it back at any cost."

Murphy twisted his good arm, trying to throw off Porter's grip. "She's a liar," he

373

shouted. "Don't listen to that little bitch. She's lyin' through 'er teeth."

Poole stared down his long nose. His lips thinned. "Tell him what he wanted to know, Miss Bohannon? You mean about the horse? You are obviously mistaken. I beg leave to doubt Lloyd Branston . . ."

"No," I interrupted again. I can recognize a denial in the making when I hear one. Dare I say my temper simmered, ready to boil? Did Poole think to refute what Neva and I had suffered? Now who was the idiot? My voice shook with anger. "Mercury is only an excuse. As far as I can tell, none of these scoundrels have made up their minds whether they want the horse to win or to lose. No, Branston is after something entirely different. You see, Neva's mother . . . you tell them, Neva. It's your story."

Haltingly, Neva complied. I can only imagine what it cost for her to recount her mother's and her grandfather's collaboration in a plot to rig races and bilk the betting public. Add in Robbie's death and it was enough to turn a grown man's stomach.

Poole's stomach certainly, as he was forced, not without protest, into belief.

My word, I wish I'd had a picture of his face when everyone heard the story of how Hazel O'Dell had picked his pocket for the money to pay Mercury's entry fee into the derby.

"But it was the notebook Mr. Branston really wanted," Neva said, then went silent.

Gratton cleared his throat. "Notebook? What notebook, Neva?"

"Oh, didn't I say that part?" Neva chewed on her lip before admitting, "My mother took the papers that prove Mercury belongs to Robbie and me. She took his race earnings, too, and hid everything in our wagon. I watched her, though, and figured out where she put them. The other night when she was sleeping, I opened her cache and took the bag. Then I sneaked off and took Mercury over to Lorenzo's camp and hid him in among the other horses. It wasn't until the next day I discovered she'd taken more than just money and Mercury's papers."

Poole snapped his fingers as though to hurry her along. "Well? What else did you find?"

"A notebook with lots of names and amounts of money. Me and Lorenzo, we finally figured out what it all meant. Sort of. But that's what Mr. Branston wanted me for. He wanted to get it back. You see —" She looked down at the road and rubbed the toe of her boot in the dust. At

375

last, she raised her head. "My mother lifted the book off Mr. Branston one day."

"You mean your mother picked his pocket, too?" Gratton's eyes flickered. "She must be good."

I wasn't surprised. I doubt Poole was either, considering his own experience with Hazel O'Dell.

Neva heaved a gigantic sigh. "Yes. She meant to take his wallet and got the book by mistake, but when she figured out what it all meant, she was glad. She wanted Mr. Branston to pay her some money, on account of all those names and dollars. A lot of money. Five hundred dollars. But then she got scared. I think she got beat up. And she told him, or maybe this guy" — she indicated Murphy — "that I had the notebook. Me or Miss Bohannon. So that's when they came after us both, because they thought I might have left those things with China."

"Blackmail." Poole breathed the word, apparently much more concerned with Branston's predicament than the fact Neva and I had been meant to die. "But why —"

"Easy answer," Grat cut in. "Branston's got gambling debts. Big ones. I expect the book is the list of his IOUs. Who and how much. How it all adds up. Sawyer Kennett, owner of the Flag of America, got put on that list the other night. If I'm not mistaken, your name is there, too. Bottom line is, Branston's in over his head."

Poole stared at him. "How do you know? He —"

Grat's upper lip curled. "Word gets around. People are saying his bank is in trouble."

Monk snorted. "We asked Bill Jackson, a retired investigator, to look into it for us."

Poole spoke so quietly I strained to hear. "Yes. I'm afraid so. He'll be ruined if — when — this gets out. There'll be a run on the bank, just when business is starting to pick up after the recession." Poole leaned against the body of his carriage as if he were tired. He appeared to be thinking. "I'm sure you young ladies never planned to open such a can of worms, but you certainly have. Trouble began the moment the coroner found that note on his autopsy report inquiring about Robbie O'Dell's cause of death. He brought the results to the mayor's and my attention. You may also be interested to learn a body turned up this morning, in a shallow grave down by the river. A boy and his dog found him. He had a broken arm, but he died of stab wounds. A jockey's riding whip was buried with him."

"Billy," Neva breathed.

Somehow, I felt better knowing we could account for Billy Banks.

"The police chief know about it?" Monk asked.

"Couldn't risk it," Poole said, "although I don't think he's part of the conspiracy. As I imagine you either know or guess, some of the higher-ups in the SPD are involved."

"Hansen, for one," I said, quietly, but clearly enough. "And forgive me if I don't feel guilty for helping bring them to justice."

"Yes. Well." Unhappiness on his face, Poole nodded. "Lloyd has made his bed, I fear. Nothing to be done for him now. He has to face what he's done."

He studied Murphy a moment then huffed out a sigh and said, "Too bad you didn't have your little dog, Miss Bohannon. You could've turned her loose to savage this fellow."

A joke? Really? I nearly collapsed on the spot! I even rubbed my ear to be sure it was working correctly and I wasn't hearing things.

All good, I suppose, if only my inner eye had stopped short of seeing Nimble bloodied and dead right alongside my own body. Because Murphy and Foghorn were that kind of men. And their boss Branston, too, at the head of the line.

Poole's carriage, parked in a rather-too-obvious position alongside the road, became Murphy's temporary cell. Monk, with Lorenzo's help, drew guard duty over him, while Gratton and Porter went off to collect Foghorn — or Les, I suppose I should call him.

Meanwhile, Mr. Poole, Neva, and I stood along the road's verge, out of danger in case Murphy were to break free. A highly unlikely happenstance, I might add, with my uncle on guard.

Besides, I still had two bullets in the .32.

The sun, bright on such a pleasant autumn day, lent a welcome warmth. Doves cooed from the trees along the verge. One of the horses drawing Warren Poole's carriage whickered softly and flicked its tail. The frail old man at the reins dozed. All calm and peaceful after being kidnapped, shot at, and rescued. So why did I have an inner chill wending a way around my innards?

After a silence that became oppressive, I felt compelled to generate a new conversation.

I'd noticed a gaping hole in the progression of our case, one nobody apparently wanted to address. But I couldn't help feel-

379

ing, by this time, the menfolk were not paying nearly enough attention to what Neva and I had gone through. Considering what might have happened if we hadn't broken free, it didn't seem right.

And I wasn't going to stand for it.

"Tell me," I said to Mr. Poole, "now we have Branston's henchmen under control, what are we . . . are you going to do about their boss? Branston, I mean."

"Hmm?" he murmured as if he couldn't think what I meant.

I didn't take the hint. "He's the one who gave these men their orders. He's the one who told them to dispose of Neva and me."

"My dear —" Those two words may have been intended to sound avuncular, but the expression on his face was anything but. "— I'm sure you misunderstood. Branston may be guilty of . . . of siphoning funds for his own temporary use, but he is not a murderer."

Siphoning funds? Is that what he called embezzlement?

"No," I said clearly, "I did not misunderstand."

"We both heard him, plain as day." Neva backed me up.

Poole hesitated. "Well, I believe that's a question for the proper authorities to decide. We'll talk to them about it when we turn in Murphy and this other man, Les, then leave it in their capable hands."

"What proper authorities?" My stomach tightened. Surely he didn't mean —

"We'll take your concerns to the prosecuting attorney. He'll be the one to organize the . . . the —"

I sucked in so hard a breath I nearly rose up like a balloon. "In other words, if I'm reading you correctly, you intend to let Branston get away with his crimes. Maybe a slap on the wrist. Why? Because of the bank? Are you going to help cover up what he's done?"

A tide of red painted his neck and face. "Now see here, Lloyd Branston is an important man in Spokane. We need more proof than the accusations of a couple overwrought girls. After all, no one has been hurt."

"I beg your pardon?" Anger infused me.

I barely heard Neva whisper, "What about Robbie? And you and me? Doesn't he believe us?"

Poole had heard what she said. I wouldn't have thought it possible, but his neck got even redder. Turkey gobbler red. I took pleasure in visualizing him in that guise. With his neck stretched across the chopping block, no less.

"Oh, he knows, Neva, but he's going to ignore us." I paused, catching his eye. "Or he thinks he is. He's wrong."

I really don't know what came over me. Anger infused my brain into a flaming torch. All the men, even Monk and Gratton, seemed almost unwilling to take Lloyd Branston on. Well, I wasn't unwilling. I wasn't afraid either.

Neither was Neva.

I spun around, marching back the way we'd come. The long drive branched off toward the mansion I'd seen from the shed. Branston's house. That's where I headed.

"Here," Poole said. "Wait. You can't —"

I ignored him.

I didn't realize Neva had followed me until she caught up just as I turned onto the other drive, avoiding Grat and Porter with their prisoner on their way down to the main road.

"You should go back," I told Neva, never pausing.

"No." That's all she said.

Behind us, I heard Poole calling — well, bellowing, actually. He sounded angry. "Miss Bohannon," he yelled. "Where are you going? Get back here."

I pretended not to hear.

CHAPTER 29

Neva and I approached the Branston home, striding up the drive as if we owned the place. A bit of an act, I must admit, since my heart pounded in my chest until I felt dizzy. Judging by Neva's white face, she felt pretty much the same.

Branston's estate showcased great wealth and status. Imposing in the extreme, the mansion rose three stories beneath a steeply pitched roof. A round turret rounded off one corner; brick and stone porches surrounded the ground floor. The house towered in the midst of a cultivated expanse of grass and a judiciously thinned stand of Ponderosa pine. To one side, even this late in the year, a rose garden bore a myriad of blooms, red and yellow, pink and white. Several impeccably tended topiary shaped into fantastical creatures menaced all who visited the grounds.

Neva caught my hand and tugged. "What

are those things?" She pointed a shaky, and rather grubby, forefinger at a rearing green horse.

The shrubbery only interested me because of the potential for ambush. "Just bushes. They're called topiary."

She frowned. "Do they grow like that?"

"Not naturally. They're trimmed and trained."

We passed one shaped like a unicorn.

"Why would anybody bother?" Her head turned to gaze at it from the other side.

I didn't answer. Walking beneath a broad portico, we reached a well-swept set of dark gray stone steps — very much the color of Gratton's eyes — which led to a double-doored front entry. Our shoes clicked on the stone as we mounted the steps. It would've been daunting if I hadn't been too mad for such things to matter.

A brass — or maybe gold — knocker beckoned.

I hammered it down. Once, twice, thrice.

"Stay behind me," I told Neva. "He may have another thug in there with him. If there is, I want you to run to Porter or Grat."

"Wish I had my club," she said, her face set and fierce.

"I wish you did, too." We'd be in serious trouble if Branston did have someone with him. Drawing the little revolver from my pocket, I hid it in the folds of my skirt. I had only two bullets left, all the others expended on subduing Murphy. These two had to count.

I banged the knocker again. Not gold. Gold would've been too soft, unable to stand up to the abuse.

A muted voice, male, spoke from behind the doors, and all such errant thoughts faded into nothing.

"I'll get it myself, Esther," it said. "No need for you to come down."

The voice belonged to Lloyd Branston.

I held my breath as the door opened, ponderous and heavy.

"Who is it?" I heard a woman say, even as I pushed on the door, hard and fast, and entered the snake's den.

He hadn't been expecting us, I daresay. The look on Branston's face was beyond price. Frightening, too, in a way. Surprise may have been uppermost, but I thanked providence — or Monk and Grat — for the gun I carried in my hand.

"You," Branston said, sounding shaken. "I heard gunfire. How did you . . ."

"Get loose from your thugs?" My smile must've been vicious. "Brute force, Mr. Branston, more of which I'm not at all adverse to using against you." I allowed him a peek at the .32. "Try me. Do."

His eyes snapped with fury. His jowls quivered. Scowling, he stepped aside as his wife descended the mahogany staircase rising from the far end of the foyer. One of her delicate hands slid along the beautifully polished rail. Her other lifted the lace over-skirt she wore just high enough over her kitten-heeled shoes to avoid tripping. She smiled as she caught sight of me, a smile that turned to puzzlement, then worry.

"Why, Miss Bohannon! What on earth has happened to your face? To your frock? Have you been in an accident? Can I help?"

She reached the bottom step, a wave of Jicky perfume preceding her. I recognized the same fragrance that had scented the note pushed under Porter's door. The note stating Neva would be blinded if —

"And who is this?" she asked, smiling kindly at Neva.

Smiling, yes, but there was something —

My thoughts seesawed up and down like a child's plaything. The perfume, the smell of it, stopped me cold.

Who had first conceived and then scribed the threat laid out in that note? Had Branston used a sheet of his wife's stationery, perhaps so accustomed to the scent he no longer smelled it as separate from her and therefore got careless?

Or had she written the message herself without giving her signature scent a moment's reflection? But she seemed so kind with the concern on her face. And there'd been the incident the other day with Warren Poole, when she'd saved Nimble's bacon and incidentally, mine.

To tell the truth, I wished she'd stayed upstairs every bit as badly as her husband appeared to do. If he, and she, too, weren't just consummate actors. Worse, I found it hard to watch both of them at once. Which was the greater threat?

I dared not risk letting my confusion show.

"Come in and sit down," Mrs. Branston cooed, although I was already in. "Let me fetch you some tea. Or coffee. Would you prefer cocoa? Perhaps a tiny glass of sherry?"

She rushed forward, her hands out, the epitome of easy conversation and gracious hospitality.

I flicked Neva a quick glance. Had time to see her letting down her guard in response to the woman before I resettled my attention on Mr. Branston.

And just in time. He was already sliding to his right, slick as a snake, where a console table stood. On top of the gold-leaf-decorated stand and incongruous in the elegant surroundings, a blued-steel derringer pistol sat on a silver tray.

I raised my own pistol. "Do not . . . ," I began. At that very moment Mrs. Branston — Esther's — feet slipped on the black and white marble tiles and swooshed out from under her.

Arms windmilling, she lurched straight toward me.

If she expected me to catch her, she had another think coming. I skipped aside. She scooted past, right into Neva. Down they both went. Esther, to my gratification, at the bottom of the pile.

Even though I avoided the collision, the commotion diverted my attention from Branston for a brief moment. His attention, I regret to say, was not diverted at all. Lightning fast, he lunged for the derringer, grabbed it up, and leveled it on me.

Neva cried, "China, look out!"

Branston and I pulled our triggers at pretty much the same instant. Our pistol's reports, louder for happening together, reverberated off the hard surfaces of the foyer, the noise hurting my already-suffering ear. Esther's scream didn't help.

A bloom of red spread high up on the front of his shirt. He staggered, sagging against the wood paneled wall.

At the same time, a searing pain scorched my thigh. Shocked, I realized I'd also been shot.

Branston remained standing, gripping one hand with the other and cursing as blood dripped from his fingertips.

Instead of a direct single hit, it appeared my bullet slid off the derringer's metal frame, giving me a "two for the price of one" shot. How lucky can you get? But now the pair of us were sort of at a stalemate. He wounded with his derringer ruined. Me wounded, with only one shot remaining.

But he didn't have to know that.

Somehow, I managed to remain on my feet and upright. I held the pistol, barely wiggling, aimed at his belly.

"We're all making our way down to the road where Warren Poole, along with my uncle and Gratton Doyle are waiting." My words wiped away the smirk that touched Branston's mouth at this news as I added, "Mr. Poole is helping keep watch over some prisoners. Your men, sir. Murphy and Les. Both of whom are more than willing to tell us everything we want to know."

Esther moaned. Not painfully, even though she was still sprawled on the tile floor with Neva sitting atop her, but mournfully. "Lloyd, how could you let this happen? You told me everything was going smoothly. You said we'd —"

"Be silent, Esther," he gritted.

Tears ran from the corners of Esther's eyes. "You'll be ruined. We'll be ruined. What will our friends think?" Her voice grew louder. "What will become of me?"

"Hush." His command didn't strike me as particularly sympathetic. "If you hadn't . . ." He stopped, realizing he was on the verge of giving too much away.

I glanced at her. "No, no, speak right up, Mrs. Branston. I'd like to hear what you have to say. But I'll give you fair warning. It sounds an awful lot like you're in on the plot."

She tried, unsuccessfully, to push Neva off. Neva, tough and wiry, though small in stature, stuck to her like a cocklebur.

"What plot?" Esther huffed little gasps in and out between pursed lips. "I don't know what you're talking about. You barged in here and shot my husband and now you're making wild accusations. You've abused —"

Her voice failed. Perhaps her corset strings were pulled too tight. Or Neva too heavy.

"That man — your husband — is a bad man and he's shot China," Neva burst out, bouncing a little and forcing a grunt from

Mrs. Branston. "He held us prisoner in that awful little shed. And he killed my brother." This last rose on a wail. I was afraid poor little Neva had taken about as much as she could bear over this last while. The drama needed to end.

What I'd said about making our way down to the road? I'm afraid that may have been wishful thinking. A kind of dark weakness spread over me, enveloping me in a slowly descending fog. I barely managed to stay standing at all, let alone walk all the way to where the men were waiting.

I'd caught a criminal, but now I didn't know what to do with him.

The darkness receded — momentarily — when Gratton Doyle's voice, rough with anger, spoke from the open doorway. "What the hell is going on in here?"

We all jumped.

"Dammit, China," he went on, apparently blind to Branston's condition as well as to Neva and Esther still wrestling about on the floor. He strode toward me. "You've been shot."

I nodded. This wasn't exactly news to me.

CHAPTER 30

My gunshot wound, though it bled copiously at the time, didn't amount to much. A minor graze, or so Monk informed me. But then he wasn't the one with a two-inch-long furrow in his flesh.

At any rate, I only limped a little the next day. Not at all, if I made a conscious effort to ignore the painful twinges every step brought about. It didn't matter. I wouldn't have missed the Spokane Derby and seeing Mercury run for all the tea in . . . well . . . China. Not even if blood were still running down my leg.

Hyperbole? Maybe, but no more than the honest truth.

Porter had agreed to act as my escort since Gratton and Monk were still on the job providing security for loyal fairgoers. Instead of hoofing it to the streetcar under a gray sky threatening rain, Porter had hired a cab and picked me up right outside the office. He even hoisted me onto the seat.

Alice, his intended, was going to be a very spoiled lady when and if they ever tied the knot.

"I could get used to this. Thank you, Porter." I grinned at him.

He blushed. "Yeah, well, tell it to your boyfriend," he replied, whereupon I felt heat rising in my own cheeks.

"He's still angry with me." Without pretending to misunderstand, I toyed with the clasp on my handbag. "He won't talk to me. Not since the tongue-lashing he gave me yesterday. And when I kind of fainted in his arms, he thought I was putting on an act to make him stop."

A bushy eyebrow arched. "Were you?"

"No! Well, maybe a little. But I was hungry. It had been hours and hours since I'd had anything to eat. Neva, either, and she said . . ."

Porter's laugh stopped my excuses.

"And I was scared. And bleeding. I had been shot, after all." I found myself indignant all over again.

"Should've thought of that before you marched into Branston's house like you headed up a whole posse. You and Neva. Worst couple of headstrong numskull females I ever heard of. It's a wonder the pair

393

of you weren't murdered right then and there."

Evidently Porter and Grat had gotten together to manufacture their speeches. I'd heard this one before.

I sat back in a huff. "How should I know Grat had sent you for the chief of police and he intended to delay the confrontation with Branston until the authorities got there? Or that he had Bill Jackson keeping an eye on Branston. He could've said something!"

To my surprise, Porter nodded. "Yeah, he could've. Thinking back, he should've. He ought to know you by now."

Before I had time to ask just what he meant by that remark, we arrived at the fairgrounds where the entire Kennett family awaited my arrival at the front entrance. A perfect copy of his father, Sawyer Jr. shifted impatiently from foot to foot, while Liddy played peekaboo with a wandering clown. Such a beautiful child is hard to resist.

Gincy wore a lovely dark red woolen walking suit. Atop her head sat a magnificent specimen of the milliner's art, evidence she'd been visiting Spokane's finest stores and spending some of the money her husband had won from Lloyd Branston. While Porter paid off the cab and departed on his own business, the Kennetts took me under their collective wing.

As we paid our entrance fees, I noticed the autumn harvest decorations at the gate were getting a little shabby. On this last day of the fair, heavy-headed sunflowers sagged on their stems and massive pumpkins shriveled after days in the sun. A stack of apples were quickly losing their bloom and beginning to smell of rot.

A different scent, that of fried food, still wafted enticingly over the grounds. Along with roasted peanuts. And coffee. And bruised grass.

The merry-go-round calliope trilled just as loudly as ever, children laughed just as gleefully — and a whole parade of noisy horse race aficionados made their way toward the track. We joined the migration, Gincy assuring her children the merry-go-round would still be there after the race.

I checked the time on my watch, recovered from Foghorn's pocket yesterday and returned to me. After washing and polishing, it had seemed clean enough to pin on my shirtwaist, although I still shuddered at the thought of him . . . well, I wouldn't let those memories spoil the day.

Thirty minutes to post time. My own nerves hammered. I could only imagine how tense Neva must be.

Sawyer lent his arm in support as the wave of humanity swept us forward.

"Will Porter be able to find us?" Gincy, clutching Sawyer's arm on his other side, gripped Liddy's little hand in a death grip so as not to lose her. "Junior," she shrilled. "Stay close."

"Yes, ma'am," the boy said, but truthfully, I doubted it would take long for him to disappear into the crowd.

"Porter said he was going to help Neva and Lorenzo saddle Mercury," I said. "Neva is rather at a loss now that her mother and grandfather are in jail awaiting their arraignment. She needed an adult to oversee the entry and Porter, bless his kind heart, volunteered."

Sawyer muttered something that sounded a lot like "Man's a brave fool," but I could've been mistaken.

"But where will she go?" Gincy, bless her motherly heart, sounded worried. "She's only fourteen."

I'd been worried too, until I learned Lorenzo and his grannie planned on taking her in. Probably, judging by the way the two kids looked at each other, on a permanent basis.

I caught sight of Uncle Monk over by the

bookie area, and waved, but I couldn't spot Gratton anywhere. Lost in the sea of people, I expect.

"Keep tight hold of your purse," I raised my voice over the background noise to say to Gincy, "and Sawyer, you'd best have a care for your wallet."

"Money belt." He patted his waistline and grinned. "And just a little cash on hand."

An excellent precaution, for whom did I chance to see but our old friend Jimsy Woodsmith? He saw me, too, and quickly veered off in another direction. Evidently, he'd made bail, although why a judge would turn him loose with the fair still underway was beyond my understanding.

Plying elbows and hips, I found myself a place at the rail near the finish line. Gincy moved in close beside me. Despite her protests, we sandwiched little Liddy between us. To quiet her, Sawyer promised to put her on his shoulders when the race started.

"You'll have the best seat in the house," he promised.

"What house?" Liddy wanted to know, scowling.

Time ticked away. Activity over by the saddling enclosure drew my attention. I picked words out of the crowd around me.

"Look, ain't that Mercury? The bay with the braided mane?"

"Think so," another voice replied. "I heard he was crippled when that boy got killed."

"Don't look crippled to me."

He didn't appear crippled to me, either, from what I could see over myriad tall forms moving between me and the horse. He danced about, hooves lifting high and dainty. His ears were pricked, his coat gleamed with good health and a thorough brushing.

I caught sight of Porter, standing at Mercury's head with a good grip on the horse's headstall. Lorenzo, hard to miss, wore a bright green shirt with a number eight tacked to the back. And Neva, her hair plaited into a thick braid to match the horse's mane and just as black. I laughed to myself. Like the horse, she was almost dancing. Avoiding Mercury's hooves here, whispering in his pricked ears there, patting his shoulder. Gripping Lorenzo's hand.

Truthfully? She looked scared — or maybe just apprehensive — or excited. Hard to tell from this distance, but probably a combination of all three. I doubt she could stop thinking about the last time the horse ran and her brother was killed. God willing, this race would be a triumph.

A stentorian bellow from an important-looking stout man caused a flurry of action. I have no idea what he actually said, but it caused riders to mount their horses. Lorenzo for one, bouncing onto the tiny saddle on Mercury's back as if he had springs beneath his feet.

Or no. Only Porter, with an almost-too-helpful heave-ho.

Then the horses entered the track, and the crowd roared.

Bookies called for last-chance bets.

Gincy smiled at me and said, "Isn't this exciting? If your girl doesn't win, I hope number five does. He belongs to my cousin Jack. He's running a reservation-bred horse."

"Cousin Jack," Liddy screamed. I guessed she was rooting for her relative. "Rider, Rider." To her joy, the horse's jockey waved to her.

The rest of the horses were passing us now, some already beginning to sweat as they sensed the tension all around them. Their riders, the crowd, their own racing experience.

Cousin Jack's horse was dark brown, tall and rangy, his finish not so fine as Mercury's. Nevertheless, if I'd actually wagered money on the race, I would've hedged my bet on Mercury with a few dollars on him. His rider wore white, a stark contrast to his brown skin.

I didn't pay much attention to any of the other runners. Only to Mercury, stepping lightly through the soft dirt of the track. The horse mouthed his bit, ready to run, Lorenzo barely able to restrain him.

The ten-horse field lined up at the starting ribbon.

For a couple brief seconds there was total quiet.

Then a collective gasp as the ribbon dropped.

Ten horses leapt away from the post.

The crowd roared, me along with the rest. Liddy shrieked with glee, her mother almost a match. The field flashed by so fast I didn't have time to see who was in the lead. I caught a glimpse of green. A dash of white. Red. Pink. Two shades of blue. Even black, although distance may have eroded my vision by then since they were all well past me and I saw them through a cloud of dust.

Someone moved close behind me then, and forgetful of my wound, I spun. The leg might've given out except it was Grat, there to catch me.

Again.

"Shouldn't you be patrolling the crowd?"

I asked, basking for a moment in his arms. I could tell by his crooked grin and the look in his storm-gray eyes he was over his mad.

He shrugged. "You think I'd miss the derby? Not a chance."

"I saw Jimsy Woodsmith," I warned him.

"Don't care." He spoke over my head, intent on the race, so I turned back to watch as well.

A matter of seconds took the horses to the four-furlongs pole, which marked the spot where a horse had been deliberately rammed into Mercury, his rider slashing Robbie across the throat with his whip. My breath caught and held. I could only imagine what Neva was going through at that moment. I only hoped Porter had her in hand.

I prayed for Mercury to win. For her and for Robbie.

Safely past the halfway point, the horses were already on the backstretch. Dust roiled. Flashes of color came through now and then. The rider wearing the green shirt seemed to be near the front. So did the white. The rest were a blur of color in motion.

"Jack, Jack," Liddy was still calling from her perch on Sawyer's left arm. "Rider."

Gincy just laughed.

Behind me, his hands on my shoulders, Grat, not so imperturbable as he'd like everyone to believe, bounced on his toes.

The horses flew around the last turn, onto the homestretch. There was Mercury. Then Jack and Rider, and one whose jockey wore red. Close behind him one of the blues gained ground with long strides. I didn't bother with the rest. These were all who had a chance.

Hooves thundered. The crowd cheered. I could hear the horses grunting with effort.

They swept past. Which horse's head passed the finish line first? I didn't know, but then a man with a megaphone, the official announcer, I guess, bellowed, "Mercury wins."

The crowd, in a single voice, roared.

Those closest to the finish line went wild, starting a chant. "Mercury, Mercury," those few yelled and a few thousand more picked it up.

Owners went out to catch their horses, winners and losers.

A beaming Neva, with Porter as escort, and Lorenzo still aboard Mercury, went out to accept a silver loving cup trophy and what I'd heard was a satisfyingly large purse.

"Gonna pat yourself on the back?" Grat spoke into my ear as we watched the celebration, causing shivers to run down my spine.

"What?"

"Mercury's big win is all due to you, you know. The horse would probably be ruined, and the girl silenced — if not as dead as her brother — if it hadn't been for you."

Eyes wide, I pulled back and stared at him. Accolades for a job well done? Or Grat's brand of an apology?

"Not to mention Branston getting away with a great deal of other people's money." He gave my shoulders a little shake. "You stuck with the job, regardless what Monk and I thought. And you were right on the button."

Praise. I figured I must be dreaming. Or else died and gone to heaven.

"Good for me," I said, trying to make light of it.

He laughed. "Yep. Good for you."

"Does this mean I get a raise?" I arched an eyebrow. "Or my name on the door as partner? Or . . . or . . ."

Grat's smile barely faded. "Means something, I guess," he said slowly. His storm-colored gaze caught and wrangled with my own.

Mercury walked past just then, blowing snot and with steam rising off his sweating chest. Neva walked beside him, one hand on the bridle's cheek strap. She seemed lit from within, looking up at Lorenzo and talking as fast as her horse could run.

A fine ending to the day. To the week. To the case.

The corner of Grat's mouth quirked up. The situation got even better when he draped his arm around my shoulders and finished what he'd started to say. "Guess we'll have to wait and see what this something turns into."

Wait? It sounded like a promise to me.

ABOUT THE AUTHOR

Born and raised in North Idaho on the Coeur d'Alene Indian Reservation, **Carol Wright Crigger** lives in Spokane Valley, Washington. She is a member of Western Writers of America and reviews books and writes occasional articles for *Roundup* magazine.

Imbued with an abiding love of western traditions and wide-open spaces, Ms. Crigger writes of free-spirited people who break from their standard roles. In her books, whether westerns or mysteries, you'll find real locales and a bit of lore taken from life. All of her books are set in the Inland Northwest. She is a two-time Spur Award finalist and won the 2008 EPIC Award for Western/Historical fiction.

Connect with Carol Wright Crigger:
www.ckcrigger.com
www.facebook.com/ckcrigger

www.twitter.com/ckcrigger
e-mail: ckcww@aol.com

The employees of Thorndike Press hope you have enjoyed this Large Print book. All our Thorndike, Wheeler, and Kennebec Large Print titles are designed for easy reading, and all our books are made to last. Other Thorndike Press Large Print books are available at your library, through selected bookstores, or directly from us.

For information about titles, please call:
(800) 223-1244

or visit our Web site at:
http://gale.com/thorndike

To share your comments, please write:
Publisher
Thorndike Press
10 Water St., Suite 310
Waterville, ME 04901